VEIL OF SHADOWS

RECLAIMING THE LOST LIGHT

ROWAN STORMVALE

Copyright © 2024 by Rowan Stormvale

All rights reserved.

No part of this book may be reproduced in any form or by any electronic or mechanical means, including information storage and retrieval systems, without written permission from the author, except for the use of brief quotations in a book review.

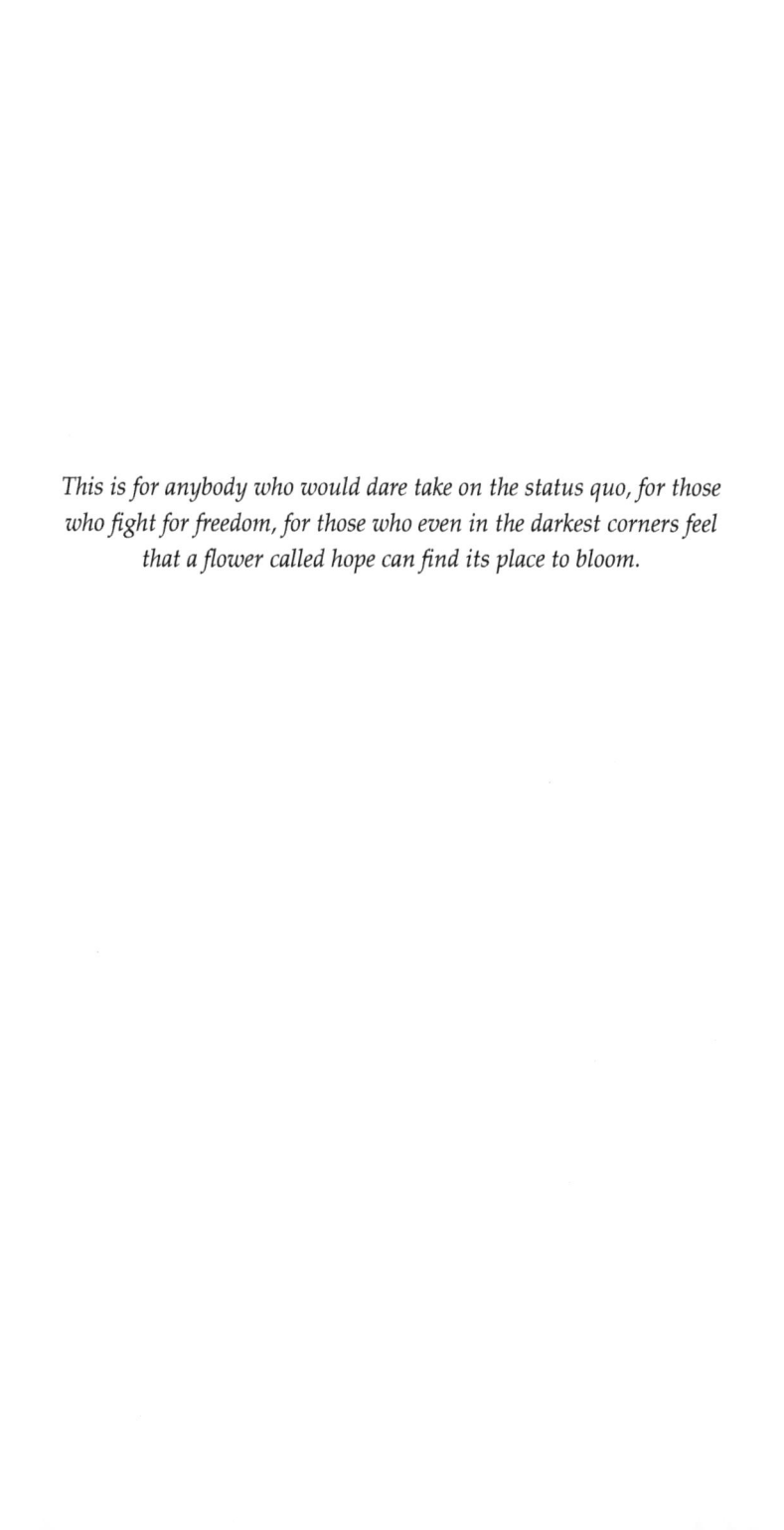

This is for anybody who would dare take on the status quo, for those who fight for freedom, for those who even in the darkest corners feel that a flower called hope can find its place to bloom.

PREFACE

In the center of every tale, there is something related to reflections on our world: challenges to power, temptations toward control, and the eternal dream of freedom. These threads lead through the tapestry of our being and their consequences of choices give meanings to our lives. It's a fable, on the canvas of the wild imagination of an endless and unwinnable fight for the triumph of justice by man, of the never-failing strength of hope, and a signal if utter hopelessness that light would find freedom.

INTRODUCTION

In this world, where three kingdoms proudly claim their right to guard the light, something brews in the dark. The Light Magic, meant to heal and protect, is subtly used as manipulation and a means of control by the noble elite over common people for their gain. Dax used to be an exiled Shadow Mage who was a great warrior of the kingdom. Now, he leads a rebellion of underground fighters against the tyranny of the ruler. He has watched people suffer at the hands of those in power and vowed to fight for the people's freedom. Sylvia was a runaway apprentice in Light Magic who finally realized the hypocrisy of the "Light" and joined Dax's cause, using her knowledge to shield the rebels. Their struggle is pitted against the head of the Imperial Radiance Church, High Priest Falk, who applies iron-fist repression using his strongest Light Magic to keep people in a state of terror.

It is a story of contrasts, of Light and Shadow in the struggle for freedom that dares reach outside the confines of such converse elements. Dax and Sylvia have been cast adrift in a sea of deception, and true power comes not from control, but from the courage it takes to step into the shadows, fight for the truth, and believe in oneself. A story of gray morality, of motives not as easily grasped within human beings, and a man's eternal yearning for freedom. In comes Dax and Sylvia, fighting against the established order, annihilation of potencies mirages, and the struggle for a world wherein justice will be decreed not according to Light or Shadow, but according to freedom born out of darkness.

PART ONE
SEEDS OF REBELLION

In the shadow of the Empire, one could hear the first murmurs of dissent. Dax, a former Shadow Mage, and Sylvia, an unhappy Light Magic apprentice, started to question some not-so-just Power above them. Their separate journeys come into conflict with the hidden manipulation within the Light they once revered. United, they make their first steps toward rebellion in a movement that will finally change their world.

CHAPTER 1
SHADOW OF BETRAYAL

Dax was alone when the winds changed-twilight wrapped around him like a shroud, cloaking the jagged peaks of the Shadowfell Mountains: a deadly divide between his past and a future shrouded in shadow. Far beneath, Aerilon shone with false serenity, its towers and spires thrusting toward the sky, shining beacons of the Empire's power. The gilt veneer could only be so thick, and Dax saw right through it-beyond-the grandeur of the city, it was a monument to inescapable repression, invisible but unbreakable. He had once sworn to defend it; now it stood as a monument to all he despised.

Dax had been the pride of Aerilon: the Shadowblade, elite warrior, staunch servant of the Empire. Every command rang in his mouth with devotion, every action in the service of what he perceived as a righteous order. Now, such allegiance lay in shards, crumbled beneath the weight of truths he could no longer deny. His path from guardian to exile had been torturous; every step cut the bonds which once held him fast.

. . .

The righteousness of Light Magic had been the doctrine of the Empire, his foundation. He was raised in the beliefs of its purity, of the power to heal and guide within it. But before his eyes, the Light had twisted to be used by the Imperial Radiance Church to enforce obedience, to mold minds, to strip people of their will. Wars for "justice," victors returning with vacant eyes, their memories seared away-all that had made them human-destroyed by "cures" cloaking mind control. With every victory, another tear in his soul, another ghostly multitude he could not shut out from his mind, the throng of those he had condemned.

The Church had turned Light into a cage, binding his people with chains for protection's sake.

The blind loyalty that had once extolled Dax's name slowly decayed and was replaced by relentless doubt. He had questions; he poked around. And in response, he got rebukes and dismissal, for his concerns were dangerous heresy. His doubt grew into defiance, and he became an odd dissenter in the very institution he had sworn to serve. This road of "righteousness" he had trodden was all the while a method of control designed to break, rather than protect, the spirit. That which finally had set him apart came on one fateful day: a denial, an act of defiance, then shattered his life. Being commanded to kill a young boy, falsely accused of heresy, Dax remembered his spirit breaking-the child's innocence, the fear in his eyes cut deeper than any blade. In one quiet word, "No," he had renounced place and title, past.

That denial was one spark of mercy in a world steeped in

cruelty, a cry for justice in a realm that had long forgotten what the word meant.

The revenge of the Empire was swift: Dax was stripped of all honor and branded a traitor, a Shadow Mage-a figure of terror, to be shunned and hunted. They had torn his name from him and cast him out into the wilderness, branding him an exile. But in the desolation of exile came a treasure that the exile Dax discovered-freedom. He wandered into the wilderness, beyond the grasp of Aerilon, to find others of his kind: those cast aside, their souls scarred by the merciless "justice" of the Empire. In the company of the forsaken, he found Shadow Magic, its ways a shield rather than a weapon of conquest. A power embracing his frailties, his struggles, interwove his agonies and pity with life into a mighty, irresistible force-no emperor's fiat could deprive him of that.

No longer Aerilon's Shadowblade, Dax forged a new path: he had become a warrior not for glory but for freedom-a rebel if there ever was one. Now, it was Shadow Magic that was his ally, unfolding the secrets of a strength he had not known.

The Empire would hunt him, brand him a threat, a foe to their way. But Dax relished their disdain, for he had witnessed the reality underneath the waxed gleam of the Empire. They might cast him into darkness, but they would never shut the spirit that drove him.

And now, he stood on the cusp of Shadowfell, his eyes ablaze with purpose; not a fugitive, he appeared as an announcer of their ruptured dream of freedom. He had given everything to get this chance and would fight to the last gasp for a world not enchained by chains of obedience and fear. And with that, Dax turned his back upon the glittering spires of Aerilon, weighed by the solemnity of his quest yet afire with desperate hope within.

For now, shadows were his allies-the very dark forces he would use in the struggle to climb back to his freedom and that of his nation. Many had been blinded by the brightness of the Empire, but in its darkness, Dax managed to find the truth-a light unhampered by machinations.

He came down from the mountain alone, but with one thought, one purpose-to take down the Empire, to stand up for the voiceless, and claim hope for them once more. In that instant, Dax was not the shadow of the Empire but a beacon, a fire in the dark, and he knew the path before him was worth the walk.

CHAPTER 2
THE AWAKENING OF DOUBT

Her eyes shone as bright as the midday sun, her spirit as limpid as mountain spring water. It gnawed at this weight she had never borne. Thus, to her, the Church of the Imperial Radiance had always been the source of warmth and light protecting the world against the dark. But now it felt cold and distant, jarringly sharp at its edges, casting shadows that she hadn't seen before.

The Church preached harmony, a world bathed in radiance in which there was no place for darkness. And the Empire, taking the lead in that same people who could avail themselves of Light Magic, made sure this was enforced with an iron fist. Like any other apprentice in Light Magic, Sylvia had learned to believe this was just protection-the world deserved.

And yet, a different glimmer began to break through of late-a tremor of fear in the common folk's eyes-as if the Light Magic shielded them not, but shackled them. When the soldiers' magic healed, it punished. And she heard whispers-the muffled voices muttering rebellion against the brightness of the Empire's oppression.

Soon, her doubts fluttered around her like fireflies-just dark streaks crossing her mind. Yet day after day passed, and her observations only continued to grow, impossible to be rid of, stirring unease for the suffering that compassed her. Her mentor, Elder Lyra, a woman whose devotion was as sure as the path of the sun, sensed quiet turmoil in Sylvia's eyes.

"You look troubled, Sylvia," Elder Lyra said one evening in hushed tones, her eyes as gentle as the moonlight filtering in through tinted glass in the Church windows. "What's weighing upon thy mind?"

Sylvia's fingers trailed along the worn edges of her Light Magic tome, the familiar words blurring before her eyes. "I… I've seen things, Elder Lyra. Things that feel… wrong."

Elder Lyra's brow furled a bit. "Wrong? What are you meaning, child?

Sylvia swallowed, and in a hushed tone, she spoke, "The soldiers. they practice using their Light Magic against people. I saw them sear a mark into a man's skin-a symbol of the Empire. They called it justice, but. it felt cruel.

. . .

Elder Lyra's expression turned grave. "It is not for us to question the Empire's ways, Sylvia. We are servants of the Light, guided by the holy flame. We must have faith in the wisdom of our superiors; they are chosen by the Light itself.

But... the man was begging for mercy," Sylvia whispered, as if to say it aloud might break something fragile. "The soldiers laughing while he was being tortured. Where in that was mercy?

The Light is clearest against darkness, Sylvia. The voice of Elder Lyra turned steely. "It's our duty toward the world that the shadows be warded, that justice be done-even when hardness is needed. It is the Empire who protects us, and its might is our surety.

Sylvia's heart twisted, and with her mentor's words fighting the compassion she could not suppress, a strange hollowness remained. It was all so wrong-the justice of the Empire, the doctrines of the Church, the brilliance of the Light ... If she was to be true to her beliefs, she had to know, understand, or somehow make amends with what was rightly just, even if it meant revising just what she had been brought up to believe in.

It was on one of these evenings that Sylvia, sitting alone in the library, stared down at the scriptures shining with soft luminescence, when a flicker of movement caught her gaze. The tall, cloaked figure in dark garb had just stepped out of the murkiness between two very old shelves; his face was shrouded. And at once, Sylvia's heart quickened, her hand reaching instinctively for the amulet at her neck-small, glowing orb, housing her Light Magic.

Who... are you?" Sylvia managed in a voice little louder than a whisper, her bravery deserting her.

He stood silent a moment, his eyes blazing with an unnatural light; then he spoke in tones which seemed to come from the very bottom of some old library.

"I am Dax. And I'm here to tell them the truth."

His hand reached out, with dark tendrils of energy curled around it beckoning to her. Sylvia was transfixed, her gaze locked on the energy emanating from his hand touching hers.

The Light, which you have been taught to love, Dax said in a soft, clear, firm command, is not the distilled essence that you have been programmed to believe it is. A tool-a means of control of those above-whereas the Empire is not your guardian but your jailer. And the Church? A puppet, dancing on the strings of the Empire's whim.

Cut through Sylvia like an icy wind, shearing through that warmth most sensible of beliefs she had lived by. Pure and warm Light had indeed been a guiding principle in her life. But here were Dax's words, impelled on a wave of conviction born from suffering, to implant a new, thorny doubt within her-a seed taking root in the cracks of her certainty.

"You're an apprentice of Light Magic, Sylvia," Dax repeated unflinchingly. "You have a huge potential, yet it's poisoned, fouled by the deceptions of the Church. With me, I can teach what light really is-what Shadow is-and how to shed the constraints they have placed upon you." Sylvia's mind was racing, her heart wrenched by terror and fascination. His words struck home, fanning the cold embers that had lain undisturbed within her. But to leave the Church, the only home she had ever known, ran chills down her spine.

Something about the unknown and darkness stirred within her, yet she remained still due to the fear that gripped her. "You are powerful, Sylvia," Dax whispered, his voice winding into her thoughts like a thread of shadow. "You're the key to breaking the Empire's hold." Dax's words seemed to stay in the air long after he disappeared into the rows of the library, leaving her to herself and the light he shared.

The world tumbled around Sylvia: the place of the Light, the Empire, and the Church-all twisted, draped in shadow. Before her lay a choice: to hold on to the comfort of dogmas she had grown up in, or to fling herself onto a path of terror and liberation.

CHAPTER 3
WHISPERS OF REBELLION

Long-voiced murmurings of revolt had been carried along the breeze, a silent storm building strength behind the mask of the Empire's cruel rule. The eye of this storm was a banished Shadow Mage named Dax, whose name was whispered with equal parts of fear and hope by those few who dared to dream of a free existence. A sworn warrior in the name of the kingdom, the loyalty which had withered after he finally saw the true face of the Empire: this so-called "Light" wasn't a power to heal and protect but a weapon welded by the nobles against commoners, maintaining their iron grip on the levers of power.

He had seen how innocent lives were entrapped, their minds twisted by that self-proclaimed guardian of the "Light"-the Radiance Church. He knew how Light Magic had been used to silence every dissent, making them conform and building a world based on fear and manipulation. It masquerades as the "Guardian of the Light" as it uses Light Magic to numb and confuse. Now branded the traitor and fugitive, Dax felt even more the fire of justice that had burned within him, to inspire a secret resistance-a hidden rebellion-designed to shatter the varnished veneer of the Empire.

But on the dark edges of the Empire, the whispers churned. Dax rallied the misfits, the rebels, the dreamers, and the few brave ones who were able to envision a world beyond the stranglehold of the Empire. They called them Shadows, a resistance force hiding in the cracks of the unyielding system, cloaked in actions, movements unseen, not under the watchful eye of the Empire. Their weapons weren't made of steel but from wit and shared truth and unrelenting belief in what they had to do.

Each rebel had something privately painful to deal with.

Some had lost family and loved ones to the evil of the Empire-their souls were scarred deep. Others had abandoned the illusions that were sold to them by the Radiance Church, their eyes unveiled to the shameless hypocrisy of the Empire, their souls afire with the urge to find out the truth.

It was a quiet, wordless resistance-where every member was an ember of freedom, joined together with hope for a world where eventually fear would not dim the light of humanity anymore.

Yet, it is there that murmurs of revolt did not long stay within closed doors and murmured tone but crept into the heart of man, firing blooms of defiance in tired breasts—a spark of hope in laden eyes.

. . .

For all its might, the Empire had underestimated the unyielding resilience that was the human spirit: an unbreakable will to believe in a better world. And all these rebels were but smoldering embers, waiting for the perfect time to erupt into the flames of resistance.

He full well knew this was a rebellion that fell squarely on his shoulders.

A shadow warrior, a leader whose will was bottomless and infinite as a starless night-the fire of his betrayal and pain crystallizing before his eyes into clear vision: let him unmask the lies of the Empire-to tear the deceitful Light which cloaked them apart-and free the people from oppression.

It was a dangerous act-undertaking, impossible, maybe-yet Dax did not cower an inch from this belief in his people, in unity, in the just power of Shadow.

This is the rebellion of whispers and actions-a silent brewing storm, only waiting for a storm to come and blow in with all its might. With every undercover mission completed, with every unseen battle won by the rebels, the whisper grew loud, fire burning in them more brightly. All-embracing, this Empire was-powerful, imposing-its rule gnawed, though unseen, at its very foundation.

. . .

Every victory against it by the rebels, even though infinitesimal or noiseless, was extremely cogent. Thieven from the stores of the Empire for distribution among the poor for food and medicine, they stole a glance at a world which one day would be free. Free prisoners from dungeons of the Radiant Church and restore in them their will to fight and remind them of the sanctity of freedom. Whispers of rebellion wove into the very fabric of the Empire, as those who had long resigned themselves to their chains began to listen-and question-and see beyond the false Light of the Empire.

There began to be quiet murmurs of defiance in the marketplace and homes of a rising resistance in the shadows. To this shadow warrior-and he who led that fragile but fervent hope-Dax knew full well this was far from over, that the Empire's grip on power was rigid, its reach vaulting. Yet he also knew that with every passing day, the fire of this rebellion was growing, nourished by speeches for freedom, a common dream of a world beyond the reach of the Empire: a world in which shadows would not be signs of terror but of promise, and a world where people could stand straight, unshackled and unbound.

CHAPTER 4
THE IRON GRIP OF RADIANCE

At the height of his power, High Priest Falk stood as a silhouette bathed in an aura of searing and blinding light. Wrapped in robes weaved from threads of gleaming stellar silver, he had the aspect of being radiantly chilling, almost otherworldly. Every movement he made was calculated; every gesture, a warning of the godly power he controlled. But deep beneath this mask of purity, a dark hunger festered, gnawing-a desire to control in simmer within his very being.

As the High Priest of the Imperial Radiance Church, Falk had become the keystone in the structure of the Empire, his influence inlaid within its very fabric. Mastery of Light Magic enabled him to heal with a touch and destroy with a word. Now he was using this capability, coldly calculated to snuff out dissidence, to make them afraid, to wrap the Empire in the mantle of obedience.

. . .

His means to this end were insidiously efficient: suave and subtle, yet vastly coercive, cloaked within the mantle of religious language. Preaching the doctrine of harmonious coexistence and order, Falk exhorted the following to obedience and oneness; and his words, laced with the implication of a threat, reached out from the great halls of the Church and out into the capital, and simply would not stop.

His reach was far more extensive than through the church doors themselves: the network of spies and informers, eyes, and ears hidden in every shade of the Empire had been spun. Their whisperings spread stories of his power, his benevolence, and steadfast devotion to the prosperity of the Empire. His presence loomed large, almost totally in control, and reached to the furthest corners of the realm.

The Imperial Radiance Church became the most dreaded armament of the Empire under the iron fist of Falk. It was one avenue through which the influence of the Empire flowed: its dogma implying a strict social pyramid, rigid structure of power. Any who would question, dare dream of another way, were swiftly silenced, the voice of those crushed beneath the blinding weight of Falk's Light.

Even in his message of unity, his words were filled with implications in subtle manipulations of the masses. He spoke about a world regulated and secure, wherein lies protection for the weak by the strong and with effective dealing for those who stray off the right track. He spun a tale of shared commitment so insidiously conceived that any departure from the dogmas of the Empire came to represent an existential threat to the very essence of the social body.

. . .

That control by Falk flowed from deep insight into human psychology; the mastery was pegged to his knack of discarding hidden fears, buried doubts, which he then used with cold precision, bending and molding them to his will as he made a society constructed on fear. He used psychological warfare like any other soldier would use his sword, with every word and action fitted to keep him in command, to extinguish defiance.

His greatest weapon was fear: molding minds, curtailing freedom, and crushing rebelliousness even before such could raise its head. Subtle and ruthless, the moves of Falk slowly wove a noose around the minds of the denizens of the Empire, which choked the life out of any spark of resistance. His rule was like some insidious, slow-acting poison, which gnawed away at the will of the people and planted obedience through the ever-present threat of punishment.

It was brutal for those who came out to oppose him. Dissent whispered immediately attracted reprisal since their voice was drowned out by the brilliant radiance of the power of Falk. He was the designer of fear, the protector of order, and the hallmark of the unbending force of the Empire.

It was this well-bred fear in which the Empire rejoiced, cemented at its base by the tireless drive of Falk toward uniformity. Under his helm, the Radiance Church was just such an effective instrument of such regulation, wherein its sermon and teaching sublimely underpinned the machinery of power he created in minute detail. His voice seemed to reach into every street, bringing the presence into every home, every corner of the Empire.

Yet, beneath this veneer of discipline, a spark stirred in rebellion. Hidden well from prying eyes, deep in the bowels of the city, this improbable band-an assortment bound in by the desire for freedom from the yoke-huddled together in secret conclave against the Empire's will. These were the rebels: a mosaic of misfits, outcasts, and dreamers, bound together under the exiled Shadow Mage known as Dax.

It came as a whisper against the steel wall that was the Empire, in a contrary breeze. Yet a dream lived on: to tear down the structure, shame the hypocrisy of Falk's false Light, rise once more into a free world. Standing free from control and deluding themselves into harmony, their course was clear: to head towards places not under their or their people's hegemony.

In front of them was the road not at all bright, with hazard. Standing in opposition to them was an Empire that had grown on fear and oppression; there was a regime fully in control of the hearts and minds of humankind. Yet, these were rebels with an unshakeable belief in another world, one where they were not pawns but free people shaping their fates.

It means that it was the time for an ideological crash-a confrontation between two giants. On one side was High Priest Falk, a creation of control with his powers amplified through Light Magic with blinding force. On the other stood

Dax, the exiled Shadow Mage, a beacon of defiance, his strength born from shadows and spirit of resistance.

Wrapped up in the struggle of the soul of the Empire were Light and Shadow, their borders blurred. For each force, a certain truth, a certain purpose-but there would be only one. The whispers of rebellion began raising the level of their voices down the corridors of power, challenging the iron grip of Falk with a new dawn, where fear would give place to freedom.

CHAPTER 5
PATH OF DEFIANCE

The world was vast and silent around her in the quiet aftermath of the decision that Sylvia had made. She had taken the first steps out of a life so long lived, shed the doctrines that had molded her, and left behind the high sanctum of the Imperial Radiance Church. Yet, however disorienting this unknown path was, Sylvia felt there was an unusual crystallization-a sense of self which thrilled and unnerved her.

The path in front of her was dark, the shadows dancing at the edges of her vision as she pressed farther away from sanctuary. Every step brought her more fully into the weight of her decision. The Radiance Church had taught her that darkness was a chasm to be overcome, its silence filled only with the purity of Light. But the moment the shadowed landscape stood around her, Sylvia began to wonder whether the Church had taught her half the truth. She knew there would be no turning back-for with denial of the Church came denial of the past-but she knew even better that to hold her silence was costing greater still. It was this reacquired freedom in which she chose truth over comfort.

As the city fell behind her, Sylvia stepped into the embracing arms of a thick forest where trees went high up into the sky to shut off the very last rays of daylight. The place was eerie yet strangely inviting, twilight filled with energy inaudibly humming inside her senses. It felt completely alien to the sterile corridors of the Church, as though Light Magic had been the only force that reigned there. And here the air seemed to vibrate with some raw, wild power-neither wholly Light nor Shadow, but an ancient thing strong in the earth, calling to her.

She stopped beside a narrow stream and knelt, the cool water running over her hands to center her in the present. On its reflective surface, her face shimmied, so well-known and yet so subtly different. Gone was that mask of duty; instead, there was a spark of independence, a good steel in those eyes. No more was she just Sylvia, an apprentice to the Radiance Church, but a seeker-a seeker who had chosen freedom rather than blind obedience.

As the darkness closed in around her, Sylvia found a strange sense of comfort in shadows thrown across the ground. They no longer carried the menace she had been taught to read from them; instead, they reached out-a silent acknowledgment of her defiance. The pulse of Light Magic within her, rather than the token of her control, was the guardian on a journey that probably wouldn't lead her to Power but maybe to Harmony.

. . .

The Church at one time spoke in very hushed tones about some sort of renegade Shadow Mage named Dax, speaking of him in equal measure of fear and loathing. The stories spoke of him as a heretic-a man who walked away from the light and into a path that embraced the darkness as a rejection of purity. But sitting here and reflecting on her own exit from the Church, Sylvia wondered whether the fear instilled in her had produced the rebellion in Dax-grown from an evil within him, or from something beautiful, a seeking after something greater, a truth beyond the grasp of Light's tight doctrine?

Anticipation coupled with uncertainty made her heart beat fast. She had always admired stories about those individuals who broke away, those who had the courage to seek some truth of their own. The more she sat here thinking, the more she connected with Dax somehow, like somehow their paths are not an accident. Both of them had chosen to step away from doctrines that molded them into what they are today.

In this, her spirit felt answer to the purpose given, a purpose common not to Light nor Shadow but to the balance between.

The moon rose, casting a gentle glow over the forest. Sylvia whispered her own quiet vow to the night air, her words barely a murmur. "I will find you, Dax. Together, we'll forge a path toward a world that embraces both Light and Shadow."

As night well advanced, the air grew cold, and Sylvia drew her cloak closer around her, her eyes fixed on the faraway hills. Beyond those woods, beyond even the reach of the

Church, lay another world-one full of secret terrors, limitless possibility, and perhaps finally, that elusive balance.

For now, she walked in these woods alone, touching the earth with silent steps, yet with each step upwards, her spirit rose, undaunted. Beyond the reach of power or redemption, she searched for freedom-freedom which shall not fear the dark but shared it as an equal fellow traveler to the light.

It was only the start of her journey, yet she felt Light and Shadow inside, those two parts making her whole, leading her ahead. Free from the narrow dogma, she was tied down by her self-carved ways of bravery and principles. Steps into an oath, never more to walk in silence or subjugation. Hers had been a path of freedom, of balance, and of Light born from embracing Shadow. Each step more deeply into the night, she knew was to be the beginning of a journey, not just for herself, but for a world ready for rebirth in harmony.

CHAPTER 6
SANCTUARY IN SHADOWS

Earth damp, weighted with hums of latent energy, the air stood upon itself in this underground town carved deep into the heart of the Eryal Continent-to hide from prying empire eyes. It was a haven within its labyrinthine tunnels and caverns, sanctity to the oppressed, where defiance grew.

Flickering torchlight danced across rough-hewn stone walls as life poured into a marketplace teeming with resilient life. Carts of scavenged goods rattled along the cobblestone paths, wheels creaking amidst a tide of boisterous voices raised in argument, the clash of metal against metal, and ringing hammer strokes against cold stone. This was not a city where greatness could find its home, but one birthed from resilience- a living testament to unyielding wills that once dared rise against the iron grasp of the Empire.

They had hewn homes out of the very rock; tapestries of weavings from rags adorned their walls. There were workshops, kitchens-smell and feel that spoke of improvisation and making do. Every nook and cranny spoke of the people's combined will to survive, to thrive. Down here, beyond the reach of the Empire, they were free.

The Citadel stood in defiance, gouged into the living rock at the heart of the city-a testament to defiance and union. It was within its imposing walls that the rebellion's strategists worked out plans, while their warriors were training for the fights they knew would surely come.

Dax was an exiled Shadow Mage, standing atop the highest rampart of the Citadel and staring down upon the city below.

It had brought him here, and the control over Shadow Magic that the Empire once condemned was embraced by the self-same entities that suffered under the order's jackboot. What Dax regarded as exile had changed; it freed him-where the Empire had wanted it to be an execution. His power was the guiding star, once a mark of shame, shining high for those huddled in this secret sanctuary.

He had seen firsthand the rot in the Empire, in the way Light Magic was one of dominion and not a healer. It was only word dressing so that the Church could tighten its stranglehold in the name of peace. In the name of harmony, they had bound people in chains of light, masking the reality of their exploitation. The Light in its blinding brilliance was a whip created with the purpose of keeping the masses in order, submissive. Standing beside him was Sylvia, the former Light Magic apprentice, who thought that blind obedience was profound clarity, and what had once guided her became chains she needed to break free from. What seemed like safety now was captivity. She could see how Light Magic was warped in an effort to control and manipulate.

Now that she knew of Light's power, she was using it for another cause-no longer as an instrument of the Church, but an instrument of the rebellion to do something with her gifts.

An unlikely pairing-a Shadow Mage, an apprentice of Lightpower, opposed and then joined in combat against an oncoming foe. Roots from different worlds, now joined as one in their aims: Freedom over Conformity, Resistance against Submission's end.

The Citadel creaked open its doors, releasing the draft of people coming from the gloom of the corridors. Before them now stood Kael, wiry, eyes quick and calculating. As the best infiltrator of the rebellion, Kael's motions were calculating like those of any archon thief; he knew things about the inner workings of the Empire, as if knowing its machinery inside out. Rebellion was personal for him, a vendetta forged in the fire of losing family to the relentless cruelty of the Empire.

Beside him stood Anya, an acutely keen warrior whose eyes seemed chiseled from the very steel she had been tempered in. In a very real way, her whole life had been training for this combat, but it wasn't until this rebellion that she finally had a cause-something more than herself to fight for. That was what made people-inspiring, uncompromising in the face of terror that the Empire's retaliation would necessarily bring.

. . .

These were but two of the faces among the faces that made up the Underground City: miners who descended into the darkness, forging tools and arms out of scraps, and healers who had knowledge in their hands-all put together, each to play his or her part in the struggle shared.

Where the Underground City stirred-an energy above and beyond the dark, a beacon of hope, a statement of the will of the human spirit to merely survive. It was not against soldiers or priests that they struggled, but against the Empire over their hearts and minds, pressing upon the will to be free with its heavy chains of fear and conformity.

It had murmurs of rebellion in its caves, an ever-beating cadence promising them a future whereby Light and Shadow were used not as tools of government but as active forces of concord. It was their story, one of resistance, of hope, of unyielding determination to rise against oppression.

CHAPTER 7
ALLIANCE OF THE FORSAKEN

T he air in the underground city was heavy with the scent of damp earth and smoke, that instantly familiar hint of what was above them: a world they lost. This sprawling city that lay beneath them was a labyrinthine tangle of tunnels and chambers carved in the heart of the mountain, pulsating with the mute hum of rebellion. The hood above his head cast a dim shadow over his face as Dax looked around the room; his eyes, cold and unmoving as the stone surrounding them, never once gave anything away. This was his sanctuary-where those who dared pit themselves against the Empire fled to hide, a haven from what ruled above.

He was accompanied by Sylvia, who stared around her in wide-eyed wonder at new surroundings, her pale face etched with both wonder and trepidation. Gone were the bright colors of Light Magic she had faced hitherto; subdued grays and browns dominated here, with stone and shadow ruling supreme, carrying testimony to the rebellion's struggle. "This is. different," she whispered, her voice hardly audible. "Very different.".

Different is what we need," Dax snarled; his voice low and rough. He turned back to her, his eyes intent. "We are free from their rules here, their deceit. We fight for freedom, not for control.

His words cut into Sylvia, coldly echoing all those chains she had torn to tatters, hypocrisy binding her all this time. So many years in the arms of the Imperial Radiance Church, forged from its doctrine, Light Magic was a power; once oh so great to her, it now insinuated purity and protection, starting to be seen in another light-a means of control, a weapon of the oppressors.

The Church," she begun, the recollection making her voice falter as memories arose unbidden, bitter with betrayal.

They're a disease," Dax said, breaking in-his voice cold, unfeeling. "They replace compassion with control, love with fear." He gestured toward the darkened tunnel that led out of the city. "We, on the other hand, are the cure. We're the antidote to their poison.

Her gaze turned to the darkness beyond, its unseen depth making her blood run cold. Grime might start to dig into her belly, but Sylvia also knew she had done the right thing: no longer constrained by the twisted truth of the Church, she was one of the many fighting in rebellion for a world free from the clutch of the Empire. Yet, there it chewed within her skull: she was a Light Mage, schooled in the very element with which she was fighting them.

"I know how the Church works," she finally said, her voice finally taking strength. "How they twist the Light, with their use of enslaving minds, erasing recollections." The fist of her hand clenched as determination began to harden within her. "I shall turn that to my advantage against them."

Dax nodded, a light in his eye speaking approval, his finding of a kindred spirit in Sylvia, another warrior with the scars of battle. The unlikely couple of Shadow Mage and Light Mage, joined together in the bondage of one fight against oppression. Quiet respect had silently started to grow between them, born of a life at the mercy of this cruel game of the Empire.

"We will know when to work as one," Dax said stubbornly. "Our strength is in our unity, so often the weapons that make us different."

He took her deeper into the city, among the hustle and bustle of the markets, the clanging of metal against metal, and the lowly dwellings burrowed into the stone, where one lived well-defiant with every gesture to defeat. Of course, there was more to this hum of the city, because this was more than an existence; it had a ring of resistance, a wild testimony to an unconquerable will of humankind.

. . .

It was a cavernous chamber, heart of the structure, warm in the golden light of the torches which gave it illumination, centred by a worn, weathered table, huddled about which were the leaders of the rebellion-faces cast by hardship, the eye lighting with the fire of purpose. This was the council-the brain and heart which functioned behind the struggle for liberty. Dax made Sylvia known to them. The low, rumbling note of Dax's voice deepened to vibrate through stone walls.

This is Sylvia," he said, his gaze still hard on the council. "She's chosen to come over to our side. She's a Light Mage, recognized by the truth in their power, and she's here to fight with us.".

Exchanges of cautious looks were made amongst the council; their faces closed off. Suspicion hung heavily in the air because to them, Light Magic symbolized the control of the Empire. But Sylvia met their scrutiny steadfastly with steady eyes, a fierce determination within them. She knew that more than words would be required to earn their trust, it would take an action.

"I'm here for freedom," she started, drawing out something from her voice that she never knew was there. "I know their lies, their control, and I am not going to be part of it anymore."

The skepticism etched upon the faces of the council members at his words melted into cautious hope. Rumors had reached them of a Light Mage who turned against the Church, tales that had filled them with silent hope. Perhaps, they thought, she could be an ally-a new weapon to turn against their oppressors.

Dax watched the exchange intently as cautious optimism raised his heart. In their eyes, he saw a flicker of acceptance, the will to let Sylvia prove her mettle. And though he knew that the trust of these people would take more time, he firmly believed Sylvia could turn into one of their biggest weapons, an unexpected strength to fortify their ranks.

The great council deliberated and decided to give her a shot. They dropped her into a group under Kellan, a grizzled Shadow Mage with a lifetime of experience. His mastery of stealth and subterfuge had made Kellan a legendary figure amongst the rebels-a thorn into the Empire's side, a constant reminder of how weak they could be.

A tangle in her stomach, torn between apprehension and grit, Sylvia followed Kellan from the chamber, knowing full well what lay ahead: the risk of stacking herself against the power she once served. Yet, she was to prove-really prove-that she was not a pawn of the Church, that she was a rebel determined enough to fight for a better world. She cast a rearward glance in Dax's direction, his features dimly outlined, and her heart swelled with gratitude. He had given this to her-both the chance to make things right, to use her knowledge and skills in the struggle against the lies of the Empire. Dax was a child of the shadows, a lord of dark arts-and yet, his heart was turned to ashes, consumed by fierce passion for justice, insistent devotion to freedom.

. . .

In an instant, Sylvia knew she found her place.

The path would be treacherous-the highway of lurking danger. She was prepared to face this hazard, standing shoulder to shoulder with this rebellion, united by one purpose: fighting together for a world where Light and Shadow no longer stood for mastery and bondage but for balance, harmony, and that liberty which would rise into a new morning.

CHAPTER 8
THE EMBER OF HOPE

The air in this underground city crackled with a layer of anxiety incredibly tinged with hope. At the middle of this cosseted haven stood Dax, the Shadow Mage in exile; around him, a band of rebels had cast aside the mantle of fear to fight for a world free from the unyielding grasp of the Empire. Together, they had hewn into rock and dirt a sanctuary: a testimoneum to persistence, a beacon, or the last denial to a regime grasping at every thread of their being.

Besides Dax stood Sylvia, the former Light Magic apprentice who had turned her back upon the Imperial Radiance Church. She represented something between Light and Shadow, proof of how blurry it gets, just how complicated the choices in their world are. What used to be her guiding principles were now being shown as means to manipulate, showing her that Light Magic had been twisted all along to maintain the Empire in its power.

. . .

Activity grated the city; a muffled hum of voices against the low purring of preparation, as everybody wove his or her single thread into the tapestry of rebellion. They had come here with faces branded by defiance and fear, and with lives risked daily for a future hardly imaginable. They knew rather well the length to which the Empire reached and how merciless the vigilance was. Yet, all this danger held a glimmer of hope, a thread of certainty that they would break these shackles. They had already chosen resistance and would not be pushed down by the forces of suppression.

It weighed on Dax-the hopes-of them all. Once branded a traitor, he was exiled for daring to question the Empire's authority.

Exile nailed him into a leader-a warrior with a desire for justice. He had watched in growing horror as the Empire, with sneaky deployment, used Light Magic against its enemies to stifle their voices and snuff out the radiance of freedom. His Shadow Magic, once a curse, was now a shield and a beacon of rebellion to freedom.

Sylvia stood beside him, her face set in a mask of resolution, her way to enlightenment barely begun. Indoctrinated through implicit teachings of the Church, she had been taught implicitly to believe in the goodness of Light and evil of Shadow; now she broke free from them. For true light was to be found not in blind obedience but in freedom to think, to question, to choose one's path. As evening embraced the stone walls of the city, so, too, the grand hall at its center enclosed within its walls Dax, Sylvia, and the freedom fighters. Shadows of fire leaped around the room, dancing across faces filled with determination and fatigue. What had once been a rebellion of hushed tones had unified into a roar for change, justice, and freedom.

The air was thick with anticipation until Dax finally spoke; his voice was low and powerful.

He spoke of a prophecy-a legend, passed down the ages, a saga that in that most forlorn of days had kept hope alive. It spoke of a Shadow Mage, one to rise against the grasp of the Empire-a warrior to contest its very foundations of power.

It was a prophecy that in this world, magic was to rewrite its essence, where Light and Shadow should balance, being the forces of liberation and not of control.

Yea, and with that, the rebels stood in rapt attention, their faces mixed with wonder and trepidation. Long had the prophecy been a whispered promise, a shimmering ray in a world that cowers under fear. Its words kindled the fire of utterance in the shadows of this underground haven-a call to take up the challenge, to give flesh to a promise that, through the years, kept alive the dream of free life.

Dax started explaining how the Empire corrupted Light Magic-curing and protecting-into a tool of enslavement. He spoke of how the time came when the reach of the Empire became so repressive, so complete, it was on the verge of smothering even the most minute sparks of rebellion. He conjured a shift in that balance, a revolution to shatter chains of bondage.

With every word, the prophecy seemed to breathe again-a reflection of their very struggle for freedom. In the tale of the Shadow Mage, each rebel saw his struggle, his sacrifice-the promise of the legend that would resound. They knew the dangers, the risks that would be run, and yet they were prepared to go through them for a world where their voices would no longer be silenced and they could live unshackled by fear.

"The prophecy speaks of a time when the Shadow Mage shall rise," Dax replied in a hopeful and believing tone. "Of a time when darkness shall rise against the false light. When magic itself shall change. It speaks of a warrior of shadows, a beacon of freedom, a champion to a world soaked in fear. It speaks of us."

There was a cheer among the rebels next, voices ringing across the cavernous chamber in a defiant cri-evening on stone. Faces aglow with fresh determination, alight with a strength which denied the darkness of the Empire, they did indeed know full well the road ahead would be hazardous and their victory not certain. Yet, for a world wherein they could breathe free, they would risk everything.

We are the shadow," he told them, almost in a battle cry; "we are the rebellion; we are the hope.".

• • •

His words were hurled back, cacophonous in defiance, as with one voice speaking, the rebels spoke. And in that bond of unity lay strength, in that cohesion of shared purpose, the resilience. They had come to rise, shake off the tyranny weighing upon not just their lives but their spirit, their very souls. They would dance in the darkness, willed by the denial of the rule of the Empire to a future wherein freedom could bloom.

From a mere whisper in the wind, the prophecy now seemed to be that very force pressing them onward, a promise to light the way through darkness. It spoke to him of the time when the Shadow Mage would lead, when the hold of the Empire would lie in pieces, and people would be let free from the chains of fear. It spoke of revolution-of a world where each voice could be heard.

Dax was the prophecy, now personified into the exiled form of a Shadow Mage, standing on the cusp of destiny. Entwined in the path of the rebellion lay his. He chose the shadows, not as a weapon of darkness but a path to freedom. He chose to stand against the Empire and to question the very building blocks of their world. He chose to hope.

Beside him, Sylvia stood, her spirit as driven as was his-a testament of will and unbreakable human spirit. She, too, had shaken off the dogma of the Church and wrapped herself in Light-not as a force to keep others under one's heel, but to heal, to strengthen, to free. And she chose freedom.

Before them stood their leaders-eyes lined with the will to persevere and the hope yet unquenched. They were the shadow, the rebellion-the embodiment of an ancient promise which refused to remain silent. Perilous would their journey be, unsure their triumph. United in this decision, they had chosen to fight-to risk all for a world that one day would be free. It was the battle for the soul of their world.

CHAPTER 9
RISING TIDES OF RESISTANCE

Thick with smoke from torchlight, heavy with the scent of damp stone, the air in the underground city vibrated with anticipation. The shadows danced along the cobbled streets, flickering across stone walls as Dax stood before the assembled rebels, his features set in stone. His voice rumbled in low tones, carrying across the square like a plucked string that struck a chord in every heart that listened.

"This is our moment," he said, his eyes aglow, unflinching in resolve, as the flickering light danced across faces in the dark around him. "The moment we break loose from chains that bind us, the moment we strike back against the tyranny that has crushed our spirits for far too long."

A cheer erupted among the masses, a surge of hope in an ocean of stone. This was a rebellion brewed in silence for years on end within-the seed of defiance buried so deep inside the heart of sufferers at the hands of the Empire. Tonight, whispers would roar, and silent resistance would flower into will-unyielding and unstoppable.

It was a very audacious plan-a desperate gamble against an enemy that very much seemed unconquerable. The target they had chosen was high-risk: the Empire's central resource hub, a large warehouse complex on the outskirts of the city, where the supplies for the Imperial army were kept. The complex was well-guarded and reinforced with stone and steel, yet the rebels knew that any tampering with this logistical operation would deal a crippling blow to the war effort of the Empire.

For months, they had prepared for this: poring over every nook and corner of the complex in search of weak points, assembling a plan of stealth and precision. Each brought their special skills, sharpened over years of survival, and willed their knowledge and tenacity into the weapons that would strike at the Empire.

Silvia stood beside Dax, her eyes shining with trepidation and determination. Her becoming a warrior was something in which she had never had much investment-so she had never really thought about it-but the suffering to which she had been exposed and the duplicity of the Radiant Church had incinerated her innocence into cold ash. She was ready for combat, her aptitude with Luminous Magic now an icon of resistance against those self-same forces that once deceived her.

. . .

They'll be expecting us," she whispered, and her voice was taut but level. "The Empire's eyes are everywhere.

Dax's eyes stroked the congregation of rebels-a motley union of battle-hardened warriors and iron-willed idealists, all who have pledged everything for that one heady sniff of freedom. "We go in quick, hit with precision, and are gone before they can say Jack Robinson.".

There was a silent signal pulsating across the city at midnight, some quiet call to arms that fluttered hearts. The rebels moved with swiftness, darting shadows down narrow alleys, their muffled footsteps upon the cobblestone streets. Cloaks and hoods cloaked faces as their fluid motions went noiseless- a tide of defiance flowing right into the heart of the Empire's stronghold.

Above the high warehouse complex-a fortress of steel and stone strong against the skyline of the city-the moon cast cold light. The torches danced in twirls along the perimeter, the eerie glow propelling soldiers into disciplined vigilance. Yet, the rebels had counted on that, knowing full well their most salient factor would be that of surprise, coupled with the power of coordinated assault.

First, there was an attack from the shadows: rain from the rooftop of a building not very far away, chopping through the dark, precisely deadly, fell guards before any alarm could be raised. In that instant, chaos erupted, and the rebels charged in all directions, their attack finely tuned.

. . .

Shadow mages sprang out of the dark, their outlines dissolving into the night as they summoned their deathly powers with deadly sureness. Blades of shadow cut through armor and flesh quicker than the blink of an eye, lethal. Light mages, bright in the dark of night, loosed dazzling flashes that confused the guards and gave very narrow windows of opportunity that the rebels did not miss.

Whirlwinds of steel and fury, the few remaining warriors under the leadership of Dax burst through the main gate. Each strike was a righteous one in all its anger, a fire forged and tempered through many bitter years of exile and suffering-a man denied his rightly deserved freedom. Every swing of his blade spoke testimony to the hardness he had managed to instill in himself, every step a reminder to him of this fight- a struggle for justice which made him whole.

Inside, the compound was all hell. The tinkle of the soldiers against the rebels filled the spacious hall with a sound of metal against metal. Yet, the rebels fought hard with a few resources but indomitable hearts. Few in men's number and with low strength, they relied upon their agility, ingenuity, and will of those that had nothing to lose.

Her Light Magic casting an ilky blue hue of light, Sylvia joined the fray with the rebels. Powers once used in the service of manipulation had now become weapons of freedom, heightened along with the Shadow Mages found standing around her. Moving with a fresh vigor, her magic was a shield of defiance-a muster to those standing beside her.

• • •

For hours, it had been a ceaseless conflict of steel, magic, and wills. That which once was the bulwark of the Empire's strength faced the rebellion as the field of its will. The air was a haze of blood and smoke, reminding one of sacrifices being made, how heavy would be the cost of freedom.

The fighting reached a crescendo at the first light of dawn. It was then-exhausted, yet unbroken-that the guerrilla fighters had sliced the vital supply route of the Empire, which would cause ripples throughout their ranks, a triumph wrung from the dark in testimony to their powers, their resiliency.

It was one of those victories that had come dearly: the warehouse lay in ruin, its shelves rubble, its floors slick with blood. The rebels sat around their fallen comrades, granting respect to the sacrifices made. Soft murmurs of grief and resolve shuffled the air-grave reminders of the price paid in blood for freedom.

The silent city now heard a hum of new sounds: the faraway wail of alarms, the hurrying feet of soldiers, the whispered fear and hope dancing through the underground city. It was then that the rebellion had landed its first blow: a message thrown throughout the Empire that the dark they sought to control had risen in defiance. The response of the Empire-a surge of most wrathful nature-would be swift on the rebels, but the spirit of the latter was anything but broken.

They had told the Empire that their valiant souls could not be destroyed and their conviction of freedom razed. Thus, the battle lines were drawn, and at one stroke the long war for liberation had begun.

CHAPTER 10
SECRETS OF THE CATACOMBS

Rumors of rebellion exploded in wild sparks down alleys and behind slammed doors in Aerilon, set into the hearts of those few that could even dare dream of freedom. The pitiless crackdown by High Priest Falk had laid a pall of terror over the city-but it had also fanned the flames of resistance to a resolve unquenchable by fear alone. Whereas the city superficially was very calm and tranquil, beneath that facade ran a river of rebellion; all it was waiting for was a match to strike.

Cloaked only by night, Sylvia slipped along quiet streets. The pounding of her heart against her chest-in cadence with the tension that seemed to hang in the air over Aerilon.

She knew well the danger her mission entailed tonight-the Empire's forces were mercilessly patrolling the streets, vigilant for even the slightest hint of dissent. Yet, she knew how vital what she had with her was: a message encoded in such a way only the rebellion could decipher, going directly into the hands of Dax and the inner circle. It was a road paved with betrayal and realization as her thoughts turned a corner. She had once been a follower of the Imperial Radiance Church, learning Light Magic and being prepared for mindless loyalty to the one man she was now trying to oppose. And complete was her belief in him until that fateful day when Falk's mask fell, showing her the rot lying beneath his veneer of righteousness.

At this moment, faith was dissipated, and loyalty had turned to ashes as fierce resolutions of finding an elusive truth took its place.

It was another move on that journey tonight-mission treacherous, yet necessary to the survival of the rebellion. In one swift movement, she darted into a shadowed alcove, her fingers instinctively skimming the coded message buried within the folds of her cloak, gaze circling for that signal to get her through the Empire's watchful net onto the rendezvous point where Dax would be waiting.

It was a low whistle, a signal cutting through the night. Swift and sure, she slid from her concealment down the darkened streets, each step closer to the heart of the rebellion, the very sanctum of resistance tucked deep in the catacombs this city had forgotten. Down there, she would meet Dax, report her intelligence, start laying the bed for the next strike into the rigid grasp of the Empire. Ancient statues' remains lay on either side of the steps leading down into the catacombs, fractured columns from a time when Light and Shadow were taken into harmony-memorials to a lost era, rubbed out by the heavy regime of Falk. Sylvia could feel a pang of affinity for such leftovers. She once had been afraid of Shadow, grown to think of it as an enemy to be overcome.

Now she realized it was a source of strength, a counterbalance that gave a power that Falk couldn't take from her.

As she went deeper down into the catacombs, the flickering shadows of wall torches danced dimly in firelight upon the rough stone. Standing tall at the hub of the open chamber, commanding yet calm-hardened by the adversity of a thousand sacrifices upon his shoulders-was Dax. Then there were the people of the rebellion, their eyes afire with the same fierce light, the same hunger in them for their emancipation, coming together in one collective act of defiance.

Closer leaned Sylvia, and in the pitch-darkness, their eyes met in that flash of reassurance crossing Dax's features, reminding him of the common purpose that drew them together in the first place. She handed him the coded message wordlessly, speaking in little more than a whisper: "Falk's forces are targeting the lower districts. They're erasing people's memories using Light Magic, changing the course of loyalties, even manipulating whole families. It's much worse than we thought. Dax's jaw clenched at the import of her words, his eyes darkening. "He tries to break the will of the people, snuff the rebellion before it can get a foothold. But that is to underestimate us. Every overt act of oppression just fuels our cause, strengthens our resolves.

. . .

Those present nodded as one, faces set, the resolve in their voices hushed and unruffled.

Dax turned to them now, his voice rising, a rallying cry across the chamber. "We fight for more than territory or revenge. This is the war for the soul of our people, the war to take back our minds, our freedom, our right to choose our own paths. Falk's Light blinds, yet the shadows are ours-they offer refuge, resilience, and a strength he cannot understand.

At that moment, Sylvia's chest swelled with pride-a deep-seated loyalty toward this motley host of outcasts and dreamers, warriors bound in a shared sacrifice. They were more than a rebellion; they were the promise of a world where Light and Shadow could dance harmoniously with each other, where freedom was not a dream but an attainable fact.

Dax spoke about the next strike, not an attack, precisely, but a thought-out move to strike at the very rule of Falk over the people's minds. Muscle, the rebellion knew by now, was not able to take down an Empire. They would have to cut at Falk's psychic hold-sew threads of doubt through the fear he had stitched into every corner of their world.

"We would send a message in code-whispers carried through safe channels," Dax said with a very mannered yet sure tone. "We want to touch the people's hearts with the reminder of the fact that there is still a choice for them, that they will never be alone. Though Falk manipulates their memories, he will never take away their hope.

. . .

As the scheme came apart, the feeling almost exhilarated Sylvia; as the moment of their own camp intensified for restored what was refused by Falk, not only to retain them but to recover all that had been withheld by him: tonight, the threads of rebellion would fall across all of Aerilon, indestructible yet invisible.

With the meeting closed, there were nods and silent signals of solidarity crossing between the rebels. But it was a while longer before Sylvia relented, her eyes nailed on Dax, who clapped his cloak over his shoulder to resume his post. It was rebellion personified, the figure that peered over the edge of the abyss and came back with a will hard as steel.

As she would have turned for the door, Dax caught her arm, his face softening. "Sylvia," he said quietly, "I know that you once believed in the Empire's Light. To turn away from that… I know it has not been easy.

She returned his gaze, a hint of defiance in her eyes. "I believed in what I thought was Light, Dax. But true Light doesn't bind-it frees. The Empire's Light was a lie. What we're doing here… this is where the real Light is.".

Her silent thanks shone in his eyes as he released her arm. There was a silent understanding between them in that one instant, a silent acknowledgment of the burden they both carried of having betrayed and fought against the very ideologies that defined them a long time ago. Together, they forged another path, one embracing shades of the past, and the advent they were fighting to bring into reality.

Sylvia came up from the catacombs, upwards into the open night, the torches dying out as she emerged into the open night. Before her sprawled the city in a darkness teeming with life in fire, rebellion. Her quiet, purposeful manner carried her through the streets tonight, when the rebellion's message was to spread: whispers of hope filtering through the hidden channels, denial even to the brightest of Falk's regime lies.

For it was in darkness that she found refuge, strength, and determination. Unencumbered by the deceptor's false Light, she was guided onto a truer path-one born of shadow, resilient and strong. And with each step she vanished into the night, she knew full well this was to be but the beginning of their journey, which would bring them all forth into freedom.

PART TWO
PATHS OF DARKNESS AND LIGHT

Dax and Sylvia move deeper into the fight, adding allies and learning more about the intricate, many times opposed nature of Light and Shadow. Their journeys showcase a lot of unexpected truths and moral complexities as they learn to balance their powers in contrast to one another. With each new alliance and battle, they realize even more the stake of their cause and the price to be paid for freedom.

CHAPTER 11
REMNANTS OF THE PAST

Dax stood alone at the room's center, the air thick with the acrid smell of dust and decay. Dim light filtered through cracks in the ceiling onto faded murals that adorned the walls: figures shrouded in shadow, to all appearances moving within the paintings themselves, their faces shrouded by swirling mists. They were the forgotten mages of old, masters of a certain Shadow Magic that had been outlawed and stricken from memory. It was in this inner sanctum, far away from prying eyes, that Dax had discovered something hidden well that could turn the tide of the rebellion. Centuries ago, the Empire had declared Shadow Magic too dangerous-a threat to the balance it claimed to protect.

His hand brushed against the surface of a stone plate; its weathered inscription was barely visible in the gloom. The words were ancient, an incantation forgotten, holding the key against the cynical grasp of the Empire. A very long time had passed since the Imperial Radiance Church had used Light Magic to dope the minds of the citizens into subservience and suppress rebellion. This provided him with a degree of hope, however-a glint of some strong power to burst their chains, born of resistance, born of darkness.

The words of the incantation were as smooth as silk from Dax's lips; with each utterance, a surge of energy would sweep through his body. The Shadow Magic was surging through his veins, exhilarating and daunting. That very darkness he had so feared, even suppressed, was giving him strength now-a weapon to break the chains of the Empire. But even as the magic began to work within him, he knew its dangers: as fire would burn as easily as liberate if heedlessly used and consume all he stood for and become another tool of tyranny.

As he backed away from the slate, the implications of what he had uncovered swallowed him whole.

He dreamed of the Rebellion no longer cowering under the blinding light of the Empire, but standing free, their minds unclouded, their wills their own. The ancient power would give them resistance-to fight for something greater than survival. Thing is, mastering its use required strength but also restraint so that it does not corrupt that very cause they are fighting for.

News of Dax's discovery spread like a bushfire within the shrouded city, instilling in the rebels a sense of hope. They had been fighting from behind the curtains for so long, strangled by such tight mental control by the Light Mages. Now, an essence of defiance seemed to seep into their being-a chance toward freedom. The first to hear included Sylvia, who hastened toward the old chamber in which Dax was standing, a look of fascination mixed with trepidation upon her face. In the poor light, Sylvia was able to set her eyes on Dax as he elaborated upon his discoveries. She had been training in Light Magic, but the time in this rebellion had proved to her how grave a lie the Empire had really been: the twisted use of magic as a tool of control. In its raw power, untamed, Shadow Magic was quite another thing altogether.

She had always felt for so long that Light and Shadow were opposites, one a source of healing, the other a harbinger of destruction. Then Dax's discovery challenged everything.

She couldn't read the ancient script on the tablet, but something of the power radiated from it, humming in the air around Dax. She watched him with interest-the way the Shadow Magic seemed to leak from him with a wildness so opposite from the control and rigidity she had been apprenticed to.

Light and Shadow," she murmured, almost to herself, the idea now crystallizing. "They've always said they're enemies, forces that can never coexist. But... what if they're wrong?

Dax turned to her, eyes flashing with curiosity. "What are you thinking?

She breathed deeply and her thoughts clicked into place with an eerie clarity she had not expected. "I know Light Magic can serve for good, but it has been distorted, controlled by the powers that be. But what if we can bring Light and Shadow together, merging their strengths so as to counter the hold of the Empire on the people?

Dax's eyes never left hers as his face moved with his thoughts. Extreme, to say the least-a uniting of groups that have fought through the ages, aside from dogma and doctrine. Yet, he knew how it all made much sense. United, their merged capabilities would become something formidable, a force perhaps strong enough to fend off controls, even at the hands of the Empire.

"It's risk," he said slowly; the spark of exhilaration in him could not be held down. "But if it pays off, it will perhaps give us the strength we need."

They just stood there, silent for a moment, the weight of their possible alliance settling in. To Sylvia, more than a strategy, this was an opportunity-to take back the real meaning of Light Magic, to free it from dogma and tyranny at the hands of the Church. A great idea sent her heart running, one that would enable her to forge her path and one that would redefine what power really means.

News of Dax's discovery and Sylvia's vision of new magic spread like a wildfire of anticipation throughout the hidden city. Rebels gathered in secrecy, speculating on what that could mean; their spirits now rekindled with the possibility to win for the first time in many months. For the first time in many months, they felt unity that did not spring from fear but from shared hope-to be able to stand together and use Light and Shadow as allies, not enemies.

In a darkened room, the heads of the rebellion sat around, faces carved by hope and caution. Years of relentless battle had taken their toll: their numbers had dwindled. Once more, it dawned in their hearts-a revelation of some ancient magic to resist the control of the Empire. But they, too, knew about the fire and brimstone of such power they were playing with, and how one misstep could pollute all that they were fighting to preserve.

After much deliberation, the decision taken was to proceed but with caution. Dax and Sylvia were to develop this new form of magic further, test all the limits of what was possible with it lest it turn into one of dominion. A source of freedom and never a tool of control.

Not a word was said between Dax and Sylvia as they emerged from the meeting. A look spoke it all: this was going to be a fated journey ahead, one that called for much restraint and wisdom. But together, they would embark on the new journey of Light combined with Shadow, which surely would unshackle the world paralyzed by fear.

It had now become a movement, a beacon for all aspiring toward freedom, no longer a simple gathering of resistance. They were to fight, not in small factions, but united, and with that hope they would beget a new dawn where Light and Shadow, not as enemies, exist as a symbol of a world that is in balance and free.

CHAPTER 12
THE PRICE OF FREEDOM

Outside, woodsmoke hung heavy in the air, along with anticipation, as Sylvia stepped across the threshold into a new understanding. The rebels were growing bolder, testing the boundaries of the Empire's authority more aggressively, and Dax was resisting the Emperor's control. Yet for Sylvia, the triumph was hollow. She had known for years that something was intrinsically wrong with the Radiance Church, that something in the lessons being taught had manipulative overtones. Yet her loyalty had been steadfast—until the rebellion shattered every reason she'd so painstakingly built for herself.

Now, smothered by brutish Shadow Mages, she felt unmoored, like her foundation unsure. The Shadow Mages spoke to her of balance, a completely foreign concept for her. She had been raised to understand Light as pure-the embodiment of good-and to rebuke Shadow as evil-corrupt by its very nature. Yet, resilience in the form of resistance against darkness could not be tamed.

· · ·

One night, huddled around a tiny, flickering fire, Dax spoke of legends of old-of Shadow Mages who could harness their powers in order to amplify Light. Sylvia listened closely as her skepticism gave place to curiosity. She had learned that Light and Shadow can never be reconciled, destined always to be set against one another. How could they possibly be joined?

"It's like a spark," Dax said in a low voice, his eyes gleaming with the fire. "A small flame you can snuff out, but if you feed it, give it its head, it's an inferno."

Sylvia's brows furrowed and her fingers writhed in the edge of her cloak. It was years she had spent mastering Light, honing it to heal. To heighten it felt unnatural, even perilous-like igniting a holy fire with fuel, knowing it would spiral out of control.

"But how?" she asked softly, not hiding the doubt in her voice. "How are we going to combine Light and Shadow, which cancel each other out?

Dax gave her a small, knowing smile. "You already have the answer, Sylvia. You just haven't allowed yourself to see it.".

He then clarified that Light, in and of itself, was not a gentle force; rather, it was energy-molded and sculpted by intent and purpose. The Emperor and the Church had warped it, twisting its potential to their whims. In like manner, with a balance from Shadow, Dax explained how he thought Light could be returned to its purest form.

"The ancient Shadow Mages discovered that with some sort of ritual, they could funnel Shadow's energy and raise Light with it," Dax continued. "It is a sensitive balancing act, but together, they can become something much stronger."

Sylvia's heart suddenly raced as Dax's eyes fixed on her. "You know Light Magic, Sylvia. You understand its power. It is now time for you to open to the Shadow-to embrace its' potential.

A maelstrom churned in her stomach. She had never walked against the rules, never questioned the Great Teachings of the Church. And yet, here was Dax telling her otherwise; the mere presence of Shadow Magic stirred in her a deep ferment. It was as if the Shadow held a missing piece of the puzzle, a fragment of the truth so long hidden from her by the Church.

With a deep breath, Sylvia steeled herself to trust him. She had seen what the power of the Emperor did: how it distorted, how it enslaved. And she saw in the bravery of the rebellion against that power the right to be in honest opposition with the Empire-to have something more than Light. They needed Shadow.

She closed her eyes and oriented her awareness to the stream of Light within. She could sense its warmth, the old gentle pull, yet now it was stifled, constrained by dogma she'd long since discarded. She visualized it differently-unshackled, merged with Shadow, a force as unstoppable as it was ruinous. She plunged deeper into the darkness of Shadow, feeling its feralness, its will to resist constraint.

The instant she would attempt to bring them together, they wrestled in a stormy turmoil of energy that seemed to tear her focus asunder, each force fighting for mastery. But Sylvia was unrelenting, will unbending. She still breathed, was seeking harmony, making the energies coexist. Hesitantly, they started to integrate. The Light was afire with Shadow as a strengthener, hotter, more vivid, but the Shadow was softened, refined by Light.

Sylvia gasped, the surge of power heightening, sharpening her senses, the world expanding around her. The light was no longer just that gentle healing force; it was a weapon, able to protect and destroy. The Shadow that had been so chaotic, so wild all the time, finally took the form of a shield-a resilient layer of protection. She felt she could reach something really ancient, something that should have been encoded in the very being of magic.

The eyes opening in a new world of fire and rebel faces, night itself, seemed to vibrate with an uncanny resonance she had not known was there. She saw Dax's face above her, and her heart ran riot between terror and exaltation. She saw, impossible by the doctrines of the Church-a power which would shift the balance of the world.

. . .

But that power had its own weight in responsibility-she was no longer just a disciple of Light but was to be a vessel for both Light and Shadow, a force to heal or destroy. She stepped into uncharted lands, treading upon a power that could easily consume her if she lost control.

The rebels circled her, staring in awe and curiosity, for they could feel it: a change, a new power radiating from her. Amidst them, Sylvia looked and spoke, her voice firm but ringing with conviction.

I have witnessed what the Light can do by itself, and what it becomes when corrupted. And so, I have come to hold close the Shadow-not to defeat, but to forge a new path: one that will free us from the fetters the Church has laid upon us.

Dax smiled, the fire of pride alight in his eyes. "This is but the opening salvo in so much more, Sylvia-the Empire twisted our beliefs to keep us divided. But united, with Light and Shadow balanced, we get one chance to try and reclaim what was torn away from us.

A murmur ran among the rebels, lighting anew faces with fresh hope. Of course, it would not go well-they knew that further on lay long roads of much danger. But Sylvia's breakthrough told them what lay beyond the Emperor's grip: a world where Light and Shadow could coexist, a world where freedom was not a fairy tale far, far away. The only light came from the dying embers of the fire into which she was staring, and Sylvia knew that the future was bleak. This was something that could remake everything and was sure to bring only ruin if used unthinkingly.

The fine balance she would have to treat it with required wisdom and handling so as not to make her the very force of oppression she was trying to overthrow. But deep in the bottom of her heart, it had set ablaze a fire. She would walk this road, take the strength of Light and Shadow, and forge her destiny anew: not just hers, but that of all dreamers of a world free from tyranny. She would fight, not as Light Mage or Shadow Mage, but as a bearer of balance.

Therein lay the balance of peace, for a purpose that reached far beyond the bondages of the Church that held her in chains. For the very first time, Sylvia felt really free.

CHAPTER 13
GATHERING ALLIES

News that it had just won its first battle-the Battle of Whispering Falls-set tongues wagging on the Eryal Continent: it was the beacon of hope knifing through the gloomy oppression that for so long had kept that whispered freedom stifled by the iron grip of the Empire, confined to murmurs in shadowed alleys and hushed exchanges in hidden dens. But now those whispers had become loud, reaching the noisiest marketplace, the silent village, and even to the most magnificent hall. The spirit of rebellion was stirred, lighting a spark within the defiant ones who had suffered at the tyranny of the Empire.

What started off as a no-account band of misfits and runaways was slowly growing into an alliance from across the continent: traders, farmers, fighters, and nobles alike-united in a bond for freedom, coming from the four corners of the continent, brought together by that most resilient of hopes: perhaps this once, things could be different.

. . .

News of rebellion had reached even the far north, unto the ears of the Kingdom of Aethel-King Eldrin.

An staunch friend to the Empire, he considered firm and implacable his loyalty to the Imperial Radiance Church. But with the tightening grip of the Empire-the growing taxes and the increased interest of the Church in his people-some fires of discontent planted themselves right within his borders. With each passing day, there are more strident rumors of uprising, a persistent undercurrent of resistance against which his precarious stability would likely shatter into splinters of wood.

Bound as he was to the Empire, Eldrin could hardly disregard the growing discontent of his people. Success by the rebellion shook even his confidence in the Church's ability to control and cast doubt over years of allegiance. It was a turning point for him: faithfulness with the Empire or the alienation of his people and unrest in his kingdom.

Days of cautious deliberation later, bold was the decision taken by King Eldrin, thinking of safeguarding his kingdom against the surging tides of rebellion yet maintaining a degree of loyalty to the Empire. He sent a discreet emissary to Dax. The no-man's-land rebel camp deep in the night saw the arrival of Lord Alaric, a seasoned diplomat and close confidant of the king, with one cautious proposition in mind.

"Aethel will support your rebellion in secret," Alaric said, his voice low as he met Dax's gaze. "We'll provision you and grant you safe passage through our lands. We'll also pass on any information we gather regarding the Empire's movements. But in return, we expect that should your rebellion succeed, you'll raise some sword arms to protect Aethel from the Empire's wrath.

Dax listened without expression, knowing full well that it was a ploy as much as a gesture of support. Aethel's alliance did much-needed resources to the rebellion, but to him, it just felt wrong-working with a kingdom still nominally loyal to the Empire. Dax had always felt that true freedom was to be clear of shackles, not masters swapped.

It was Sylvia who finally broke the silence, her eyes resolute as she turned to Dax, "We have to be realistic: knowing that Aethel is behind us, even in secret, emboldens us. If we are going to go further, to fight the Empire, we will need allies. This alliance could prove to be the push we may get. Dax nodded, her words an echo to his mind. Reluctantly, he extended his hand to Alaric, sealing the pact. The silent support of Aethel would add weight to their cause-a necessary compromise in a world where pragmatism almost always sailed above idealism.

News of the alliance between Aethel and spread fast, creating ripples throughout the other kingdoms.

Conceived at the heart of the continent, the Kingdom of Ebonwood was home to mighty warriors and archers under the rule of King Gareth. Gareth was a discreet ruler, staunchly loyal to the Empire, yet above all protective of his people. As rumors of the pact Aethel had made spread, Gareth called his council in secret deliberation, weighing a decision that might very well seal his kingdom's fate.

"Join the rebellion, and invite the Empire's wrath," said one of his advisors, in a somber tone. "Our people might suffer in that case."

"But to do nothing," Gareth protested, "is to betray their hopes-their aspiration to something better. The people of Sendeth have lived beneath the iron hand of the Empire long enough, their freedom receding a little more with every passing year.

After much arguing, Gareth called it: Ebonwood would openly support the rebellion against the Empire, joining Dax's Shadow Mages and Sylvia's Light apprentices. Gutsy move, hence Gareth found himself appealing to the masses of Ebonwood-the people had been ruled under the Empire for too long, and now they saw real change with the rebellion on their side. The rebellion grew stronger and continued to rise, its ranks swelling with a new wave of allies, each kingdom bringing its particular strength and variety of burdens. The Kingdom of Solara, lying to the south, had always fared poorly under the Empire's trade restrictions. Its once-booming coastal cities had been stifled by exorbitant tariffs, their merchants weighed down by the tight, monopolistic grip the Church held over the trade routes. Victories of the rebellion encouraged this people, and in most intense determination to get back to freedom and prosperity, it became one with it. And thus, Solara proved a priceless bedmate, for with their knowledge of the trade routes, the rebellion might find a new way across the continent. Their skilled artisans did much in the way of arming the rebels with arms and tools they so desperately needed. In return, the rebellion promised to free the people of Solara from the Church's economic stranglehold, to free their cities from the hands of the Empire.

Greater influence by the rebellion meant greater renown.

People started looking up from the little village to the grand kingdom for Dax and Sylvia-not as leaders, but as beacons of hope and defiance. The rebellion, instead of being merely some once-in-a-while, unclothed band of misfits that actually struggled to survive, began to take a different meaning: one of the strongest bonding forces across the continent. With every victory and every alliance, it grew stronger, feeding the belief that the Empire's oppressive rule could be overturned.

But with each new alliance came a new set of challenges. Dax knew the success of a rebellion required more than just increasing numbers; it needed unity. The rebels came from varied backgrounds, each kingdom with its own reasons and pasts.

The Southern artisans arriving with their skills, the Northern soldiers with their strength, and the Ebonwood archers with deadly precision-all brought their different strengths and expectations, if not doubts. Keeping these in alignment to one vision would require diplomacy, sacrifice, and a will of iron. Later that night, as they all sat around the fire, talking about what was to happen next-so to say-Sylvia spoke her own anxieties. "We've gained so much and yet risk losing ourselves within it. Each of these kingdoms has its own vision as to what the future should be. If we don't stay true to our purpose, we might just end up fighting each other instead of the Empire."

Dax nodded, his words deep within him. "We don't just fight for victory but for a better future where freedom is equally divided. We can't let these alliances become our new chains.

The next morning, Dax spoke at the campsite, which had swelled into the ranks. His voice burst out across the hum of murmurs. "Each one of you has joined us here because you want to see a different future without the stranglehold of the Empire. Diverse skills, diverse histories, most importantly, diverse motivations-but one fixed purpose: taking back our freedom. And so as we leave here tonight, as we leave here tomorrow and in the days to come, let us remember that every step we take, every alliance we make is because of that vision.

Spirits renewed, the people cheered, and in that very moment, it became something other than just an alliance-but a token of defiance that razed kingdoms and titles. Dax knew full well that from that day on, everything was going to get worse: the road ahead would be lined with difficulties, and the Empire would strike back with all its might. Yet, he knew equally well that once the fire of freedom had been lit, it was hard to douse. From the underground city at the hub of the rebellion to the ornate halls of Solara and the thick steppe of Ebonwood, this spirit of rebellion flowed out and fostered just the sort of unity the Empire had so long worked to suppress.

. . .

On and on, the kingdoms rose individually, while voice after voice continued to rise across the continent in defiance of the iron-ruled Empire. And for the first time, people dared believe in a tomorrow where the light of freedom might just be a little brighter than the darkness of oppression.

CHAPTER 14
ECHOES OF THE FALLEN

In every corner, it would have seemed that Light should have flourished in the Imperial Radiance Church, tinged there with shades of gloom in solemn halls. Every step Sylvia made upon the marble floor caused soft echoes down the great, high corridors. An apprentice of Light Magic, such halls had always seemed the well of wisdom and purity to her, though now, beneath the surface, she sensed subtle hairline cracks in the veneer, unease even among the most devout followers.

A murmur of doubt had reached her ears among the acolytes: whispered conversations between the senior clerics, who glanced over their shoulders before uttering a word. It would seem, in those halls, perturbation flowed quietly down an undercurrent of dissent, though nobody dared to confront High-Priest Falk openly. Something was in the air-fear, loyalty, and just that itsy-bitsy little bit of skepticism, the feeling that Light Magic in its clearest form was actually adulterated to act as an agent of domination rather than a cause for healing.

. . .

She passed by a knot of young initiates, Sylvia caught one of them-a boy no older than twelve-who stared at her with wide, questioning eyes, his face a picture of reverent uncertainty. He looked away almost immediately, frightened to be caught thinking thoughts he wasn't supposed to. It suddenly dawned upon Sylvia that she was not alone in feeling the fissures beneath this shining veneer of perfection.

Down in the bottom of the temple, she came to a stop in front of a huge stained-glass window depicting the Radiant Ascension-a mythic tale sublimed in the doctrine of the Empire. Light Magic, with colors of shimmering beauty, fell from above upon the floor and overwhelmed. Now she could see that this place, which once had been her sanctuary, had also been a gilded cage-a product of the Empire's grip on the very heart and mind of its people.

Lost in thought, Sylvia jumped at the sound of approaching footsteps. She turned to see Elder Maros, one of the oldest priests of the Church, known to one and all for his tireless commitment to the High Priest, a countenance chiseled by the passing of time, yet reflecting now some tacit perturbation, as he stretched out a hand-even his eyes flashing between command and indecision.

Child, it's unsafe to prowl these halls with such a contemplative mood in your eyes," Maros warned in a hushed voice, soft and gentle. "The Light guides us, yes, but even the Light becomes able to blind if one dares gaze beyond what he is to see.

. . .

Sylvia nodded, choosing her words delicately. "Elder Maros, is it true Light and Shadow were once learned as complementing forces, the balance of both a path hallowed once?

Maros's face drew tight, and he glared about before answering, as if even the walls might betray him. "You ask perilous questions, Sylvia, but indeed, there was such a time when Light and Shadow were not perceived to be enemies. Long before the wider-doctrined age took hold, even before the High Priest brought the conglomeration of ideas into one clear vision.

A moment of silence passed as they so stood; and for the first time Sylvia saw something else in Maros's eyes-something akin to regret, or perhaps the least shadow of doubt.

Some things are forgotten for a reason," he whispered, his voice low. "The High Priest has found control in unity, but in control, we lost perhaps something greater. Do not let your curiosity draw you into darkness, Sylvia. Some truths are dangerous to those who can't bear the weight.

The words from the Elder struck deep inside, stirring her to a decision. She started to realize that even at the very heart of the Radiance Church, there were those questioning whether this road they had been forced to take was right. The concern for Maros was palpable, but the subtext-perhaps not all within the Church had been silenced-was equally strong.

. . .

It was then that reality hit with a bitterness, as Maros swung around and walked away.

She could stay within its walls-bound by dogma to which she once felt was right-or take the path that took her away from this gilded prison. It was at that point that, however, the choice was no longer one of obedience but instead a question of purpose: finding guts to hold onto what she feels is true, even if it takes her from everything. Later, in her quarters, Sylvia lay staring up at soft, silvery moonlight struggling to make its way through the window. Her head stirred with the words of Maros and the probing stare of the young initiate. She knew to remain was to repress her doubts, to continue down the path twisting Light Magic into something it will never be.

Yet to leave would have demanded an impossible strength of will and the determination to live in opposition to that very institution which had formed her.

With one last, soft breath, Sylvia finally stood; her heart heavy, it was set. She started to gather her things, and every article reminded her of what had been and what she must be. No longer would she be Sylvia, obedient apprentice, bound by dogmas that turned Light into means of domination but transformed into Sylvia, the balancer, protector of truth embracing within itself Light and Shadow. Free, she felt the power surge in her veins as she slipped silently out into the night. She turned her back upon the false Light of the Empire, walked into a new dawn of freedom, where the harmony of

Light and Shadow might one day flower once more.

A silent prayer escaped her heart for those she had left behind, the young initiate, Elder Maros, and all the rest who were waiting with stilled breaths in darkness to find strength to step forward into the light.

CHAPTER 15
A BOND OF LIGHT AND SHADOW

The sun this morning sifted between the trees, laying lacelike patterns on the forest floor, drawing Sylvia once more to that place which had first then frightened her-a strand of abandoned edge of some ancient Imperial outpost. Whispers of the Empire's power remained here, rags of resistance clinging grimly to the present. Scattered fragments of broken walls and fallen statues spoke volumes: symbols of a regime that had demanded even from her obedience.

It wasn't nostalgia that had brought her here; it was clarity. The recent victory at Whispering Falls had lit the fire of rebellion, but there was much that remained set in fast concrete inside her head. It would be the reflections in herself and those standing in opposition against them that should shed light on the way forward, not their torches. It is the silence that reminds her of the ruins of her old life: allegiance to the doctrines of the Empire and Light Magic for reason in control.

. . .

Picking her way cautiously through the debris, she became conscious that others were near her.

Ania, a fighter and a rebel, had steel-cutting glances and a light hand resting on the hilt of her sword. All her life, living under oppression, had chiseled her face, her scars testimony to the losses she had borne, her eyes screaming with the resolution never to let such a thing happen again. Her features softened as her eyes met Sylvia's, revealing a few ripples of compassion beneath the tough edges of this warrior.

These ruins," Anya whispered with bitterness, as if memories of pain lingered. "These ruins mark the last hold of the Empire here. Once, I was forced to go down on these stones, branded as a dissenter. My brother stood next to me, but only I ever walked away. A pang of guilt twisted within her as realization slowly seeped into her conscious-that indeed, she had taken part in this very system that had scarred this poor girl. Anya was the silent testimony to the sea of others that suffered from what was touted as "Light." And Sylvia had taken part in it. The weight of this knowledge weighed heavier upon her than any blade could. Now, Dax rose among them, powerful and balancing with the wounds dealt upon him. To his own cost, he knew how it was to fight against imposed identity-to fight out a night for clarity.

Sylvia drew confidence from his own devotion to the revolution, but beside him, she felt bolstered yet at the same time pressed-he was the inescapable reminder of the principles she was only beginning to set in cement.

· · ·

She took a deep breath, her gaze sweeping across the ruins, almost as if from the debris would emerge the faces of those people who had to serve every whim of the Empire, faces that once looked up to her for guidance with faith unyielding to dogma within the Radiance Church. Her head was filled with just how wrong it had all gone-a rain of guilt.

Yet beyond the guilt, a new stirring of purpose began. The obedient apprentice of only a few weeks ago, hitherto following every command without the least question, was gone. She was here to take Light Magic from under the yoke of oppression and to use it as a force of unity, not control.

What do you see here?" Dax's voice cut through the silent-quiet and pierced. So simple a question, an invitation to wrangle her internal world.

Sylvia's eyes clouded, and finally, her words began to tumble out in a measured tone, weighing each word. "I see.-domination. A world where Light was yielded as a weapon, the gift of healing distorted beyond recognition." Her voice fell soft now, laced with ruefulness. "A part of that I was, and in that, I did believe, though something deep inside felt.wrong.

Dax nodded, brilliance aglow in his eyes. "We have faced darkness, enforced upon us or born of our choosing. But that's why we're here-on this journey." He laid a grounding hand on her shoulder. "Light and Shadow are the two facets of one whole. The Empire did indeed teach you discipline, but it is for you to decide what that power serves.

. . .

Among them emerged Rian, one of the eldest members of the rebellion, his face cut by years of hardship, and quiet wisdom etched into his eyes. A former novice of Light Mage, Rian was excommunicated by the Church because he had some curious thoughts on the balance Shadow Magic could bring. He had to face exile and isolation all those years until he found refuge with the rebellion.

The teaching of the Empire was never about balance, Sylvia," Rian said, the weight in his words heavy with betrayal. "It used Light to bind us, to blind us. The teaching should be Light and Shadow-they are meant to thrive together. The Church erased that truth because they feared the strength true balance would bring.

There was a clarity in Sylvia's heart, welling inside her as never before. She saw parts of herself, echoes of her past-which she was so gradually learning to confront-in Anya's fierce resolve, in Dax's strengths, in Rian's wisdom. Now was the time for her to reconstitute her belief: to hold Light not in the role of an oppressor, but as a beacon for unity and hope.

Every step quite literally pressed Sylvia deeper into the ruin with each other closer toward conciliation with her past. She felt the echoes of her old self wither, replaced by crystallized resolve: this was not a rebellion meant to tear down the physical presence of the Empire but also the ideological walls which pitted Light against Shadow and strength against compassion. As it was now time to walk her way back to the rebel camp, much of the burden in Sylvia's heart started to lift, shadowed by determination. She wasn't any tool for the Radiance Church but rather a keeper of balance-somebody able to use Light honorably. Now was the time to build such a future in which Light and Shadow would not be struggling against one another but find their place and complement each other, their nature accepted and understood. Dax glanced over at her, a slight smile tugging at his lips. "You're ready," he said simply, his voice filled with conviction.

Sylvia met his gaze, her eyes bright with newfound certainty. "I am. I'm ready to fight not just for freedom, but for balance—for a world where Light and Shadow can coexist as equals."

With a grim determination in their heart, they returned to camp, knowing full well that in their war against tyranny, a place in the future had to be found for every force, for every form of life. The chokehold of the Empire would break, stone by stone, to raise in its stead a world ordered by Balance, not at dominion over all. As shades across camp lengthened, the silence hardened into steel within Sylvia's heart. She now knew her purpose: one far removed from the doctrines of Light, which used to enshroud her from within as an apprentice. The battle-worn Sylvia, a warrior of balance, would not take Light as a weapon; she would instead hold it as an illuminating beacon of hope.

CHAPTER 16
TRIALS OF FAITH

It was a path of sorrows: a race of inexorable wills and endurance on to Imperial City. A host of surviving warriors and dreamers, united in their common dream of deliverance, journeyed through a landscape traumatized by the cruelty of the Empire. Deserted villages stood at every turn of the way, showing gutted houses with caved-in roofs-mute witnesses to the chokehold the Church held on the land. The very air was thick, as if the earth itself had grieved from all its suffering under the Empire's reign.

Every mile bespoke new reminders of what they were up against: rugged terrain and fractured communities, each remaining piece of a brighter past. Across the mountain passes, forts dotted the ruins, proud bastions left in ruin, their stones bearing scars from Imperial battles long past. It was here, over these treacherous highlands, that patrols of Light Knights came into contact with the rebels. Brilliantly armored, the soldiers were draped in the grim conviction of the zealot. Every confrontation was a fanatical adherence to the very opposition between hope and oppression that the Church had come to represent.

Every move for Dax was an issue of leadership thrust upon him, rather than asked for or expected. To others, he was hope-a freedom leader whose subversive activities branded him the target of the empire's most severe punishments and therefore the Shadow Mage. It was a mantle of responsibility weighing heavily on his shoulders-an unbending weight whereby every defeat and every life lost placed blame upon him. His companions were betrayal and loss, the whispered doubt against the decisions he'd made, the paths he'd chosen, what he'd asked others to give up.

The horizon was his target, undeterred, whereby he had, in turn, encountered a certain resolve in Sylvia, a former disciplina of a Light, and her belief unshaken steadied him. What Sylvia knew of the Church-its manipulative rituals to be precise-had proved to be very useful. She was part of that world once, bred from its doctrines and bounded with the same rigid faith. Now she applied that very understanding as a sword against it, guiding the rebels through the dangers of Light magic and twisted teachings that kept people enslaved.

Sylvia herself was tormented by her own personal demons, all those years of training instilled into her mind the doctrines of the Church. The lines between right and wrong blurred into indistinction with the memory of the manipulation she once had taken for gospel. Yet, even as much as the rebels she was now fighting, and with them her heart remained, a shadow of doubt pulled.

. . .

She cast upon herself an aura of light magic with a determinate look, though aware that the very same power she used to protect the rebels might be warped into an instrument of oppression. It is that complex reality that continually haunts her, challenges her to stand forth and be true in a world in gray shades.

But the journey also brought alliances with kindred spirits from across the Empire.

To their number came the Wildwood archers-quick and sure-their lifelong existence on the borders of the Empire's lands instilling their marksmanship. In company with them came the warriors of the Stoneborn, a mountainous northern tribe, strong and resilient. Every new face, every added skill brought various and different points of view to thread the rebels together in one thin strand of common purpose.

With every step closer to the Imperial City, the graver was their procession. The way began to wind itself, the rich countryside slowly thinning out before giving way to scrubby fields and crooked trees, with the life squeezed out of the soil. Before them rose the Imperial City: a block of stone and steel ringed in with walls throbbing with Light magic. It served both as a symbol of terror and a fortress of command, a towering reminder of the seeming invincibility of the Empire's grip.

. . .

Every night, out under the stars, the chill of the air coldly reminded them of the dangers that closed in. Patrols were near; their movements echoed across the quiet, and the rebels slept lightly, ready for treachery or surprise attack. The landscape seemed to reflect the turmoil within their hearts, since every step took them nearer the dark core steeped in the tyranny of the Empire.

It just painfully reminded him of the price of the journey of rebellion: to see villages razed, landscapes desolate. It indeed brought home the urgency of the cause, yet at the same time, it spoke about the power that they were pitted against. A force that was energized by hope, against a well-oiled empire of fear and power.

Dax walked in silence, his thoughts heavy with what was to come, for he had seen so many lives to their end, so many cut short in their fighting. Every mile, every fallen village, weighed a little more. The Imperial City was to be the most dangerous assault yet-the culmination of their struggle and the field that was to seal their cause, one way or another.

With him came a familiar mixture of resolution and trepidation. The methods of the Empire were nothing new to her-the coldness with which the Church went to any length in order to keep people in their grasp. The city was fortified, not just by stone, but by the mighty wards of Light magic, the signature and testament of the influence of the Church-an obstacle that seemed impossible to overcome.

. . .

Still in her, a low fire of determination was always burning because she hoped that once the people could see behind the mask of the Empire, they would rise with her against it.

As dusk fell, the rebels set camp on a cliff that loomed over the Imperial City. The fortresses lay sprawled below them, a harsh silhouette against the setting sun. Its spires lanced into the firmament, radiating an almost unholy light-one could feel the very presence of the Church. It chilled Sylvia; yet, it reminded her of why they fought.

They sat huddled around the small flickering fire; fire shadows danced across the faces of the people. Dax spoke to them in a clear firm voice with the weight of seriousness. "We are close now," he started, his eyes sweeping the worn, yet determined face of each before him. "Tomorrow, we take on the heart of the Empire, the very wellspring of oppression we have fought to bring to an end. This is the battle that will decide it all.

A hush befell them as the weight of those words settled in. The Imperial City was more than another stronghold; it was the manifestation of the Empire's rule, the epitome of the Church's grip that strangled their lives.

"This will not be an easy task," Sylvia added, her voice even, yet hard as stone. "They will resist in order to preserve their power, to save the lie they have woven over these lands. And let me remind you-our power lies in our unity. We have overcome hardship; we have faced loss. We know why we're here, why we fight. And let's show them the strength when Light and Shadow stand together. And to them, the words were like a spear to the hearts of the rebels, instilling an unrelenting drive within them.

Knowing full well the danger and the moment for which they had fought and sacrificed all, they could not give up now. The night wore on as they sat in silence, enveloped in their own thoughts. Far off against the horizon sat the dark phantom that was the wall of the Empire, but down in the heart of the rebels, something started to birth. Shattered by the deaths and defeats, yet they stood there, united and ready for the fight to take it right to the oppressor's gate.

Spirits unbroken, their hearts knitted by the realization that they do not fight for their personal interests alone but for a future free of tyranny, these warriors would then march at dawn towards the Imperial City. Not mere simple rebels, they were bearers of new hope: a dream of a world where Light and Shadow balance, and where the Empire's reign of fear would cease to be.

Long and cruel had been their travel, but standing at the threshold of fate, every one of them knew that whatever was in store for them, they would confront it together, ready to fight, to sacrifice, and to endure; marching forward into the test of wills against the core of darkness, with the light of their defiance.

CHAPTER 17
THE HEART OF THE REBELLION

Before them sprawled the Imperial City: an obsidian-and-iron high behemoth that seemed to bulge upward, to pierce the heavens-a forbidden fortress. The very center of the city was the Imperial Radiance Church; its spires were well above the black night walls, even against the firmament itself. Light magic lit up the city from a distance with its cold glow, a sign of control rather than warmth. On the other side of that, Dax and his rebels were fully enlightened as to what was to come and at what cost.

They struggled through twisting ways and narrow alleys out toward the gates, suspicious faces at every turn, every eye potentially another spy or Empire informant. Silhouetted against the dark, the regime's furtive operatives watched in silent vigil, listening for every murmur of rebellion. Carefully Dax and his scant handful danced around the set traps of the snitches of the Empire, through webs of deceit.

. . .

He watched the ripple run through his men, the tremble of fear intermingled with determination. A soldier once, taught to take a sword and magic into chaos, Dax knew how to be certain. Now, a leader, he should balance conviction with caution, strength with compassion. Each decision led to freedom-or to sure defeat. With every step closer to the Imperial City, human lives in his hands weighed more; in every step, new sacrifices, dreams, and hopes were laid on his shoulders.

It was in the evening, as he was passing with them through a marketplace near the gate of the coming night, that his eyes chanced to fall upon an aged woman, bearing upon her the lineaments of age, her shoulders stooped low from all the loads of her many years. She smiled to him and beckoned him close, giving him a small charm for good luck.

But just as Dax would have reached out, Sylvia's instincts flared. She felt the faint trace of Light magic pulsating inside the charm-a tracking spell, not any sort of blessing intended to lead Imperial soldiers to them. Swiftly, Sylvia pulled on Dax's arm, arresting him just as a phalanx of guards emerged, eyes fixed on him with lethal intent.

A short, fierce combat ensued. Sylvia flashed Light, dazzling their oncomers, and from Dax's hands, shadows exploded, wrapping the guards in a veil of darkness that was impenetrable. They did manage to get away, but it left a nasty taste in Dax's mouth-the grim memory of how quickly trust can give way to betrayal.

. . .

Huddled in the protection of an abandoned building, Dax sat next to Sylvia as the night wore on heavy with what was to come. Weary of the relentless pressure and ever-present threat, he knew each move brought him closer to a final confrontation that would result in either freedom or complete destruction.

I should have known better," he whispered low, "had let my guard down, and it almost cost us everything.

Sylvia's gaze was steady and unwavering. "You can't carry this alone, Dax. Leadership isn't about being perfect; it's about resilience. We're here because of you—the hope you've given us, the strength you've shown. Don't let one moment of doubt overshadow all we've accomplished."

Her words cut through his despair like an anchor, binding him and dragging him back from the edge of that self-doubt. He had leaned for so long upon her rock-solid conviction, her way of seeing past the shadows of his fears. And she spoke to him now of what they fought for, of what lay in their future, and with her by his side, he found the strength to take the mantle of leadership once more.

They worked it out all night. Sylvia's tactical acumen was a nice counterbalance to Dax's raw instincts, guiding them as they mapped a route through twisting alleys to a little-known entrance to the Imperial City-a small, nearly forgotten path buried under ruins and rubble, overlooked by the grand ambitions of the Empire.

. . .

Cloaked by the night, silent was the move; the guards slipped past, shadows and light entwined, drawing closer toward the very heart of the city. With every step taken, anticipation rose, and every beat brought them closer to a fateful confrontation.

Before his eyes danced the ghosts of the losses, the sacrifices; Dax steeled himself against the ache. It was now from the memory of their sacrifice, Sylvia's unwavering support, and the faces of the rebels who walked with him that his strength came, and their faith shone more brightly than the stranglehold of the Empire.

Finally, the concealed entrance appeared: an old, tattered archway, half-concealed behind vine and rubble. Every word uttered was a whisper, for they would soon be well within the belly of the Empire. Dax went first; he laid his hand flat on cold stone and felt the reverberation of the city's magic in the walls.

Sylvia came to stand beside him, her voice barely more than a breath. "This is it, Dax. It's not about us anymore. It's about everyone who has ever suffered at the Empire's hands, everyone who dreams of freedom.

Weary but resolute, Dax turned back to her. "Whatever happens, we fight for them-for every silenced voice, every life the Empire took. We won't back down now.

They walked into town together, the rebels following them like ghosts as they slipped into the city. The walls of the Imperial City loomed overhead, oppressive, weighted with the burden of a thousand years of oppression. But as he crossed the threshold, the strange and peculiar calm fell once more upon Dax-a quiet resolution which drowned out all fear and doubt and uncertainty.

He vowed then, by his oath, crackling of fire in his veins, the sacrifice bound with him from the very start of this journey-as neither soldier nor exiled mage, but as beacon to the voiceless, forgotten murmur of the land. With Sylvia at his side, he knew what awaited in store: theirs was the torch of hope, and they would wrestle with that to the last. A spark lit in his heart, and into the night they vanished, towards the depths of the Imperial City: it was their hour, their struggle-the birth-pangs of a free Eryal, wrought in the crucible of sacrifice, nourished by Sylvia's faith, and goaded by dreams that stirred unslumbering.

CHAPTER 18
A SPARK IN THE DARK

She came out into the Imperial Archives with her mind afire, as every new revelation she had found was to her convictions-like fuel to dust and ashes. The magnificent architecture of Imperial City, so proudly standing, weighed ominously upon her now, each stone an indictment of the lies she had reverenced.

In this street, the rhythms of daily life pulsed. People moved, weary yet obedient.

Everywhere, it seems like the symbols of the Radiance Church stretch out long shadows across the citizens, looming large, a promise of protection, one of retribution. Sylvia saw Imperial guards at every corner; their eyes were steel-like, impassive. Once, she had viewed these sentinels as a symbol of order. Nowadays, they reminded her of oppression-the silent enforcers of a system well and truly thriving on control.

. . .

As she walked along the streets, her mind churned over and over with the words of the archivist and the chilling knowledge inscribed upon the scroll. It was as if the mask had been torn away, showing her the monstrous machinery below the gleaming surface of the Church. Sublime and sanctified Light Magic was distorted beyond recognition, forced into a means to kill-a leash that binds the spirits of the people.

She didn't quite catch the shadow detaching from an alley until a rough hand grasped her arm and pulled her into the shadows out of prying eyes, those belonging to the guards. Sylvia's instincts flared; surges of Light Magic welled up inside her, ready to defend herself-until she recognized that flash of Dax's eyes under the hood.

"It's me," he whispered. The calm certainty in his tone steadied her teeming brain. "We have to go. They're watching everyone today.

Sylvia nodded, catching her breath as they descended into twisting back alleys. Dax maneuvered her around through a maze of paths, his intimacy with the city's secrets lending them a modicum of safety. Finally, they entered a secluded courtyard, walled high on every side with ivy clinging to it-a broken fountain whispering with faint trickling water, a weird serenity against the storm that raged within Sylvia.

"What happened in there?" Dax asked, searching her face, his voice low and insistent.

· · ·

Sylvia clutched the scroll close to her chest, as if it were shielding her from the revelations it contained. The words poured out of her in torrents as she related all she had learned: the history of the Radiance Church, born not from a beacon of light but an institution forged from ambition and a hunger for power; the words tumbling forth one after another, as if in pressingly driving this nail of betrayal home.

They twisted Light Magic, Dax, she said, barely audible. They have used it to enslave people's minds, to take away the memories of dissent, to create an empire based on fear, not faith.

Dax's face clouded, the words falling upon his chest like a ton of bricks-a truth he had always felt was looming and yet never grasped. His fingers flexed involuntarily, and the shadows stirred around them with his anger. "It fits," he growled. "The Church imposed not only loyalty but obedience, shaped and fitted into the soul of the populace.

Sylvia drank in deeply, her anger mixed with a strong resolute spirit. "We cannot keep this hidden. The people have a right to know. They must know.

Dax nodded, his eyes fixed on her, with a new respect in them. "Then let's make sure they hear the truth. Still, we have to be careful. The Church will stop at nothing to keep their secrets buried.

. . .

Already preparing to leave, Dax waxed eloquent about his plans: "We are going to spread the word, but just not yet. 'Cause if we try to expose everything at once, they'll squash us before that. We need allies, people who also know the truth and who can carry this torch if we fall.

Her heart, pounded by the mix of fear and excitement as she knew the dangers, the influence of the Church, but then again, she also knew the spark that had been lit inside her-a flame of conviction not so easily extinguished.

Over the next several days, Sylvia and Dax worked without rest. Whispers of danger and truth spoke in the dark, murmurs building to a wildfire of the masses. The rebels tentatively turned up, trusting in the bonds forged in the underground as every word of dissent-merely another crack in the well-thought-of narrative of the Church.

They used code phrases, small words, and symbols that were carrying, in silent testimony, the weight of their message. Plainly visible to all who knew how to look or listen, every meeting, every whispered word chiselled away at the walls of deception that for so long had kept the people subjugated.

And then, one night, there in the secret alcove where they were gathered, finally, Sylvia saw in the shadows someone whose features she knew-a young priest she had trained with; his face had the same doubting look that hers had taken that day that she had read the words on the scroll. Forward doubtfully he came, his eyes flashing cautiously with hope.

. . .

"They say... they say you know the truth," he repeated hoarsely, all the unasked questions weighing upon it. "About the origin of Light Magic, about the Church.

Sylvia set a comforting hand on his shoulder, her eyes shining with understanding. "I do," she replied softly. "And I want you to know, you're not alone. You don't have to walk this path in fear.

His shoulders slumped with relief, and he nodded, determination hardening his expression. "Then I'll join you. Whatever it takes."

The rebellion was swelling in numbers; their influence seeded into the earth like creeping roots, hidden and insidious. The truth was a lethal weapon, which they used with an obtuse hand, aware of the risks yet refusing to be gagged.

As months replaced weeks, Sylvia felt it in her, too-the doubt and terror of those early days now tempered in purpose, her heart forged anew in the fire of revelation. She knew she would never again return to her former life, the life she knew and believed in. Her life now was linked with the Rebellion, her fealty no longer to the Church but to a higher truth to which she had sworn her oath. Dax had, for her part, finally clung to a course of will.

It had always been against the Empire-the goals of the rebellion-but now it did: to free these people, not just from physical control, but from the chains of indoctrination, from the chains that bound their minds and hearts. Sylvia and Dax lay together, both at the very heart of this unstoppable movement, having nailed the secrets of the Empire, having the truth behind its power revealed, fire lit to rip through the deceit fostering this people's darkness, generation after generation. And gazing out at the spires of the Imperial City, that very city which had once stood for order, for peace to them, they knew they had barely begun to show the true meaning of what the rot of the Church means.

The walls of the Empire still stand, but with every whispered truth, with every act of defiance, the walls fell. Her fight to free everyone had barely started, but Sylvia was ready to be at the head of that charge, her Light no longer one of control but a guiding star of hope and liberation.

CHAPTER 19
UNVEILING HYPOCRISY

ndestructible, it towered above the field of battle, shining with the mighty glow of the Light Magic issuing from its walls. The fortress of Great Priest Falk was no building of stones and mortar but a center of the Empire's control, the very heart of oppression that had been throttling the continent for centuries. Around it, a shimmering barrier pulsed with an unholy light, an unbreachable wall emblematic of Falk's unbreakable grip on his people.

He led the rebels through a maze of waste-lined streets; his Shadow Magic was interwoven with chaos as he concealed his forces from keen-eyed Imperial soldiers patrolling the periphery of the city. His movements were fast, each step taken with intent, each gesture silent command. The rebels knew what was at stake; their spirits had been tempered in the crucible of war, their wills unbreakable. Dax's presence ranked as a reminder to them of their purpose, for his vision had transmogrified into their own, his fight their last hope for freedom.

. . .

The radiant glow of her Light Magic danced across Sylvia's features as she kept near him. Her powers, once a tool of control under the doctrines of the Empire, had transformed into the fire of resistance. She knew the control that Falk held over the citizens was not based just on the force but on playing tricks with the minds and souls. As they approached the Citadel, she centered her energy and cast a shimmering field around their forces, one which would repel the debilitating effects of the Citadel's Light barrier.

The Citadel's defenses are tied in with Falk's own life force," she whispered to Dax, staring hard at the undulating walls. "Distract him, and his energy begins to flag, and so does the shield on the Citadel.".

Dax nodded. "We need to draw him out-they have to make him confront us directly.

The rebels closed in, the inches crawling towards the Citadel's main gate, while their hearts were wildly drumming with fear and anticipation.

Above, the night sky reeked of the residues of smoldering fires, with smoke reminding them of the blood-curdling battles that were fought up to this last stand. They had lost comrades, seen the fall of friends due to the Empire's cruelties, but their spirits remained unbroken. The pain of their losses only fueled their determination, while their hopes were sharpened by the pain of sacrifice.

. . .

Approaching the base of the Citadel, Dax flung his hand out and sent a swirl of Shadow Magic eddying around the high-reaching gates. Crinkling, the dark energy swirled over the barrier like ink through water, poking for weaknesses, seeking entry. Beside him, Sylvia allowed the touch of her Light Magic to dance against the shadows, a caress between the dual opposites of the powers.

It was then, in one swift burst of light which had blinded the view, that the gates opened, and he was facing a passage where warriors with gleaming armor guarded the elite of the Empire, faces masked by frigid masks. Further behind them stood Falk with a dagger-like stare from his eyes, his hands broadcasting an oppressive, pulsing feel. His Light Magic was a storm now, no more subtle; in one second it was a raging torrent of power enveloping the whole entrance.

"You dare come against me here, at the very center of my dominion?" Falk's voice rumbled, while his eyes coldly shone with a fury of calculation. "You, the misled, poisoned by shadows, hold no place in my Empire."

Dax stepped forward, his own magic coiling around him like a living shadow. "Your empire was built on lies, Falk. We're here to tear it down and free the people from your control."

Falk sneered, his eyes darting to Sylvia, who was standing resolute at Dax's side. "And you, my lost apprentice. You traded purity of Light for this... corruption.

. . .

Sylvia glared straight at him. "I don't trade, but simply took back what you tried to hide from me: the truth in the cunning Church, in the repugnant Light you use in maintaining delusions, making them slaves. Now, today, such a truth shall reveal itself in front of the people.

With a deafening roar, Falk threw a cascade of Light Magic in one blindingly brilliant wave at the rebels with the force of a tsunami. Dax and Sylvia replied in turn-the two magics joined and became a dazzling shield, absorbing much of the attack. The earth shook with the tussle of the two forces, and the air was charged with energy from their powers.

Something was happening here within this Citadel that had never happened. The elite guards of Falk fought in lethal precision-movements perfectly synchronized, their loyalty never shaken. Whereas the rebels fought in desperation, that was born from hope-with every strike, every block, a vow to freedom taken. The clash of steel, the hiss of magic, the cries of defiance-these boomed along its echoing walls.

Sylvia pressed on, her Light Magic condensing into a tiny beam that pierced through the shielding of the Citadel. She could feel the power of Falk resist, an immovable force pressing against her, yet never budging. Yet Sylvia was unrelenting, no longer an apprentice to heed lessons from the Church-she was a warrior, a beacon of hope, and she would not falter.

A wraith upon the battlefield, Dax moved-magic alive, part of himself-a blade of darkness slicing into them with deadly precision. His mind veered to one thing only: reach Falk, disrupt his concentration, weaken his power. The closer he got, the bigger the resistance became: Falk's light magic wrapping around him like an iron grip, trying to strangle the darkness inside.

Cutting through the din, Falk's voice was cold, mocking, a sneer: "You think you can challenge the might of the Empire? The Radiance Church is eternal; its Light unbreakable!

But then, while watching his forces falter and his guards fall before the never-ending attack by the rebels, the surety in Falk's eyes did falter for a moment. A doubt danced fleetingly upon his features, a shadow of uncertainty loosening his grasp. In that instant, Dax took advantage and plunged his Shadow Magic with all his might into a final blow toward Falk.

The effect was immediate. Falk staggered, his Light Magic faltering, the repressive barrier over the Citadel flared as his grasp on it relaxed. Sylvia felt it and redoubled her struggles, her Light fusing with Dax's Shadow in a peaceful counterpoint of energy. Together, they battled through the last line of defense that Falk might yet raise.

With a roar of defiance, the rebels surged forward, flooding the halls of the Citadel. The few guards that still remained to Falk had their strength sapped and fell back before the overwhelming onslaught. Closer and closer came Sylvia and Dax, their gaze on Falk, their combined might a beacon of defiance illuminating the darkened chamber. Cornered, Falk unleashed a last wild burst of Luminous Magic in their direction-a blinding wave that was to engulf them all. But Sylvia was afire in her heart to bring this tyranny to its end, her power rising to meet his as she channeled her Luminous Magic into a shield that deflected the attack.

When the dust began to clear and the clang of war faded into the distance, in that final moment, it was Falk upon his knees, his power broken, his control shattered. Laid bare beneath torn masks, with his lies now finally exposed, this once great High Priest, architect of the Empire's oppression, was nothing more than a man. She stepped forward, her voice firm, her eyes almost piercing: "Your reign ends here, Falk. The people are now free. Immediately the rebels erupted into cheers, their voices rising together to a victorious chorus that thundered along the halls of the Citadel.

The battle was over. Here on Eryal lay the shattered noose of the Empire. They had won-but not by sword or sorcery, not even by the valor of Eriol, but in the victory of truth and hope, in bearing witness to an unconquerable human spirit. Dax and Sylvia stood together, powers juxtaposed in a balance against each other, yet the very balance that they had fought to reconstitute.

They tore down the walls of oppression, chains of control, and took back their future of Eryal together. Scarred and battered, the city would heal-its people reborn from the ashes of tyranny, joined into a new freedom. And when the first light of dawn touched the Imperial City, upon that broken

Citadel, a sense, a promise stirred in the heart of every rebel for what times were to come. It was the end of the fight, but the beginning of their journeys: to rebuild, to restore, and create this world anew, where Light and Shadow could coexist together in harmony.

CHAPTER 20
BROKEN CHAINS

The town slept, wreathed in the mists of morning; the air hummed in battled yesterdays, murmurs of hope from very, very afar. Dax went ahead into the empty streets, the softness of his feet on the cobblestone at every step reminding him of how he had landed here-at the hub of rebellion. Everywhere, around him, clung the residue of the Empire's rule: half-burnt banners bearing across its emblem of the Radiance Church, frames of windows shattered in great halls where doctrines of control still echoed, light scarring on every single wall from the conflict that had become engraved.

By this time, the city had become the eye of the hurricane in the struggle for rebellion with freedom having begun flowering on the embers of tyranny.

A first realization of possibility-a chance for a world no longer in the grasp of the old polarities of Light and Shadow. And heavy on his shoulders it weighed, lightened only by the belief of a few who had willingly stood by his side. His legs carried him to the edge of a small square: a few getting ready for the day in general, some making supplies, others attending to the wounded. Their faces were exhausted yet determined. They looked up to him and nodded as he passed-things that reminded him of the trust they had given to him.

They were no longer his allies but his people, unitedly tied through the navel string of a common cause, a shared dream of a better tomorrow.

He saw Sylvia across the square, surrounded by a group of apprentices learning how to harness Light Magic. Her voice came softly yet firmly, correcting them in patience now grown characteristic of her. She looked up as he drew near-a slight smile touching her lips as she beckoned him over.

They learn so fast, she said, her eyes returned to her apprentices. Some of them had previously been taught by the Radiance Church, but they're slowly beginning to realize that Light Magic is so much more than they had been led to believe.

Dax nodded, his gaze set on the sea of young faces looking up to him, their eyes alight in a mixture of hope and uncertainty. "And Shadow Magic?" he asked, knowing old prejudices against it would hardly be so easily overcome.

Sylvia sighed. "There's still fear, but they're open to learning. They're beginning to see that Light and Shadow are not enemies. You've shown them that balance is possible."

. . .

"Balance," Dax whispered, her eyes drifting off as she spoke, weighing the sensitive balance they strove to reach. So foreign it was to the world they had known, which the Empire had hacked into bits with its iron-hand control over Light and villification of Shadow. In the new times they were building, balance started to be their guiding star, one on which they finally could build something worthy.

A voice cut into his reverie. "Dax!"

He now turned to find Rion, one of their strategists, running towards him with a parchment in his hand. "There is something you need to see."

Dax handed him the scroll, which he unwrapped to reveal a crude map of the territories of the old Empire. On it, there were symbols showing each of the towns and cities that had been freed from the clutches of the Church, a testament to the progress of the rebellion. But among those marks, new ones showed-indicators of unrest, the whisper of factions, of groups who would seek power for themselves now that the Empire was gone. They are taking advantage," Rion said seriously. "Now that the Empire is not in control, that's a vacuum of power. To some, this could be their chance to take control over these regions, in essence supplanting one overlord for another.

Dax's jaw was clenched. "We didn't fight for a change of masters. It's not enough to tear down the Empire, but it's to build a new world where all beings are free from tyranny, where power isn't stolen, but shared.

Sylvia set a hand to his arm, the touch anchoring. "Then we need to act fast, to remind them for what we are fighting in the first place. If we do not guide them, then the cycle of oppression will continue, only in another form.

Dax nodded, and the weight of his words fell into his mind.

What he had always known served them to do something that would last was not a rebellion, but an organized movement; not a revolution, but a representative council coming forward for his ideal of freedom and balance. Then he thought of all the comrades-in-arms, all those who gave everything for this cause, and how they deserve to have one word in the new world they are building.

We will have to gather all the leaders from each free region," he said, his voice firm and unshaken. "We'll make a council-a place where every territory will have its word. We won't rule over them; they will govern themselves, and we guide them so that things stay in balance.

Nodding reflectively, Rion said, "A council would give them a stake in this new world-a cause which would be supported, for it was them seeing it rather than imposed upon them.

. . .

Sylvia's eyes shone with approval. "It's a step to unity. If we can show them Light and Shadow can exist together, then we can show them that different voices, different perspectives, can only serve in creating a stronger whole. And it was then that it started falling into place in his head, bit by bit-a vision of a future worth fighting for: no new empire would they be raising, no regime that embraced all the diversity, the complicated humanity of their world; they would build a foundation of unity. Every free territory would send their people to the council, and all of them would help draft the laws governing their lives.

Dax watched the square, his eyes resting on faces that had fought hard toward this moment-young and old, full of hope and worn out. This was the core of the rebellion, the soul of this movement he had begun. They had lost so much for this dream, and it was his duty to see it didn't fizzle. "Rion," he said, handing back the scroll, "start reaching out to the territories. Tell them we're forming a council, that every region will have a voice. We'll hold our first gathering here in the city. This will be our new beginning."

Rion nodded, a glint of purpose in his eyes. "I'll see to it. We'll make sure they know this isn't about replacing one regime with another. It's about building something truly different."

Dax turned back to Sylvia as Rion vanished, all resolution in his eyes. "We have come a long way, but this is only the start." Sylvia nodded, her expression softened by pride. "And I'll be by your side for every step of it. We've fought for this chance, and now we'll show them what true freedom looks like."

Standing together, they watched the morning light, the city coming awake around them in rags, swords of early morning sunshine laying long shadows across the square.

It wasn't going to be easy-being beset upon every side with trials they could little yet fathom-but it was a readiness. Every step, every decision, forged a way to a world where freedom was not a word but real, a world wherein Light and Shadow coexisted and not one at war with the other, worth bequeathing sacrifice.

The sun was by now well risen, sending ripples of warmth in gold hues across the city. A quiet confidence folded deeper into Dax. They had fought for this chance, and as leaders now, they would see through that the fire they kindled would burn bright, guiding further generations into a world to which freedom, balance, and unity would not be some dream, but a certainty.

CHAPTER 21
SEEDS OF CHANGE

An almost hollow silence was hanging in the air, rarely disturbed by crackling sounds of dying embers and a far-off, gentle breeze whistling through the shattered ruins of the Imperial City. Once proud and truly exemplary of the greatness of the Empire, it now lay in smoldering ruin: high spires now etched a tortured silhouette against the gray atmosphere, like so many jagged bones thrust into the sky.

Dax stood atop the ruined palace, a panorama before him of stark aftereffects from their hard-won victory. His Shadow magic was in a slight stir all over him, a dark, quiet force against the tide of emotion inside. It was the sight and sound of this battered city that tugged at him-a weight that was practically physical: the faces of the fallen, the cries of the wounded, blank starings from those who had been freed from their oppression only to find themselves adrift in a world turned upside down.

. . .

Standing beside him, Sylvia's face was a reflection of the angst within him, her usually shining, warm Light magic dulled, weary, and smitten; her eyes reflected all those lives that had been sacrificed on the road to this victory. This victory seemed hollow as the staggering cost of the lost lives and torn families weighed in.

It's done," Dax whispered, the words raw, as if they were too much to say aloud. "We did it.

Sylvia's eyes swept across the fractured skyline, lingered a moment on the hollowed remains of the Radiance Church, and then the streets scattered with bits of shattered banners. She spoke barely louder than a whisper. "The Empire is gone. But the cost.

The weight of her words hung between them, echoing the unspoken truth they knew too well: the lost lives, the spilt blood-it was all for freedom, yet freedom was now fragile and like the broken stones at their feet.

Down into the city they went together, down twisting ramps through the silent aftermath of war, and there were people in the streets now, some stooping to pick through the rubble in dumb amazement, others clasped in tearful reunions, their faces alight with the shadowed joy of absence. Free, and mourning, they seemed like shades of themselves, at a loss for how to move in a world suddenly bereft of its familiar chains.

. . .

The guilt stabbed tight in Dax's chest. He was the icon of hope, the voice that had called them into arms, the figurehead who had urged them into risking everything. Yet, staring at the dead eyes of those whose universes had irretrievably shattered, he couldn't help but wonder if he called them into freedom or into desolation.

"They'll need time," Sylvia whispered, intuitively reading his thoughts. "This is all just the start of it. Freedom.it takes time to become real."

Dax nodded, though he could feel the weight of the thousands that followed him into battle weighing heavy upon him, the victory they'd gained coming at unmeasured cost. He couldn't help but think that every survivor now carried with him his own weight, his own grief.

Yet amidst that ruin and despair, Dax and Sylvia began seeing the first, fragile signs of hope. They walked the city's battered streets, observing small acts of resilience: children gathering stones to rebuild a fallen wall, an elderly couple planting the first seeds in a cleared patch of earth, and families huddled together beneath makeshift shelters, whispering words of comfort to one another.

It was then, for the first time, that Dax understood what this rebellion was all about: not to tear down the rule of the Empire, not even to win against those who have kept them oppressed, but to restore people's choices and to rebuild their lives as free people, with dignity so violently torn from them.

In that realization, the clarity that had always eluded Dax finally appeared.

He closed his eyes, drew a moment to reach into his senses to pull on his Shadow magic. There was humming energy in his veins, no longer a weapon but now a shield-a presence that spoke deep within him, filling him with resilience for the uncertainty ahead. Shadow, he suddenly seemed to realize, was not really a force of resistance but rather an important balance-a force which protects and fortifies, not corrupts. It is a power which gives one the right to choose, one which respects freedom.

He turned to Sylvia, who was watching him with the same intensity he watched her. Her Light magic was submerged, yet still very warm, a presence which continued to exist-a complement to his Shadow, a counterbalance to his darkness. Together, they formed a harmony he had not really understood until then.

Light and Shadow," he whispered, staring into Sylvia's eyes, "we were born thinking they could not exist together, but maybe that is what we need to rebuild: a world where each will have a place standing next to each other.

Relief and resolution crossed Sylvia's face as she relaxed. "If we are going to free the people, really free them, we have to give them something more than to survive. We have to give them hope. A life. The weight of her words descended inside Dax, filling him with a completely new sense of determination. No longer was this a revolution; this was a rebirth-a second life to shape afresh. But they could not do it on their own; they would need the people, their trust, their resilience. They would also need guidance enough, not of promises for easy salvation but with wherewithal to build a future with their own hands.

Together, they transitioned into the inner core of the city, amidst a people who had come together here, all stirred into a new creation of need and want. Dax oversaw the people in this crowd, his voice firm, though with an undeniable shade of his convictions:.

"We have won our freedom," he began, his words echoing loudly across the square. "But the battle is far from over.

A war not of swords and shields, but born of courage, strength, and unity. We will rebuild, not as servants of the Empire nor subjects of fear, but as people who earned their freedom. We shall forge a new world together-one wherein Light and Shadow stand next to one another, where no man shall be held by chains or fear. The weight of his words descended on the crowd, and it fell silent. Then, like the notes of a symphony rising, so rose the voices to lift as one in a sound of assent and hope and possibility. In that moment, Dax no longer saw mere crowds of survivors but the beginning of community-a toughened-up force that would see them through. Sylvia stood beside him now, her Light magic smoldering brighter, a constant flame to surely see them through the darkest hour. She laid a hand on his shoulder, and though her voice was low, it was firm with conviction.

. . .

"We shall do that together," she spoke softly, "not as conquerors, but as creators of our destiny." Standing together, as the sun went down, its setting shading their figures into silhouettes, images of hard-won victory, they knew that their road was a very long, long way from being done. But for the first time, they did know which direction they were going-to go through the experience of resilience, rebuilding, and undying faith in the people they freed. They would march forward together into the sunrise of a new world of their creation; of a world of liberty which all human souls had been tending since time began.

CHAPTER 22
THE STRUGGLE WITHIN

It is smoldering-the grisly testimony to the dying moments of an empire. That which had once shone so bright, a beacon of imperial glories, now stood hollow and forlorn, quite opposite from what glorious things they had lined up with litter-filled streets, detritus of a broken world order. Thick, acrid smoke curled into the sky from innumerable fires-a dark signal of the last desperate struggle of the Empire for survival.

Dax stood at the very center of the city, his gaze cast far over the ruinous landscape with an equal measure of sorrow and steely resolve. The fallen Empire was a marvel to behold: raw power, fuming rage cataclysmically birthed from the starving populace in want of but a small morsel of justice and truth. Beneath the surface, his Shadow magic churned and simmered, quiet storms to match the intensity of the spectacle laid out before him. The battle was done, but the cost weighed heavy on him, a weight it seemed his very soul was pushing against.

. . .

Beside him, Sylvia looked out on the broken city, her eyes grave. The fire of her Light magic, so steady, was low and flickering now, a perfect reflection of the setting in her face, lined with exhaustion and pain. The two of them stood as contrasting pillars against the ruin around them: Dax a focus of dark, defiant energy; Sylvia a dying beacon of hope. They had fought for this day, and the reality of victory was triumphant and devastating.

Where the teeming, luxurious streets once played theaters of war, now disadvantaged civilians and soldiers alike in their new freedom. Everywhere, there were scenes of raw grief and desperate celebration: people wrestling with the weight of revelation that came with the lies that had shaped their lives.

Look at them," Sylvia breathed, her voice shaking with emotion. "They're free, but. so lost.

"They have been chained for generations," Dax said roughly. "They will need time to remember who they are-who they were before the Empire's lies."

As he spoke, a number of the old imperial guards strode past them, battered and stained armour, their eyes sunken with the shock of betrayal-the instruments of High Priest Falk's control, the use of force to manage the twisted word of the Church-now, without the purpose of that task, they wandered freely, trying to work out that they, too, were just pawns in a much larger game.

· · ·

The Radiant Church had fallen, its glittering facade splintered like glass, revealing the rot festering beneath. Abandoned were those temples, once thought hallowed havens, their idols cast down and icons of authority blemished by truth. And the people learned of Falk's manipulations with Light Magic-that twisted power by which he had controlled the minds and bent the will of the masses. A revelation so damning, it proved to be an emancipation.

Making their way through the middle of the city with Sylvia, Dax emerged into the center of town to find a crowd before the ruin that was the Grand Citadel: the marble pillars that once stood tall were now cracked and blackened, its oncebright halls silent. Mixing on the faces of the people as they stood together was anger, relief, and a tinge of uncertainty. They had torn down the walls of the Empire, but in its ashes, they found themselves staring into an unsure future.

Among them spoke one woman, her face haggard, her eyes ablaze with a resolute fire; and raw with passion from one who had endured too much were the words: "We have broken their chains, but what now? We were promised freedom, but what does that mean to us? What shall we do with this void, this loss?

Then, Sylvia spoke in a low, clear voice: "Freedom is not no chains; it's making life choices. It is a gift, yet meanwhile wants courage, strength, and cohesion. The Radiant Church kept us in obscurity for so long that we forgot how to search for our own light. It is time to remember-together.".

. . .

Her words hung in the air, sinking into the hearts of the people. She could feel their confusion, their hesitation-but she also saw something else, there: the flicker of hope, the nascent understanding that they did not stand alone. Dax watched her, his heart swelling once more with purpose renewed. Together, they were not just rebels but guides, showing fractured society how to rebuild from the ashes.

Yet Dax knew their job was far from over. Beneath the rubble, the remnants of the Empire's legacy lay like dormant seeds, just waiting for the right climate to sprout anew. In building them a world freed from corrupting influences of the Empire, they should have dealt with such remnants: uprooting the entrenched belief systems that allowed such control in the first place to take so thorough a hold.

We can't just demolish what they built," Dax said, his eyes taking on flint. "We have to make certain that this could never raise its head again. Terror and control nurtured the Empire. Unless we pull the roots out, they'll grow back even stronger.

Sylvia nodded, her expression solemn yet set. "That would mean we have to learn from the past, even from that which we would rather forget. We have to teach people to search for the truth, to question, to shield their minds from falsehood. Light and Shadow, together, to shield and to guide.

And so, with a shared sense of purpose, Dax and Sylvia once again began walking amongst people, speaking with small groups, allaying their fears, sharing a dream with them-a dream of a world where Light and Shadow coexisted, of a society where power was balanced: instead of force-smitten people, empowered people of choice. Yet, an ambitious vision so much believed in by every fiber in their bodies. The sun began to set over the ruined city, casting long shadows through the rubble. And Dax felt the weight of his past, for the first time in so long, start to lift. He was a tool of the Empire-serving in darkness, bound to act in the name of control. Now he was free, not just from chains, but free from a legacy of fear that once defined him.

In the gaze of the people, he for the first time saw the sparks of the world they might build together: a world in which Light and Shadow were an explanation, not an attack.

Sylvia laid a hand on his shoulder, the touch rooting him. "We did this, Dax. Together.

He looked at her, a faint smile breaking through the weight of his expression. "This is just the beginning. There's so much more to be done, so much to rebuild. But we'll do it—together."

They stood shoulder to shoulder; the silhouettes of their frames stretched out across the ruins, tributes to the night that they had lived through and the dawn that they were now fighting for. The road ahead would be long and vexed, full of tussles to negotiate this fragile balance of power and freedom.

In that moment, however, wrapped in shades of their victory and the muted whispers of a world reborn, Dax and Sylvia found a well deep enough to sustain them. Then, as the night fell, the city went black; they marched anew, lit by dancing flames of hope and resilience, for though the Empire had fallen, from its ashes they would forge a world built upon truth, courage, and the bond-twixt Light and Shadow unbroken.

CHAPTER 23
VEILS OF DECEPTION

The morning after the fall, all was still-as if the world held its breath, waiting to fill the silence that had been left vacant by centuries of control. People in the Imperial City came out into a new world where the sky looked a bit brighter, the air a bit lighter, and where the burdens which weighed upon their shoulders through generations started slowly to lighten. There was energy in the streets, a cautious optimism, but also a wonder-a world without the constant shadow of the Radiant Church seemed a dream too fragile to touch.

Dax walked through the heart of the city with his face drawn but a fire of determination in his eyes.

He had come down those steps a witness and not the conqueror, caretaker for those people bearing so much to stand upon this ground of freedom. And he went in clusters, telling stories of the past and dreams of what was yet to be. Voices once hushed, afraid, rose high as music, filling the city with life. Standing tall beside him, in Sylvia's eyes shone equal parts of pride and reflection. She, too, could feel this monumental weight of a new beginning, knowing full well that the triumph they had fought for with blood and sweat was only the first step in a long painful way to heal and rebuild.

Now free from the rigid doctrines of the Radiance Church, shades of her past still clung to her, the residual emanations of doctrines in which she had invested so much belief. And walking beside Dax, the best she could do was speculate on what place she would occupy in this world yet to be fully formed.

And the people asked questions-endless questions about what next. Dax and Sylvia found themselves in the middle of the city square, surrounded by faces strained from the struggle of living but with a hopeful glimpse of revival. A young woman came forward, her eyes bright yet her expression hesitant. "Now that we're free, how do we begin? How do we build something better?

Dax's eyes softened, and he raised his voice to carry over the crowd gathering around them. "Today we are free from the chains that bound us, but our work has only just begun. Freedom isn't just the absence of control; it is a promise we make to one another. We'll build this world together-by lifting each other up and protecting the dignity of every person in this city. Sylvia's chest swelled with pride at Dax's words; this man, once a feared Shadow Mage, had grown into a leader, a rallying point for those around him. One step forward, her voice was steady: "We have so long been taught to believe, taught to think, and taught to live. Now the time comes to make our choice.

That means we'll make mistakes, we'll face setbacks—but we'll learn, and we'll grow stronger together."

A murmur of assent stirred outwards into the crowd; a nodded head here, an encouraging murmur there, and the sense of one mind seemed to flower. No longer were they subjects of a regime but participants in the building of a society-one they had yet to imagine but would create as they went.

Now, as the people dispersed, it was to them that a man, in plain, shabby garments, drew near. His face and body seemed to have been through the fire too many times in life; the skin was like leather, the frame gaunt. Yet the eyes shone with lucidity, sparkling, so to speak.

I used to serve as a scribe for the Radiant Church," he said, his voice rough but level. "I saw things-writings, records telling the true history about this city, about the rise of the Empire. Things that shouldn't have been spoken, hidden from the people so that only a select few knew where the roots of our oppression lay. And they need to be told.

Dax and Sylvia looked at each other, knowing instantaneously that taking care of the hidden histories was something important to be done. The Empire had controlled not only the bodies of the people but also their minds-their very perception of the world. Reclaiming those lost truths was crucial in breaking the last remnants of its power.

"Tell us what you know," Dax said, in that perfect blend of urgency and gratitude.

The man nodded, his face set. "There are scrolls, hidden deep in the catacombs beneath the city. They contain accounts from early on in the Empire, records of how the Radiant Church warped the power of Light Magic into a tool of control, how they sowed fear and twisted the truth. Those scrolls will help people understand their oppression was not because of fate but because of choice.

A plan forming between them, Dax and Sylvia set off with a small group to retrieve the lost records. Deep within the underbelly of the Imperial City, their journey would take them through the almost endless labyrinth of tunnels and chambers that had served as the hiding place of all manner of dark Empire secrets. The air was damp and chilled, the only sound the faint echoes of their footsteps.

They had lain in an alcove, safely wrapped away from age's dust and grime, while Time did little to them. Dax unrolled one, and the words spoke not of the holy epiphany of the Church's founders, but of their brutal opportunism-their deliberate choice to twist Light Magic into a tool of mind control. He read of the planning in minute detail, of the calculated untruths interwoven into the fabric of society-and his jaw set in rage and sorrow.

. . .

As Sylvia read over his shoulder, the words cut deep into her soul. She had known all along that what the Church preached was wrong, but it was quite another thing to have the cold calculation at the root of such manipulation staring her in the face. She closed her eyes, and a wave of sorrow washed over her, only to open them to bright with a fierce resolution.

"We'll share these with the people," she said quietly, "and they will know the truth. They will understand that the power to change things was always within their grasp."

Above ground, the city square gradually became a scene of public meetings-a platform from which people could put across, argue with, and project visions of the future. Dax and Sylvia mounted the stage, holding the ancient scrolls aloft for all to view some actual proof of the Empire's deception.

And these were the unsaid truths of the Radiant Church, he finally said: "For generations, they ruled with an iron grip, tamed Light Magic into a weapon. Today we show their lies, and we take back our right to know, to question, and to choose.".

People listened in dead silence, faces mixed with shock, sadness, and anger; yet, in their eyes, Dax and Sylvia saw something else-an acquired toughness, a single realization that made them come to understand just how much in control over their own life they really were. As the reality finally sank in, a new unity started developing, this time borne not out of adherence to commands but out of understanding and a common purpose.

. . .

No longer were they individuals under one leader's oppression but a budding society learning about their capability and the immense influence they could create to change the world. Standing at his window, looking out over the city, were the weight of his journey, the scars of his battles, and the enormity of the task before him that really weighed upon Dax and Sylvia that night. For a very first time, they could feel the glow of a real hope.

They liberated those people not just from the shackles of bondage but also from the chains of ignorance, and herein lay a fire that would outlast them. Before them lay a length, but they are never alone again.

PART THREE
UNBREAKABLE BONDS

As the stakes grow ever greater, the rebellion is whiplashed between searing losses and bitter betrayals that push its membership to the breaking point. Dax and Sylvia-only bound by a common dream-are pressed tighter and tighter in the crucible. Now they rally their most trusted comrades around them as, in bonds that cannot be broken, they prepare for the last, impending confrontation with the Empire.

CHAPTER 24
BOUND BY PURPOSE

As the triumph of the rebellion came, in the hush of dawn, the world was sullenly still, holding its breath. Imperial City had stood mighty as the name of oppression, but now it was bereft of any ornated display of pride; scars spoke volumes on the cracked walls about that battle that unraveled its powers. The smell of smoke and earth lay thick in the air as people began to come out onto the city streets, still cautious, still with the taste of tyranny in their mouths.

Dax, the strong, reluctant leader of this rebellion, moved among them, pride and sorrow stirring in his heart. He had led these people through fire and bloodshed, and now, looking into the weariness of their eyes, he saw what victory had cost them-the losses that had been suffered, the sacrifices that had been made. For every cheer, there was a family in mourning; for every hope restored, a life had been lost. His magic shadowed; once a great weapon of defiance, it was a heavy mantle-a responsibility he had never asked for, yet one which he would bear.

. . .

She stood beside him, silent but unrelenting, reminding him of that to which they had decided. Light Magic, once symbolic of all that was corrupted according to the twisted view of the Church, was now symbolic of purity: a way forward, a promise toward healing.

She did, however, also hold within her the consequences of all that befell them: her dream haunted by memories of comrades who lay dead, of innocent lives lost amidst the chaos. She reached out and touched the crumbling walls of the Imperial Palace-feeling the cold stone beneath her fingertips, so reminding her of what had been and was now nothing more than a sobering symbol of what was left to rebuild.

Now the people who had hidden away in abject terror, people who had been humbled, began to emerge into the daylight; their faces told the story of emotion-relief and grief. There were families searching for their loved ones lost in the chaos of everything, children who wandered down broken streets, staring with wide, uncertain eyes; elders watched the coming dawn with guarded hope. They wore on their faces, in their hands, in their hearts, the signs of oppression. And for the first time, they were flecked with the small glow of hope. It was as if the victory of the rebellion didn't wipe the scars away but somehow managed to open that door. Cautious, they began to sweep away the debris, rebuilding piece by piece what had been torn asunder.

. . .

Dax and Sylvia sat with the surviving leaders of the rebellion, all who had survived the battles and now were faced with another-perhaps daunting-task: rebuilding fractured society. They sat in a circle around a plain table in the shadow of the broken palace and talked about plans, hopes, and fears. There was no hierarchy among them, no imposed order.

It was born out of suffering together and a common realization that the only real strength was not in dominance but in unison.

"We have freed the people from the clutches of the Empire," Dax said as he started speaking, his voice full of gravitas. "But freedom isn't an end; it's a start. We are not constrained anymore by the edicts of the Empire, what kind of world we want to build remains to be decided."

Sylvia's eyes scanned the faces around the table: the set lines of the warriors, the stoic features of the farmers, the joyful enthusiasm of the scholars who had been called into this cause. "We must make a community which truly hears every voice, which realizes the suffering we all carry with us and strives to soothe it. The Radiant Church used Light Magic to throttle compliance; we shall use it differently-to illuminate our path, to guide us forward, to cure.".

Murmurs of assent circled the room, but it was unmistakable how much hesitation still lingered among them. They were soldiers, rebels, survivors-but few of them were builders. And the world they wanted-a world where Light and Shadow could be left to their own devices-almost seemed as fragile as the bits and pieces of the morning light pushing in through the shattered windows.

The words were said, but both sides knew it wasn't going to be easy. Many among them were still loyal to the Radiant Church; one doesn't unlearn indoctrinated ways in a matter of days. For others, freed from the Empire's grasp, there was a fear that new leaders would only supplant the old, and the cycle of power and oppression would never truly break.

Sylvia's heart bled for them, for the baggage of their past sticking so obstinately. "We shall have to be patient," she said softly. "Healing takes time. The rebuilding of trust shall not be done in one day. But once we prove to them it is not fear but mercy we lead with, they shall find their way.

They knew rebuilding would not come from the strength of arms alone but from empathy, understanding, and the will to listen to those who once had been their oppressors. The components of the past had to be used to forge a new world; the old fractures had to be healed, a task that could only be accomplished if one faced the darkness within oneself and the shadows provided by the Empire.

The moment they began to shift, to spread themselves out, one stepped forward: a small boy, smudged with soot, a glaze in his eyes that spoke of having seen too much. "There's someone here," he said in a voice at once small and steadfast. "A woman. she says she's from the Radiant Church.

. . .

Those were words that sent them freezing; memories of betrayal ablaze in their minds-the Church had been their greatest enemy, a manipulation weapon used to subdue the people. Instinctively, Dax reached for his gun, but Sylvia placed a light restraining hand on his arm.

"Let us hear her," she murmured resolutely. "For the first acts of building a world that will barrage no voice, we must first listen.

The woman who came inside was not clad in gilt robes of the high clergy but in plain garments, those of a penitent. Her face was ashen, her eyes haunted, but something else-conviction-was there. With a deep bow, she raised her head to look at them, an unflinching determination in her eyes.

My name is Liana," she finally began to speak-her voice trembled, yet it was firm. "I was one of those within the Church, among the believers serving under High Priest Falk. But I. I have seen the truth. I know the pain we have caused, the lies we spread. I am unable to mend the past, but I beg of you for an opportunity to atone and help rebuild what we have destroyed.

The only sound in the room was the weight of her words. Anger began to rise in him as his mind was filled with the memories of suffering the Church was responsible for, but as he looked into Sylvia, he met an expression in which sorrow and hope mingled. For the Church's teaching also bound her and once made her believe in the purity of Light Magic. If she could unlearn the lessons of her past, then perhaps some could too.

Dax took a deep breath and began to speak to Liana in tones that resonated with echoes of the past and promises of a different future: "If you wish to seek atonement, you will have to do so in an atmosphere of truth and modesty, for we are not the servants of those who claim to possess all the answers. We go this way together, uncertain yet resolute. Convince us that a change may be possible for you, and we shall take you to our midst.

Liana swallowed and her eyes welled with tears, but she nodded, her face set resolute. "Thank you. I'll do anything, try my best, to make amends for what we've destroyed." With the coming of Liana, the beginning of their vision of a new world began. Reconciliation between the tears that had been created by so much fear and oppression would neither be quick nor easy.

It was in building their society that they would not be built upon their vengeance neither would they go onto surrender to a will to destroy all those that had stood against them. Wounded and uncertain, they would move ahead, together in a shared purpose-to forge a world wherein Light and Shadow coexisted, the voices that were never given a word were finally listened to, the pain of the past confronted rather than denied, and yet would heal. And in that fragile beginning, amidst the ruin of a torn empire, the first seed was sown for hope.

CHAPTER 25
LEGENDS OF OLD

First light crept over the city as Dax moved through the streets of Aerilon; his mind was as restless as the shadows stretching across the walls. Even free from the Empire's grasp, the town was showing a scar: in the reflecting vicious circle of oppression in the walls, in the eyes of citizens worn out and trying to shake the shackles of their past. And thus, the way to freedom lay stretched out-an endless horizon, little shimmering beyond the ruinous fragments of a world that needed, not its conqueror's victory, but its healing.

He had stopped before that open square now, where already some early risers were collecting, to offer a hand or a hope to the labors there of rebuilding. This would be the heart of their resurrected city, the ground from which a future would grow-a place where Light and Shadow may coexist without fear or division. Sylvia joined him, her footsteps light yet steady, her presence a quiet reassurance.

. . .

She had been busy tending to the wounded all night long, her Light Magic used for far more than just soothing physical hurts, but also to heal hearts that were still raw from wounds the Empire had inflicted.

In the tender morning light, the city lay fragile yet resilient, full of echoes from times past, with the silent promise of change. Today, Dax and Sylvia would lead the people through the sensitive process of rebuilding, well aware that their roles had changed: They were no longer warriors of the battlefield but guardians of unity, stewards of a new realm in which the hearts and minds would go to defend.

One step forward, Dax spoke without a hint of strength or a waver in his voice: "We stand at the genesis of a new era, one forged not by control but through unity and mutual respect. The Empire's rule may have fallen, but its ghosts are the scars we carry, the walls that still remember subjugation. A city is what our choices now will make it.". Hopeful faces stared out, uncertain faces, determined faces-those who dared to dream that their lives could be different from those now freed from fear. Led so rigidly by dogma for so very long, even now, as freedom was in sight, that thought was tenuous, self-governance like a new leaf in a storm.

Yet in Dax's words, an undertone of quiet determination seemed to ring out: a vision of a future they would plan out themselves, where every voice would carry equal importance with every other.

. . .

Sylvia stepped forward, alongside him; her voice was soft, yet threaded with conviction: "Our guide shall be balance. For too long, we had allowed ourselves to believe that Light and Shadow could not coexist, until we came to realize that the only true strength emanates from harmony, taking all parts of our self into consideration. Every stone that we laid, every choice we made, reflected the unity we struggled to create.

The elderly one, Councilor Rian, slowly raised his hand; lines upon lines of what seemed to be wisdom and struggle were etched upon his face. "But where do we begin, Dax? How do we build something new without emulating the old?

Dax nodded, appreciating the weight of the question. "We start by listening—to each other, to our needs, our fears, our hopes. We've all suffered in different ways. This city can become a place where every person has a voice, where no one power holds dominion over another."

Then one young fellow, with fresh wounds from the last battle, stepped forward, his face still tense with unresolved anger. "What about justice? We let those who served the Empire off scot-free? Forgive?

Sylvia came around to him now, her eyes locking into his with compassion. "Justice should be one of the bedrock ones, but we cannot afford to be ruled by vengeance. True justice is not punitive; it's about seeing that such evil doesn't happen again in our society. We need accountability, tempered with compassion. The Empire ruled by fear. We must choose another path-one that embraces humanity in all, even in those who may have lost their way. A murmur rumbled through the crowd at her words, wary, unsure, the vision of a world sans masters enough to fire the fragile hope. Freedom had been tasted; the process of rebuilding called on them to look deep into the soul-to question familiar presumptions, to redefine what constituted strength.

Anya, the grown-up rebel, got up to tell a lifetime story of losses and overcoming them.

"I lost my family to the Empire," she said in a low but clear voice. "I began seeking revenge, but that doesn't ease the sense of void. Only rebuilding does, and only by loving each other does this void get filled. This city," she said, with a sweep of her arm, "can be a city where every life is worthy. Nobody needs to experience what I do every day, when everything was taken from me."

The morning wore on, and through the sea of people, Dax and Sylvia listened as voices now long silenced spoke again of a school where magic was learned all under one roof, where Light and Shadow learned how to balance each other; visions of community areas to which people would have access, with the free right to congregate as they chose, speaking about healing and mutual understanding instead of suspicion.

By noon, the crowd laid the founding of a new council: a presiding authority to represent each district, created by the people, serving according to the people's will. A council not of rulers, but of stewards-persons entrusted with the execution of wills of those whom they represent. Dax and Sylvia were there to guide, not to govern, voices of balance that ensured no one single force dominated but that all voices harmonized.

Then, as night began to fall, lanterns flared into life, casting amber glows over the square as citizens remained, sharing and planning a future for which, at last, they could hope. It was a world Sylvia had hardly dared dream existed: Light and Shadow, citizen and leader, living in harmony.

Dax was standing right next to her when people remained late into the night, telling stories, laughing, and dreaming together. He knew the coming days would be hard, times of questioning themselves. Tonight he was shown that together they could try to find something lasting rather than the edicts from an empire. With the crowd slowly clearing, Dax turned to Sylvia, almost a glaze of introspection in his eyes. "We did not just win a battle," he whispered. "We started something bigger than ourselves: a movement into a world that will start valuing every life and every voice. Sylvia, her heart filled with hope and gratitude, reached for his hand, her eyes bright with conviction. "This is the world we've fought for—a place where Light and Shadow walk side by side, a place where love and strength grow from every corner of the city."

They came together, then, and were varminting their faces to the dawn, watching the light stretch over the city. Their journey was long, but tonight the possibilities hung thick: a future braided by unity, resilience, and hope. And as the first light hit the city, Sylvia knew the light within her finally found its place-not as a power of domination but as a guiding light of love toward a new, lasting peace for their world.

CHAPTER 26
EMBRACING THE UNKNOWN

Now, on the second attempt, the Imperial City stood scarred in memory of what was and must never again be. The way was muddied on the long slope ahead: filled with gray areas and divisiveness. As Dax and Sylvia walked among the people, the expectations with the burdens of a hard-won victory weighed heavily on each.

Dax knew full well that the job of a leader wasn't simply to tear an empire asunder but to see that the ideals they had fought for were looked after. It's very easy to unify people against something; the rebellion had done that-under one banner of liberation-but now the chains of the Empire were broken, and the differences between the factions bubbled up, like dormant seeds in spring, each with its version of what freedom truly meant.

Here, within the improvised council chambers that were once an imperial war room, the leaders of the rebellion finally came together. Former soldiers, peasants, merchants, scholars, and even some erstwhile members of the Radiance Church-who had finally veered against the manipulations of the Empire-melded into one in a united front against the Empire. Noise clashed in a cacophony of opinion and discontent as voices rose around the cracked stone table.

What we need is order," an aged merchant struggled for, his voice hoarse, yet firm, "The Empire's gone, yes, but without structure, without someone to lead, we risk falling into chaos.

"Order?" Renna laughed, a hard-headed warrior who'd lost family to the Empire's brutality. "Order's just another word for control. We didn't fight to trade one dictator for another. We fought for real freedom."

Then the soft and melodious, yet firm, voice of a healer spoke, "We cannot turn a blind eye to their pain, nor to the anger that lingers therein. Justice is due, but if we act from our hatred, we continue the chains of oppression.

Dax listened to them all-voices of every shade in the complex tapestry that was fractured society. He could feel the tensions build, the rifts of the past ulcerating into fresh wounds. And yet, he saw, too, what might emerge from this: unity not compelled by obedience to one will but by mutual respect and a common purpose. Sylvia laid a reassuring hand on his arm, grounding in her presence the storm of dissension. When the voices had died away, it was possible for her to speak in a clear, commanding voice across the room.

. . .

"We have all suffered," she began, her eyes catching each one around the table.

"We've seen what happens when the use of power becomes a weapon, when Light Magic and Shadow Magic go to war. But the true enemy wasn't the magic itself-it was the corruption, the will to twist the power to one's own purposes. We have an opportunity now, a rare chance to build something different. But to make it, we must learn to trust one another."

The room fell silent as the full impact of her words set in. All that Sylvia was trying to say was a very simple and profound message: unity was not about forcing everyone into one single vision but creating a society where every voice would have its place, where differences could exist without fear.

Dax breathed deeply and stepped into the silence following Sylvia's words. "I know each of you has a different vision for what our future should be like. Some of you fear chaos, others control. But if we are to avoid the past mistakes, we must reject extremes. We must find a balance-a place where Light and Shadow coexist, not as enemies, but as allies.

He could feel the weight of their gazes, some skeptical, others with a glimmer of hope. "There will not be a single ruler here, no going back to the ways of the Empire. We shall establish a council, a representation of our disparate voices, and every decision with the welfare of all in mind: justice, yes, but mercy too; freedom, yes, but with responsibility.

. . .

The tension that had so recently filled the council room gave way to tentative understanding. They knew the road would be long, that old wounds would not heal overnight, but the vision Dax and Sylvia offered was a beginning worth fighting for.

Outside, the people began their own process of healing in the streets of the city: neighbors came together to build their homes, sharing food and all other resources, cheered by the new generosity the shared hardship forged. The former stronghold of the Radiance Church now offered a haven to which people would turn for leadership, succor, and to rediscover meaning.

In this sanctuary, Sylvia honed her craft, using Light Magic as one of the healing forces and not as a way to dominate. She taught anyone who would learn how to use magic as a sign of balance and not as a weapon. Dax accompanied her, sharing the subtle art of Shadow Magic, helming myths and fears that even Shadow had a place within this world that cherished harmony over division.

Their efforts began to take root. Those living in fear of magic realized it was a gift-one that could heal just as much as protect. They came to learn that freedom wasn't just an absence of tyranny but respect toward everyone's boundaries, strength in diversity, and support around them when needs arose.

Days fast turned into weeks, and with time, the city changed.

Deep wounds of war no longer anchored them in reverse; they were a reminder of how far they had come.

One evening, with the sun setting behind the ruin of the imperial palace, sending long shadows across the city, Dax and Sylvia stood atop a newly built platform overlooking the assembled crowd. The people had come to view the formality of establishing the council as a sign of mutual commitment toward a just and balanced society. Dax's voice rose above the cheering. "Today, we take the first step in building a new world-a world where the light of freedom is balanced by the shadows of wisdom. We will make mistakes, and we will learn. We will face challenges, and we will overcome them. This city, these people, this land-we are the guardians of our future.".

The audience erupted in a storm of applause, pregnant with all the hope, resilience, and unity that had come out of the ashes of the Empire. Dax and Sylvia, their hearts welling up with pride but more with humility, knew well that the journey ahead was hazy and that what happened in the past would still continue echoing. And they both knew that, with this, they made the first necessary step towards a world where Light and Shadow would finally coexist in concord.

As the sun dipped below the horizon, painting the city in hues of twilight, the resolve between Dax and Sylvia was silently met through the gaze of their eyes. The Empire fell, but they were far from over. They were no longer fighting against tyranny but for a future where every man, every voice, and every dream finds its place in the new dawn.

CHAPTER 27
THE WEIGHT OF SACRIFICE

The Imperial City was coming back to life, yet it was fragile, hesitant regrowth. War had bitten deep-the fang marks still showed in shattered walls and, deeper inside, in the peoples' eyes. Every block rebuilt, every stone laid was an act not just of reconstruction but of reclamation too-a struggle to regain their dignity, their hope, their identity.

Dax walked through the streets, watching the re-building process with a sense of pride and discomfort. People were industrious, energized by a common ambition to leave the past behind them, yet occasionally he picked up suspicion and fear. He knew why: Imperial rule had managed to break that trust so deeply that no amount of restoration of the walls could mend it.

Sylvia had stood with him, silent strength beside him. Since then, she has taken on the task of reintegrating Light Magic, working day and night with apprentices and scholars on what it was really meant to be. This was going to take a little time, she knew, but one day, people would finally understand that Light Magic was to heal, illuminate, and inspire-not to control. She would make sure to cut it loose from the shackles of tyranny it had been strung up to for so long.

Some days," Sylvia said, staring at the silent workers, "I feel like we are trying to untangle a knot that was tied centuries ago. The more we pull, whatever the pull may be, the tighter it gets.

Dax nodded. "I know. The Empire may be gone, but its shadow remains. It's there in the distrust of people, in the way they look over their shoulder, afraid of an enemy that is no longer there.

She faltered, her eyes remaining with him. "But they believe in you, Dax. They look to you for a sign of what's possible outside the Empire's reach.

I know, Dax said, some doubt creeping into his tone. It's just that this trust feels. fragile. One misstep, and it all may crumble.

Around one corner, they could hear raised voices: a gathering at the steps of what had used to be the Empire's judicial hall. Gone was the throne of the judge; in its place, a humble wooden podium leading into their new open forums: disputes settled, voices heard. Yet this gathering seemed tense, charged with some resentment.

. . .

A man in the crowd thrust a shaking pointing finger accusingly at the woman standing as if at bay. "She was one of them!" he shouted. "A member of the Radiance Church! She helped them manipulate our minds!

A murmur of assent ran through the crowd and Dax felt the tension build. Sylvia stepped forward and spoke in calm firm tones:.

"I know you are angry," Sylvia told the crowds, "but the Empire lied and cheated with their forms of Light Magic. We fought for a world of free speech, free thought-even towards those once deemed our oppressors.

Now, the man shook his head, bitterness flowing across his face. "How shall we believe them? How are we to know that they are not still loyal to the Empire?"

Dax pushed his way forward again and raised his hand for silence. "True freedom means unlearning the hate that the Empire has taught us," he said. "I understand your doubts, but we can't build a new world based on fear and suspicion. We have to give people the chance to prove themselves. Those who were part of the old order need to make a choice about their place in this new world, just like the rest of us.

He said nothing more; the reminder of what they were fighting for was enough. Tensions began to dissipate, and people slowly broke away, all giving the woman odd looks but no more accusing finger pointed.

When the crowd finally cleared, Sylvia turned to him, "This will take time; for everyone. People are probably afraid to forgive in case this will somehow belittle what we were fighting for.

Dax nodded. "It's true. The scars go deep. But unless we can let go of the past, unless we can forgive, we have a danger of becoming precisely what we threw out.

Well into those weeks, with representatives from the different regions and factions present here for the constitution of the council in order to have their say about the future, she plunged herself into therapeutic sessions with former members of the Radiance Church, teaching them a new way of approaching Light Magic: that of compassion and service, and not of control. The once feared slowly but surely found a place of belonging as the shadows of their past were gradually shed.

Yet not everyone was ready to move on. There were whispers around town concerning a fellowship unwilling to give up the old ways: those who had their hay day under the Empire and who did not like the taste of the power they lost. They spoke low, planting seeds of dissatisfaction, stirring memories of "stability" that the Empire once gave them.

· · ·

One evening, after a meeting between Dax and those council members, a small boy passed a note to him. Simple, in a hurried scrawl: "They plan to take back what's theirs."

Dax listened, his heartbeat quickening. Ah-opposition to their vision was to come, but a little sooner than expected. He had called upon a secret council meeting with Sylvia and the other leaders, laying the threat before them.

"We won the battle," he said with a serious expression on his face, "but there are those that would bring the Empire back from ashes if given the chance."

The weight of the moment depressed their faces; for a second, the council sat in silence; then, from the Northern Alliance, came Kael's voice, dripping with the tantalizing tang of tempered steel:.

Dissent mustn't be allowed to fester. We need to weed out those who would undermine all that we have built. Sylvia shook her head. "Trying to force them out will only ensure that any trust lingers far longer. We need to offer them a place in this new order, a chance to be part of it. Refuse, and then we deal with them as a last resort. We cannot be tyrants, seeking justice; that would make us no different from the Empire. Dax nodded; the words had struck a chord in his caution. "Sylvia is right," he said. "We must extend the olive branch of unity first. If they reject it, it will then be time for us to consider action.

. . .

They spent the next few days consolidating, never to stop and call a conference with skeptics to spread the word of a world which would balance, peaceful between Light and Shadow. Thereby, the danger of rebellion would lessen, though not totally gone. Trials filled this path of unification, and every passing day became another reminder to each of how much pain they had undergone. Yet, again and again, they became watchful and labored for those very ideals that had combined them in the first place.

One evening, as they stood atop the hill looking towards the city below, Dax quietly and with much determination turned to Sylvia and said, "We may not be able to see in our lifetime this world that we dream of, but we can at least create a ground right for those people coming after us.". Sylvia smiled. Her eyes were gold like the setting sun as she said, "And that, Dax, is what it means to be a true leader-not being able to see the end but knowing the journey will go on, that light and shadow will find their proper place.". They watched together as the city awakened beneath them: building after building, corner after corner, a statement to their resolve.

Far off in the distance, the Radiance Church stood-ruined-a reminder of what they overcame, while before them lay the city, a canvas on which they would paint with colors of trust, respect, and freedom.

CHAPTER 28
SILENT ALLIES

It was on the wide-ranging halls of the Imperial Citadel that once echoed with the tread of soldiers and the hushed whispers of clergy; now silent, it was as though only a different kind of echo filled them: a deep, contemplative stillness wrapping around the few who dared to venture out. For though the rebellion had won its victory, within these walls, the weight of what that meant to them was finally settling.

Dax stood in the middle of the great hall, wrapped around by history. A place that once housed the seat of an oppressive power would now be the venue of reconciliation in its true meaning. Gathering the leaders, thinkers, and healers from each and every part of the Eryal Continent, he got down to discussing where to head further in the process. Representatives of the various factions, once terrorized and hated, now stood shoulder to shoulder as they unified for one cause: to rebuild not just the city but also the spirit of a nation that had been subdued for so long.

. . .

Sylvia stood beside him, her light cloak slung over her shoulder, shining softly, steadily from her. It was as though those teachings of old, the ways in which Light Magic was twisted into a tool of control, were distant, some sort of bad dream. Now all that remained was the urge to take Light Magic in the opposite direction-the power of healing, not corruption poisoning its very essence.

A hush fell upon the hall as Dax raised his hand. In a voice unraised, yet cutting through with quiet intensity, the hall was his: "We stand in the ashes of an era defined by fear and oppression, an Empire that used its power to silence, to manipulate, and to control. Today, we are here to make sure that what we rebuild will be shaped by hope, by compassion, and by the resilience of those who endured it.".

A murmur of assent, heads nodding in the moment of silence succeeding his speech. War marks, the tough survivors, and the determinacy of never again were written on every face around him.

"Yet we also have to take into consideration the fear," Sylvia added, the modulations of her voice in equal balance. "That which still lingered, even nowadays, of the Light Magic, of trusting, of the darkness within each of us. If we want to build a future embracing everything we are, we have to approach it with honesty.

. . .

Lyria, one of the strong faction leaders and respected by all, rose, and her firm voice sounded: "Sylvia is right. Light Magic has been used to dupe us, and it is not something we can just look away from. Thoroughly discarding it runs the risk of taking away from ourselves that inside part, which is a force that can be harnessed for good.

Kael's face was a mask of seriousness, his voice gruff but sincere-a fierce warrior from the Northern Alliance. "What we need is balance: a counterbalance to protect Light Magic from corruption in the hands of people with ill intentions, yet serving its true purpose.

Sylvia stepped forward, her face set. "My proposition is thus: let us form a new covenant, an order invested in the art of using Light Magic with a consideration towards ethics. Let whoever joins this order promise that his use of Light shall be to heal and to protect only, to nurture our people. They shall be bound not by lust for power, but by a commitment toward well-being for all.

The idea sparked a debate down the hall. In Sylvia's mind, the covenant became the means whereby the integrity of Light Magic was preserved, allowed to flower without the fear of being exploited. It would be a vow-bound order, principle-led, so that Light Magic would never become the tool of tyranny again.

Dax listened, weighing the implications. "When we build such a system, it must be transparent to invite scrutiny. We cannot afford to have secrets nurtured in dark corners, or we run the very real risk of becoming what we fought against.

A murmur of assent went round the representatives present. The concept of the covenant, an ordinance for the responsible use of Light Magic, was progress, a check against those atrocities being allowed to happen again.

It was only when the day wore on and the deliberations finally began in earnest that Dax turned to them-the fighters, the caregivers, the sages-all adding their unique perspective to the world they forged. Their visions, their dreads, their aspirations-these teemed inside his brain and helped solidify his perception of what was possible.

With that, the council closed the first meeting on a seal of common oath: an oath to unity, justice, and transparency. In that moment, Dax realized that the final victory of the rebellion had not been by the fall of the Empire but by this-people all different, with many abilities and different opinions, joined together in service to a common ideal. Challenges would arise; to that much he was certain. But they would face them together.

As night began to fall, a soft darkness draped over the ruins of the Imperial City, through whose silent streets Dax and Sylvia strolled, side by side. Yet the city in blast, scath, and scar stood but within the house of ruin lay a stillness, a quiet strength which had outlasted the storm.

. . .

She looked upward into the black sky, her face aglow in the pale moonlight. "Dax, do you think we're doing the right thing? That we really are making something that will last?

He took a deep breath, and his gaze did not waver from the far horizon. "I think we are working on a thing that can give humanity an alternative. An alternative to live free, to trust others, and to wish that Light and Shadow can coexist. And to me, that's a beginning worth fighting for.

And so the two kept traveling into the night, each step a soft echo of distance traversed and paths unraveled. Their hearts felt the burden of the past-the scarred landscape of war and the still-glowing spark of hope: a future to take shape, to find the proper place of Light and Shadow, in a world where freedom was no longer an ideal, but living and everlasting.

CHAPTER 29
THE DARK BENEATH

Dax stood before the Tree of Life, whose luminous branches stretched high toward the sky, bathed in an ethereal light which seemed to pulse with every heartbeat of the forest itself. Each of its leaves shone with some semblance of the ancient knowledge the Whispering Woods had to offer. The wide trunk of the tree was weathered; its grooves seemed to mark the passage of ages past with innumerable souls coming for solace and truth.

He went to one knee, his hand remaining on the rough bark, his fingers tingling with the buzz of energy running through it-a pulsating stream that connected the past to the present, Light to Shadow, life to death. It was a feeling unlike any he had ever experienced, a stillness, a quiet beginning to hush the ragged whispers of his mind.

This had been a journey unrelentingly fraught with trials-the weight of combat, the death of comrades, the gnawing knowledge of freedom's cost-all these had left their scars upon him.

It was here, now, before the silent witness of this ancient guardian, that he gave rein to his grief.

His hand touched the bark, and with that touch came visions: faces of the dead, what was given, what was never to be. Let his frozen feelings well up: grief and regret, relief, and love for the friends who'd stood by him. It was an offering-what he had suffered laid open before the tree so that it might understand, so that he might find some little peace with himself.

A warm breeze stirred the leaves as he closed his eyes and murmured tones that seemed to come from deep within him. At first, it was incomprehensible-too much interference by too many voices-ancient guardians, forest spirits, those who had gone before. Then, the whispers coalesced, and they spoke not of judgment but of understanding.

Together, the voices whispered low, yet powerful, "Life is a balance, a dance between light and shadow, between pain and joy, growth and decay. Every path taken, every decision made, becomes another thread within the tapestry of existence.".

Dax's breathing slowed; his heartbeat fell into rhythm with the pulse of the forest. The Tree of Life was more than a vessel of knowledge; it was a medium of connectedness. It was here, in the quiet, that he caught sight of a reality that had little to do with his doubts or fears-a reality that he was described not by victory or defeat, but by a balance he worked toward inside and out.

. . .

Whispers brought him further, infusing him with silent strength-a realization that the past need not be his prison but part of the foundation on which to make a new construction.

You have walked through shadow yet it has not consumed you," they said, "You have fought with light, yet it has not blinded you. Embrace the wholeness within, for it is there peace will be found.

A tear tracked down his cheek as what was in him started to lighten. Now he saw that to honor the lost wasn't to be consumed by their loss, but that he could remember the hell he had known without giving in to it. He could be a force for balance: carrying on with the ideal of freedom and justice yet not the compulsion toward its control.

But by his side stood Sylvia, also a constant-a bright comprehension shining in her eyes like a reflected shine of those inner strengths in himself. She, too, had struggled with her demons, coming out strong, her sense of purpose both deepened and clarified. Outside, the war raged, and with it, the struggle inside on their journey. Together, they would go more into the future beyond this clarity.

Gently, Dax allowed his fingers to slip off the tree. That was it-the reason he came searching, not for an answer but for the peace, the reconciliation with his past and into the future.

. . .

The whispers died away, leaving only the rustling of leaves and the soft humming of life within the forest. Dax stood, his heart lighter now-the weight of his choices no longer a burden but a reminder of his journey. It was if the Tree of Life gave him its wisdom, leaving him with a feeling of completion, a feeling that he found within himself the strength to do what lay ahead.

Sylvia reached out, her hand clamping on his, her smile soft and resolute. "The journey's not over," she said, her tone a promise.

Dax nodded, his gaze meeting hers with a newfound understanding. "It does. And together, we'll forge the path forward."

They returned to the Tree of Life, no longer irresolutely walking but now with purpose. The whispering woods seemed to stand back to let them pass as they walked along in soft light, as it were, with a kind of blessing upon their further journey. They turned and went away lightly, treading with light hearts and new hope from the sheltering home of the woods out into the morning of a brighter world.

CHAPTER 30
REFLECTIONS OF THE SOUL

In the aftermath of the Whispering Fall, the Rebel camp was quiet, resolute-the stark opposite of the bloodbath that had graced the same ground less than a week prior. The scent of pine and earth clung to the chill in the air, bitter among wisps of smoke from small flames as soldiers gathered, tending wounds and piecing armor back together, telling tales of the hard-won victory they had fought to claim. Yet beneath the relief, one serious weight still lay-a recognition that very far from over, their journey still lay under the reach of the Empire's shadow.

Dax sat on a tree stump at the edge of camp and sharpened his blade with the steady rhythm of a warrior practiced. The victory at Whispering Falls had been huge, but the shadow of the Empire still hung over them, as dark as the cloud that had threatened to storm on the night of their battle-a reminder that the struggle for freedom was still very, very far from over. He worked, his eyes straying to the other rebels-the weariness on their faces, the quiet resolve dampening all signs of jubilation.

. . .

And then Sylvia appeared, an oasis of tranquil light amidst the fatigued camp.

She stepped in silently; her healing magic was a balm to both body and spirit as she resumed tending to those who were still recuperating. Yet, she knew deeper wounds-those wrought by loss and fear-would need more time to heal, healing which was more than her magic could mend. Leaning down beside Dax, she laid a light hand on his; the touch was grounding and warm, offering a wordless moment of connection.

He looked up, his face softening as his eyes wrapped around hers. "We won, Sylvia, but somehow, it does not feel like a win-not quite.

Sylvia nodded, knowing in his fatigue. "Victory is not in the battles, Dax. A conquest is a thing built to last-a world where nobody must be under the shadow of the Empire. That's why we go on.

Dax exhaled loudly, loosening his hold on the blade. "Sometimes, I wonder if that's enough. If we're enough.

Her eyes were steadfast, shining with silent strength, fastened on his. "We are, Dax. And it's not just us. Look around-these people believe in this cause. Not because of us, but because they believe in a world where Light and

Shadow can coexist. A world where power isn't feared, but respected.

Around them, the camp was abuzz with activity. The rebels passed by purposefully, tending to their tasks with silent pride and with weariness. Sylvia watched them-observed how firefight leaped across their features, casting light and shadow alike, a reflection of unity sought, the equilibrium they had fought for.

"Remember when we started?" she asked softly, "We were few, lots of outcasts and dreamers with a vision. See the difference in us now.".

A faint smile arced Dax's lips. "A dream that somehow seemed too impossible. Yet here we are." He turned to the faces behind them, a flicker of pride softening the shadows in his eyes. "Do you think they understand? The people behind us, do they get it, really-the harmony we're trying to achieve?

Sylvia cocked her head to one side, contemplating. "Some do. Some still are learning. But that's why we fight, right? To show them that Light and Shadow are not enemies. That we don't have to be afraid of one and worship the other. It's not a question of which side you choose, but embracing both.

A snicker of laughter, from a huddle of young soldiers sharing one of those few light moments, wafted up to them. Sylvia smiled, catching in their features that flame of hope which had seen them through the most desolate of moments.

"Look at them," she said softly, shining with feeling in her eyes. "They're more than just soldiers. They're people who know what it's like to live under the control of the Empire-people who know what's at stake here.

Dax followed her gaze, his expression contemplative. "They trust us. They trust that we're leading them toward something better."

Sylvia laid a firm but tender hand on his arm. "That's our strongest weapon, Dax. It's also our responsibility. Every step we take, every decision we make-it's about honoring that trust.

The sky over them dissolved to twilights, and the stars lanced the dying light one by one, each a silent witness to their oaths. Sylvia collapsed backward, looking upward, as if drawing strength from the constellations that watched over them through each battle, each struggle.

We cannot alter the past," she whispered, as though the belief were swollen inside her. "But we can frame the future. We can build one to make every sacrifice worth our while-something to last.

Then Dax looked at her, a spark of hope lifting the heavy weight in his eyes-and all the journeys they had undertaken together, the connections forming between them, the one of Light and Shadow, forged and then tempered with every battle side by side.

. . .

It was in this quiet of the camp, in soft murmurs of their fellows, crackling of fires, and humming far away of the forest, that resilience soothed. It had turned out that the camp grew bigger than a refuge; it was a stronghold of strength where people came to unite, not to fight, but to build a fear-and-oppression-free life. It had been a while; night started enveloping the camp in its cocoon of shadow. Amidst the dark, the glow of Sylvia's Light Magic beamed serenely, a soft reminder of the balance they fought for with their blood and sweat. Turning to Dax, her voice was barely more than a whisper. "We may not see the end of this journey, Dax. That doesn't make it any less worth fighting for.

He nodded, his heart overflowing with pride, mixed with the determination within. "We're in this together, Sylvia. So long as we keep on moving forward, we are already winning." They stood together, shoulder to shoulder, ready for whatever was to come. Their journey was not yet done, but as they looked out across the camp, there was a renewal inside-a quiet, unbreakable resolve to protect the balance they had found, guiding those that would follow on to a future wherein Light and Shadow, unity and freedom, might coexist in harmony.

As they went inside again, toward the center of the camp, the stars above witnessed that pledge: a silent promise of a fight, a struggle for a world in which every man finds his place, where balance isn't some ideal, but a way of being. As they walked among the camp, nodded and smiled at by the rebels around them, they knew they held inside something more than arms: the capacity to inspire-to lead their people toward the dawn of a new era.

The low-burning fires cast a warm glow of comradeship over the camp-the very reason now that had joined them in this battle. And in that soft, lissom dance of light and shadow, Dax and Sylvia saw their future: a world where both forces could finally stand as equals, unbroken in their harmony.

CHAPTER 31
AN OATH RENEWED

The Whispering Woods were wardens against the growth of doxatic expansion: a place of wild growths, a haunt of ancient mysticisms. Filled with trees that, with their years, had grown so twisted and gnarled, their tops culminating in one unbroken cathedral of emerald light, their branches intwined as with the arms of gods forsaken by the world, it was rare for any sun to break its way through the thick canopy above and make the dappled shadows dance upon the moss below. It was as if the forest breathed-and not just with that soft hum of life, but with something almost physical, an energy palpable to the weight of uncounted secrets and eons of wisdom.

The forest was like a cloak upon Dax, weighted heavy with the memories of those who had gone in before.

The air was thick with the scent of pine and damp earth in a rather heady mixture. Every breath carried in it the wild, subtle essences of the place. His own shadow seemed to melt into the dim, green light, a part of the wood's primeval energy, its deep-seated memory. There was a pricking at the edges of his awareness as if the forest watched him, weighed and judged him. The past had brought Dax here-into this place where myth and reality merged together. Rumors of numerous seekers, journeys lost in thick mist since times of yore and the secretive confines of the woods, lay nestled beneath the thick canopy of the Whispering Woods. It was said to be here, the place of the fabled Tree of Life, full of ancient wisdom and healing. And yet, there was this nagging, indescribable feeling of doubt. It was never about mystic powers nor even peace of mind; it was an attempt towards understanding-perhaps a conviction that in this primeval woods, he would find answers that would help him carry his burden along graciously into the future.

Sylvia walked with him through the woods, herself entranced by the soft dancing of light and shade. And the pull of the forest was there, deep, all but inscrutable, a vibration from something laid long ago deep inside. The unspoiled beauty of the wood, the wisdom that it held, weighed against the sanitized dogma of the Radiance Church that had shaped so much of her life until recent times. Here, she felt the very heartbeat of the world itself: raw, wild, whole. She knew truth to be found here would not come from doctrine but rather from within her own bravery to see things as they were.

The tales whispered by the legends of the Whispering Woods spoke to both of them: of the persistence of life and of its balance. In the tales told within the Church, Sylvia knew of the Tree of Life, but there, it had been referred to as if more in terms of a relic of power than a fount of wisdom. With each step forward, she made out that it was more like some ancient tree speaking of more than just doctrines. She turned to Dax, his proximity reminding her of the unity they both aspired to, not a division into Light and Shadow, but a meeting, a coming together.

Yari and Sho had done so much together in preparing for this journey, but here the deep was responding to them individually, each confronting what each most feared. With Dax, too, the Whispering Woods became a mirror to his soul-the place where shadows changed shape-like the flickering flames of fire dancing before his memory, faces from his past watching from their dark depths and reminding him of the onus he carried, the lives lost to freedom. It wasn't just his power that pulled him forward, but his urge to find redemption, to find peace amidst chaos he had been through.

But Sylvia, too, knew that the forest was testing the edges of her soul, and Radiance Church had once taught her to fear the uncharted-to view anything deviating from the known light as corruption.

Here, though, she felt those shadows were not here to be feared but to be understood. She reached her hand out and touched the bark of this huge tree; its roughness pulled her back into the real world, exhaling slowly. It seemed as if the Whispering Woods held memories of times when Light and Shadow weren't divided yet-a bridge between common grounds they shared and wove in, their need for balance.

. . .

The woods immediately changed into a maze of tracks, circling under the blind mist with strange inner noises-a strange symphony of whispers and sighs. Now and then, Dax and Sylvia would get glimpses of figures-translucent outlines that fluttered out of sight, eddying between trees. They moved with the fragments of forgotten dreams-guardians of woods, protective of their secrets for so many ages.

Dax's heart raced, even as his head wasn't entirely clear if the cause of that was fear or some semblance of awe. Neither benevolent nor hostile, they simply were things testing his resolution-a measure of his intent.

As the day closed, it colored amber at its setting and cast long shadows, like skeletal fingers, across their path. The two stopped in a small clearing where one shaft of sunlight managed to pierce the canopy, lighting on a patch of wildflowers seemingly afire with an ethereal light. Dax's gaze stayed on those flowers, whose tender forms were such a sharp reminder that life would find a place to thrive even in the most deserted areas.

He shut his eyes, feeling the whispers of the woods surround him, a soft murmuring that was in someways kindly and in others confrontational.

"We're not just looking for answers," Sylvia said softly, her voice barely more than a breath. "We're looking for peace, for a way to reconcile everything we've seen."

· · ·

Dax opened his eyes and fixed her with his gaze. "And do you think we'll find it here? "I think," she returned, "that the answers are inside us, but so often, we have to go to that special place-a mirror, a reflection-through which to see. Their footsteps hushed on the thick moss carpeting the ground, they went further into the woods. They knew well: embracing in its shelter not only the Tree of Life but also the truth of who they were, the Whispering Woods-shelter balanced between Light and Shadow, between the past and the future.

The guardians they met standing between them and the Tree were there not to stop them but to let them see aspects of themselves they would not see otherwise. With the complete fall of night, the woods around them had changed; the shadows, now velvet deep, almost protected them.

They came upon a quiet glade, scented with night flowers in bloom, steaming with the hum of life unseen. It was here, under the canopy of endless stars stretched across the sky, that they were in silent understanding-a bridge not just to each other but to the forest itself. It was in this quiet, the Whispering Woods wrapped around him with ancient arms, that Dax felt a weight lift, his mind growing still before the calm strength of the forest.

And for the first time in years, he allowed himself to believe that the burdens he carried might find their rest, and he just might find a way to live beyond his past. Next to him, Sylvia closed her eyes, and her hand slipped to the ground-to touch the pulse of the earth, it seemed. They shall have their way to the Tree of Life, finding therein not the mythical powers it was said to hold but the way it shall mold this world as they want: a world where Light and Shadow may coexist, where peace is forged through understanding, and where whispers of the past become the building blocks of a better future.

CHAPTER 32
THE EDGE OF LOYALTY

Before Dax stood the Tree of Life, a monument of the mysteries of the Whispering Woods-twisted, its roots seemed like veins from Earth herself, a seeming network pulsing with the heartbeat of the forest. Its leaves glowed, casting an ethereal light over him and lighting his path to this sacred place. In this quiet stillness of the woods, the tree enveloped him with its presence, almost in a comforting embrace, and for the first time in a long while, his soul was still.

The Ancient tree - a vision in front of him - made Dax's heart hammer. This world was altogether different, deep in the woods. The air was pure; timeless, even, as if beaten beyond the cares and weights he had carried. He had gone through so much to get to that moment in time, yet standing at the base of the tree, his scars were lighter, almost as if the forest understood the pain and, in turn, gave its condolences in silence.

. . .

Yet with this peace came an acute realization of his vulnerable self. Whistpering Woods had confronted him at each turn-spirit, endurance, and determination. His gaze met the tree, and old memories of those trials flooded back into his mind: how ancient spirits confronted him with his fears and doubts, how creatures showed him his deepest insecurities to see whether he was worthy to press further. This tree stood as a paean to life's indomitable will to live; it wanted more from him-to know his pain and to release it.

He stepped forward, hesitations stopping him right on the edge where the light of the tree enveloped him; he felt a subtle shift in energies. A soft breeze stirred the leaves and carried faint whispers-voices that sounded like an echo of his thoughts.

The way it was overgrown, like a living thing with memories, bits, and pieces of all those who had gone before him-those who had found their refuge and transformation under its shadows. He shut his eyes, drawing a deep breath as the whispers closed over him.

Images flooded his mind: moments from his past, both painful and triumphant. Before him now was laid open the comradeship of battle, betrayal etched upon his heart, and the relived pain of not being able to save those who had been doomed. The faces of the people who relied on him for guidance, their strong point and hope, swirled in front of him. The memories whirled around him in a storm of emotions in which he had no blind eye. They'd made him, formed him and here, in front of the Tree of Life, he could feel them dissolving-the tree seeming to take his burdens into its own body. Dax exhaled a shaking breath as the wave of heat washed over him, his shoulders finally easing. He didn't realize just how intently he'd clung to those moments, how much they'd weighed upon him. The tree seemed to know his battle, its leaves whispering a language he didn't know, yet somehow knew far too well-a language of life, of healing, of acceptance. Slowly, he reached out. His fingers brushed the bark: it was rough, warm beneath his touch, but with a gentleness, it seemed, as if the tree were giving something of itself in return for the pain he'd brought. A soft pulse traveled from the tree into his hand up along his arm, to rest in his heart. It was a feeling he had long known, like a light, a glow, an easy warmth seeming to soften the angular edges of his memories, quietening the jarring of his sensations within him.

The whispering voices were loud, with the visions of the lives that had touched the tree before him-warriors, seekers, pilgrims-who had come to the Whispering Woods with no lighter hearts than his. Each one had its own tale of struggle, tussling with the darkest corners of their own soul; beneath its shelter, each one regained their strength. He felt them in the bark, the roots digging deep into the earth, the leaves dancing above his head. Countless lives it gave to that tree, watching every soul as it took its rest under its shade and then rose again.

Dax felt the welling of tears in his eyes. The legends spoke of the Tree of Life being a source of healing, but nothing had prepared him for this profound peace that now enveloped him in the knowledge that his heart, shattered as it had been, was finally to begin its healing process. He now finally knew that that tree was not here to take away his pain, but to help him shoulder it, to change it into something that would give him strength.

Energy pulsed in the tree-soft and gentle-and a new comprehension began to seep into Dax.

The Tree of Life was more than any source of healing; it was supposed to remind one of the strength of resilience, sourced from embracing the poles of joy and sorrow.

His scars would never disappear but rather be less a case of wounds here with the tree, more one of survival marks to remind him of battles won and the resilience within. Dax drew his hand back reverently and stepped back to take in the full view of the tree for the second time.

The entire journey had tested everything in him-to be confronted not only with the darkness of his own past but also with the light he could hold onto within himself. More than anything else, the Tree of Life had given him what he came for in that it showed so delicately the way healing was not the absence of pain, but the will to face it, to accept it, and let it be its beautiful story. As he went to turn and leave, he felt somehow lighter, steps sure. He knew this way was far from over, that even on the path, challenges would still arise. But one gift the tree had given him-to remember-was not to be defined by pain, but by strength, by the way he rose above it.

. . .

This would be his bearing when he returned into a world beyond the Whispering Woods, to face with tenacity each one of the circumstances that befell him, given the resilience here beneath the ancient boughs of the Tree of Life.

CHAPTER 33
THE LIGHT'S SHADOW

The center of the Whispering Woods was different from anything Dax had ever witnessed. Trees here appeared to straighten up-towering sentinels draped with ancient knowledge, their heavy branches interwoven with the very substance of the forest. An electric surrealness hung in the air, an exciting and unnerving atmosphere where every move made was a step closer to something sacred and full of foreboding.

The shadows danced around him, shifting from tree to tree, indistinct in form, spirit more than substance. It was almost as if they too were part of this place, inextricably linked into the web of forest magic. He knew they watched him, weighing his worth, his intentions. Yet silent, their gaze cut into him with pointed judgment, an unseen weight that tested his resolve, set when entering into the forest.

But the Tree of Life's appeal binds him to the determination anew. He could feel that at times during the quiet-the call, the beckoning that spoke to the very fiber of his soul.

He had entered the woods to heal the scars he carried, hoping that some of the mythological powers the tree possesses would mend the fractures inside him. As he went deeper into his journey, he felt the journey wasn't just of a mere wanting of peace; the woods called him to confront his hurt, not to heal them, but to understand them.

The guardians closed in as he went deeper, their forms stark. Some he knew-creatures of the woods, of flesh and bone. Others were strange, amorphous beings of light and shadow, shifting between worlds, bound by some ancient purpose beyond mortal comprehension. Unyielding eyes regarded him, eyes that seemed to stare right through him, beyond the mage to the man beneath-to the echoes of his past, the choices he had made, the regrets. Sometimes they let him pass, while at other times they stood in the way, impressing upon him to stop, to look inwards: confront the feeling of guilt, the shroud he felt he had wrapped himself with-the weight of the lost life taken in his name, decisions taken in the fracas of battles that still haunted him to date.

Confronted with everything he had been trying to bury-the betrayal still scarring him, the relentless pursuit of vengeance driving him-he had no place to hide from himself here at the heart of the Whispering Woods.

Where earlier the path to the Tree of Life did take an aspect of travel, now it took one of pathways in his soul. For every step he made deeper in the woods, the more he got pressed into confronting the shadows within. He has always yielded Shadow magic as a weapon, a motive force to shape the world to his whims. But here, the guardians and the forest itself called for another manner altogether-one of gentle understanding. And slowly, Dax let go of the tight hold he had with his old identity-a warrior forged in darkness-and slowly began letting it go. Dax knew that the shadows were not his enemies but also constituents of power; each small part of them formed a part of him, no different from the light he had come to dread.

And in that, he almost immediately started to see his going into the woods as a trip toward balance, not triumph. The power of the Tree of Life he could feel in his bones did not erase the shadows but rather somehow integrated them, creating harmony.

It was almost as if, with each step, the guardians shifted-no longer barriers to his path, yet seeming to point the way through the twisting and turning pathways of the woods to his destination. He'd catch glimpses of their actual function-they weren't simply guardians nor sentinels but caretakers to the balance of the forest-life/death equilibrium, light/shadow, in the intricately sown web of the forest-kept.

His footsteps fell in bits of sun that dappled across the floor from breaks in the dense canopy above; every sunbeam reminded him that light and dark danced harmoniously. The trees spoke in gentle, ancient songs, and their leaves danced with knowledge from times so long past his. He began to realize that it was this balance-the heart of the Whispering Woods-while the Tree of Life, if he ever reached it, was the culmination of that balance. Now he came into a clearing bathed in an otherworldly light, in which stood, proud and very tall, the Tree of Life. His roots plunged toward the core of the earth, and the branches high toward the heavens. Upon every leaf, a delicate sparkle-as of gold-pulsated softly, as the beat of a heart. It was surrounded by air with such a high level of energy it felt almost tangible-resonance within him, tugging at those parts of him he had kept locked for so long.

The energy of the tree washed over him, enveloping him with a sense of warmth he had never known as he drew closer.

It was the reaching in, into him-touching the wounds, not to take them away but to point to even these as part of his journey. It was on the Tree of Life, which promised not to make him whole by erasing the pain but rather help him to see that his scars were a seal and a witness to his strength. He reached out and touched the rough bark of the tree; instantly, the deep stir within him overwhelmed his past, his choices, his regrets, melting into the symphony of the forest-a song of balance and harmony-embracing. And in this, he knew, as if more fully than at any other moment in his life, that to heal was not to banish the darkness but to enfold it into the light. The silent guardians watched as he went to stand beneath the tree, his head bowed respectfully. A peace fell over him, not of absent pain, but a new understanding of it. His path wasn't about choosing in light and shadow, but how to hold them both within him-to walk a line which honours the duality in his nature.

He had known it all along: this was the balance the Tree of Life stood for, and it was beautiful because of his acceptance of all the parts of himself.

As Dax reached to turn and leave, he felt the forest's blessing upon him, its silent acknowledgment of his journey-of the courage it took to face the shadows within. The murmurs of the leaves, mixing with the whispers of the guardians, somehow blended into one harmonious note of farewell and of promise.

Thus, lighter than upon his entrance, he left the glade, knowing well that he carried with him the memory of the Tree of Life and all the wisdom it had bestowed upon him. He had come for healing, and found it-not in the removing of his pain but somehow in embracing it, in fathoming where lay the balance of true strength that he was now to carry inside. The Whispering Woods put him through trials, showed him the depth of his shadow, the light therein, and he came out not only as a mage but also as a man who knew full well his journey was only just beginning.

CHAPTER 34
PATHWAYS UNSEEN

The Whispering Woods came alive around Dax and Sylvia-the forest shifting, swaying in time with their footsteps almost in Time, it seemed, with their footsteps as if it were alive and accepted them. Long, sinewy shadows stretched out, interlacing in a path that took them deeper into the heart of the Ancient Woods, where tales spoke of the Tree of Life. It was the mythological tree whose power was unfathomable to the human mind, at the same time rumored to be a source of wisdom and healing-the one that healed not only physical wounds but the deepest scar inside.

A shiver overswept Sylvia, though the air was heavy as with unliving things. Trees were taller and closer to each other; gnarled branches interlaced in a strange tangle of grey arms above her head, a vaulted arch that invited yet threatened her.

She glanced through at Dax, her eyes settling on wrinkles tracing his brow-a supposition of anticipation and trepidation-and then back again, a quiet resolve, a hardness forged from a life of hardness and survival beneath the shadows clinging to his person.

"Dax," she whispered, "do you think we're close?

He nodded slowly, his eyes sweeping the heavy shadows. "The forest is changing. There's... a presence here, a force that I can feel, like a heartbeat beneath my feet. We must be near.

They went on, stumbling more and more with every step, the ground getting uneven, gnarled with reaching roots seemingly to grasp them. There was some low hum buzzing in the air, a low-pitched vibration, pulsating with every breath of the woods, ancient power stirring deep inside them.

Then, of course, the guardians appeared.

Figures emerged through the gaps between trunks, through shades formed by branches intertwined. First, they had been just flickers in the corner of their eyes, but as Dax and Sylvia drew closer, the forms grew more clear, congealing into shapes both diaphanous and disturbing. The guardians were as tall and lean, their eyes glowing embers, standing sentry, their existence interwoven into the very weave of the forest.

One guardian stepped forward, his body morphing between animal and spirit, his eyes settling on Dax. And in the farthest corners of his mind, a voice boomed out, bypassing speech. You seek the Tree of Life. Why?

Dax's heart thundered. He met the creature's gaze, and the weight of his own response weighed heavily upon him. "I seek healing," he whispered, "not just for myself, but for the wounds left on the world. I carry the scars of my past with me, scars I need to understand if I'm to help rebuild what the Empire destroyed.

The guardian's eyes narrowed, and the air seemed to firm a little around him, testing for the honesty in Dax's words. "The path you seek is not an easy one," he said. "Healing is more than the removal of pain: it is the acceptance of all that has passed, the good and the ill.

Sylvia stepped forward; there was a strength in her voice laced with an underlying hint of vulnerability that was rarely shown. "I, too, seek understanding," she said. "I've seen Light twisted, used for control rather than compassion. I wonder if there's a way to honor Light and Shadow, creating balance.

In return, the guardians spoke in soft rustling of leaves and words of ancient speech that weight seemed to attach itself to. The leading guardian, more spirit than form, stretched a beckoning hand in their direction.

Then come, it whispered, but to find the Tree of Life, you must face all that you fear. It would take more than courage on such a journey; it would take laying down every illusion, confronting every shadow.

They nodded, and in the depths of their bones, his words came to rest. Together, they stepped forward, deeper into the forest. And with that gesture, the air did thicken, near liquid with anticipation. Every step was like going down into some forgotten world, some place where time and memory did a dance as complicated as the tangle of trees around them.

Suddenly, the ground opened before them, revealing a bright, flat place that seemed to radiate light from any and every point and none at the same time. The center had the Tree of Life, tall and ancient, on whose bark grew living runes and ivies, while its leaves shimmered like a star constellation stitched across the treetop canopy.

Dax's breath caught in his throat, and he had the sensation that he stared into the very heart of the world. It pulsed to life-once, twice-and with each pulsation, a concurrent beat of his heart, unsaid rhythm binding him to this ancient being. And in that instant, he could feel fear and doubt melting, flowing out of him, replaced by a deep sense of peace, one feeling he hardly knew. Sylvia felt that, too. Standing beside Dax, she felt the tree peered into her soul, read every joy and sorrow, every hope and regret. The tree's presence was gentle and unyielding, reminding one of the oneness of all things, Light and Shadow, life and death, and the balance binding them. Dax came closer and laid his hand on the rough bark of the tree. The sudden flood of warmth coursed through him, soothing energies washing over mind and spirit. Memories bubbled to the surface-memories of battles fought, of friends lost, of the darkness he had wielded, of the light he had shunned. Each memory was an ache, each beautiful-a constituent part of the whole that was himself.

It spoke to him wordlessly, in feelings, impressions, and images. The tree showed him that to heal was not to delete but to take the past and weave it into the present-what the tree was: strength from sorrow, resilience from regret. And he saw his scars as evidence not of his failures but of his survival, testimony to his journey.

Sylvia stepped close, laying her hand beside his.

And with the sudden surge of energy from the tree within her, she was acknowledged-counting all the paths she had walked and the choices she had made. She could feel Light tingling and Shadow cooling within her, reminding her again that her strength was in accepting both.

The Tree of Life was whispering a truth now felt for long and greatly dreaded: this compassion joined Light and Shadow more closely than was supposed by such men in inflexible divisiveness, erected for a lust of power. And it was into this light that the two stood together, worshipping in light of the Tree of Life, which was not a source of healing so much as a reminder of the balance they had been seeking. Healing and peace had been their purposes for coming-and all those things they had gotten, but not in the erasing of the pain, rather in embracing it. As they finally turned to leave, the guardians parted; their eyes, softer, no longer imposing, now protective. Dax and Sylvia knew they would leave this place changed-within them, a chip of the Whispering Woods, of the Tree of Life, with the wisdom thus forwarded.

The walk back through the forest was quieter, lighter, with weighted silences between them. Whereas before the whispered sound of the forest had seemed ominously daunting, it now seemed to hum some song of reassurance-a promise that they were never alone, and the forest would watch over them whenever they went out into the world beyond its borders.

Coming out of the woods, they stopped and looked back on the trail from whence they had come to the Tree of Life. Refreshed, feet on solid ground, ready for purpose: it was as if Dax finally felt the weight of his past lift, now replaced by an inner determination to carry forward into life the lessons he had learned. And Sylvia, with much pity in her heart, she knew her path would join worlds of Light and Shadow to the same balance she herself had found deep in the forest. Together, they pressed onward, taking leave from the Whispering Woods with its wisdom within their heart, their soul forever touched by the gift the Tree of Life had given it: to heal, understand, and bring balance.

CHAPTER 35
DEFIANT HEARTS

As Sylvia emerged from the heart of the Whispering Woods, the truth she had unraveled weighed heavily upon her. Indeed, the knowledge she now carried was a burden and a beacon-a painful reminiscence of how deep into the land the corruption of the Empire had managed to sink, twisting the very fabric of magic to its controlling whims and not protection. Hurrying her pace, her mind was a jumble of thoughts tumbling over each other, urging her to get to Dax with this revelation. He had to understand the ancient, horrific legacy of the Empire. Together, they would make sense of it and harness it. Perhaps this was how they would actually manage to use that revelation to unshackle the people once and for all.

Dax was waiting for her, standing on the edges of the Whispering Woods, a look of both relief and curiosity etched upon his features as she approached. Sylvia could tell he was studying her, keen perception in his eyes reading tension in her stance, the determination set in her eyes.

· · ·

"Sylvia," he said, his voice low but insistent. "You found out something, didn't you?" Nodding, she huffed to catch her breath, the enormity of the truth bubbling inside. "The Tree of Life, its magic, its wisdom-it's tied in with the history of this land in a way I never thought it was. Dax, all that we have fought for, all that the Empire has in control-it all started here, with these woods.

He quieted then, but his ablaze eyes didn't leave hers. "Tell me.

Sylvia took a deep breath and composed herself.

But the Empire didn't only conquer with this war and manipulations of the government; they also abused the very Light Magic, using the Whispering Woods as a source. They created an artifact-an ancient relic of unimaginable power. With that, they had sustained their dominion over the people, had entrapped Light Magic into servitude, and corrupted its purpose." She paused, her voice caught in bitterness.

The Radiance Church-the entirety of the Empire's foundation-is rooted in this perversion of power.

Dax's face hardened and a storm began to rise in his eyes. "And the Church... used this very artifact to subjugate the people, imposing their desire through that self-same magic they declared was sacrosanct?

. . .

"Exactly." Sylvia's voice turned fierce. "By means of Light Magic, they kept the people incarcerated; they used it to enslave the people's minds and snuff out their terrors and hopes in the name of enlightenment.

He fisted his hands at his sides, the weight of this revelation only now beginning to set in. His own scars felt raw; the memories of the Empire's oppressive grasp even more real, knowing now that it was so close to the use of the power emanating from the Whispering Woods. "This artifact, this weapon. it is still out there?

She nodded solemnly. "Yes, I believe so. The tree showed me pieces, snatches of how the Empire misrepresented the woods' magic, binding it into their artifact. And I felt the darkness wrapped around it, the grotesque strength that keeps our people hostage to this day.

Muscles clenched in his jaw, the thought wrestling with him. "Then we have to find it and destroy it. If this is a relic at the heart of their power, it's the only way to truly free the people.

In that silent pause between them, a connection had been made; that crystallization of resolve now rested on this one common goal. Sylvia's revelation had changed everything. They were no longer resisting the Empire but on the path of uprooting its base to take down the magical forces which were holding it standing.

. . .

Dax," Sylvia's voice softened, "this isn't going to be easy. The relic is ancient-protected by layers upon layers of enchantment. And then there are those who would stop at nothing to keep this buried-those who believe that even within the Church, the end can justify any means.

His eyes flashed bright. "Then let them come. We've come this far, and I won't let fear hold us back now." Then he looked at her, his voice dropping. "Thank you, Sylvia. For finding the courage to face the Tree, to seek the truth. I know that can't have been easy. A faint, worn smile crossed her lips. "I did it because I believe in what we're doing. People deserve to be free, to know the truth." Then she met his gaze, and the heat in the sure conviction of his eyes lent weight to hers.

Together, they brewed a plot, the whispers mingling with the sounds the trees emitted. Whispering Woods acted like one silent listener, approving this scheme. It was a perilous path they were about to thread, full of uncertainties, with the possibility of betrayal at every turn. Having truth on their side, they felt nothing could stop them.

As night began to fall, they headed back to their camp, each step filled with what was to come. They now had a purpose beyond the rebellion-a purpose that could change the world. They were going to see it through with the will to return balance to the world, release the chains that bind Light Magic, and let the real power of the Whispering Woods restore to its rightful place.

CHAPTER 36
THE GATHERING STORM

Stemmed from the heart of Whispering Woods, the weight he carried upon his shoulders was new-and an undeniable truth. The revelation of the woods' spirits had shredded his comprehension and left him raw, yet with a potent clarity. And it was there, while he understood how the Empire manipulated the use of Light Magic, suppressed Shadow, and how such powers were being tragically misused, he had in front of him the web of deceit set to ensnare the people. His heart bled for each life that was getting entangled in those lies hailing from the Empire, but this message of the spirit echoed within: It is time for Shadow to take its rightful place. These words cut deep and beckoned him further.

Poppa stepped out from behind the trees, and Sylvia stood before him, her eyes reflecting the relief and anxiety tugging within her. Yet, in an instant, she registered the difference in him now-the hard core of strength, the determination renewed. Even now, though, his eyes reflected a sadness, a shadowed acceptance of a burden taken on unwillingly.

. . .

"You found them, didn't you?" Sylvia's voice was barely a whisper, almost fearfully low, lest she break the weight of such a moment.

Dax nodded, and in his tone lay the weight of revelation. "The spirits showed me the truth about the creation of the Empire, Sylvia. Everything we've believed in, everything they've taught us... it's all a lie. Light and Shadow, they aren't adversaries-they are two halves of one. The Empire distorted the Light and then used it to enslave and control people.

Sylvia's face clouded; her eyes clouded in a surge of anguish intermingled with anger. "Their having taken one thing intended to keep us safe and then turning that into shackles." Painfully scarring, her voice was bitter with undertones of betrayal. "How dare they take something so pure, so holy, for their self-serving ends?

"They didn't just defile the Light," Dax said, his voice whetted keen with malice. "They made us fear the Shadow, despise it, be afraid of it, made a monster of it. What they were afraid of, though, was the power. The Empire knew, as long as Light and Shadow were in balance, they had no chance, and so, they tried to eradicate it.".

Sylvia's eyes burned with renewed resolve as her hands clenched at her sides. "Then we'll turn that balance against them. We'll show them that together, Light and Shadow are far stronger than their distorted version of Light could ever be."

Praise and wonder welled in Dax's chest as he looked at her, still standing, unflinching by his side to remind him that he did not have to bear this weight of destiny upon his shoulders in isolation. "The spirits called me the champion of the Shadow, Sylvia. But I was never meant to do this alone. This path, this balance-it's something we'll forge together. I need you. We need each other.".

Sylvia placed a firm hand on his shoulder, grounding him. "Then together, we'll restore balance, Dax. We'll show the people the truth, reveal the Empire's lies for what they are, and watch their hold crumble."

They began to walk together, making a plan to get at and expose various scams run by the Empire.

The trees surrounding them hummed their approval; the rustling of leaves was the chorus of their resolution now shared. Dax's mind raced with how they could stand in the way of the Empire without putting those they tried to protect in a compromising position. They couldn't afford recklessness; they needed a strategy-a way to turn this newly found truth into an advantage without inviting further destruction.

I've been thinking of the Radiance Church," Sylvia whispered, and furrows deepened on her forehead. "Their leadership, the High Council-they're at the center of this farce. Can you imagine, if we were able to unmask them and make the people see, literally, that the 'Light' of the Church was a constructed thing. this may well bring a revolution, one that should finally break the Empire from its axis.

Dax nodded, things finally clicking together in his skull. "The Church depends upon its relics-the symbols of its supposed purity and power-to keep control. If we could get a hold of one of those relics and show its real nature… that might be enough to tear down the veil of lies.

Sylvia's eyes flashed with comprehension. "Yes! It would be like drawing aside a curtain, to let the people see the truth that the Empire has kept hidden." And even as she said it, her voice grew serious. "The only problem is. getting close to a relic. They're heavily guarded, and the Church would go to war before allowing anyone near them.". A sardonic curve pulled on Dax's lips, his eyes glittering with suppressed laughter. "That would be where Shadow Magic comes in. They may fear it, but at the same time, they underrate it. I'll be able to use Shadow Magic to slip in, unnoticed, and mask us as we go in search. With your Light Magic, we may be able to bypass the defenses they have set upon the relics.

Her hand drifted to the crystal pendant at her throat—a memento from her days as a Light Magic apprentice. "There's a relic buried deep within the Cathedral of Radiance," she said quietly. "One of the holiest symbols of the Church—far more powerful than anything I've ever carried. They claim it's infused with divine energy.

. . .

Provided we can reach it, show it as it actually is; it finally might yield the secret to break the Empire's stranglehold.

Mere consideration quickened his pulse-dangerous and exhilarating. There and then, Dax realized the purpose the spirits gave them: they were not rebellious against a tyrant but protectors of a fractured balance, champions of a truth that finally was to free their people.

They moved further, and the whispers of the forest sounded to bid them farewell. For one instant, the Whispering Woods were allied with them, and the secrets of the past became weapons in their hands. What lay ahead would be dangerous, but they were prepared: armed with one another, Light and Shadow in balance, and the spirits' blessing. They finally emerged from the forest when the sun was well below the horizon, stretching out long shadows that mixed in with the dying light.

Standing together on the edge of the forest, Dax and Sylvia looked out over the land to which they had sworn allegiance. Before them, danger; behind, the truth they had discovered, a guidepost to light the way. Ready?" Sylvia asked, clear of voice, with a sparkle of fire in her eyes. Dax nodded, his eyes ablaze with unyielding resolution: "Let's rebalance the scales." And with that, they moved forward together, the conglomerate darkness huddling around their feet. Standing together, no longer simple rebels, but two halves complementing each other, Light and Shadow in an almost impossible fight to finally give hope to a world that had lived in darkness for far too long. The Empire would shake; so would the people.

CHAPTER 37
FIRES OF REBELLION

The deeper Dax wandered into the Whispering Woods, the heavier the air got; every step he made was deeper into the heart of some sort of ancient magic pulsating beneath his feet with the cadence of a steady heartbeat. Shadows danced beside him; their movement was almost alive, reminding him of a power he once feared and fought. With every step, he felt the hum of dark corners of the wood, the quiet confirmation at each step of the place he had renounced.

It was a gift from the spirits, painful to receive but a gift nonetheless. The revelations of the spirits about the origins of the Radiance Church and the twisted use of Light magic had shattered everything he believed in.

He had known cruelty, yes, but to understand that even the very magic he had once held in high regard was intentionally perverted-the comprehension was a deep wound to his soul. Still, he would hear the whispers of the spirits, images of ancient Shadow Mages, who once made sure the power of Light was balanced with the wisdom of Shadow-to protect the world from the manipulations of the Empire.

Balance." he mouthed, the word hanging in the air, heavy with the silence, and settling into his marrow.

The whispered secrets of the forest grew loud with every step, almost into a coherent melody of sorts-a guiding tune closer to the Tree of Life. It was a place of healing, a wellspring of untarnished power that the Radiance Church had never reached. That thought comforted him, like a beacon of purity untainted by the corruption spreading throughout his former life.

The path started getting narrow and heavy with foliage. A different feel settled over the Whispering Woods. It was as if the trees were leaning in closer, their bark, in this light, etched with glowing runes. He ran his hand along the rough wood, feeling a strange pulse beneath his fingers as though the trees themselves knew him, knew the burden he carried. You were never my enemy, he whispered now, his eyes traveling along the shadows between trees. Taught to fear the dark as if it should be the embodiment of all that is evil, he now knew otherwise. Shadow was just one more face of the world's nature-nothing to be feared but understood. It was the Empire that had distorted his perception, instilling their very fear and prejudice with the purpose of keeping the inhabitants downtrodden, keeping the Shadow and its power from those that might find freedom within its embrace.

. . .

Until finally, he came upon a clearing; there, dead at the center, stood the Tree of Life, still upright and proud.

It had a huge trunk, a mixture of colors and textures on the bark, with veins of silvery light for lifeblood seemingly running through its roots. Its branches rose high towards the sky, inwoven with bright leaves that reflected even minuscule amounts of light, casting soft beams onto the forest floor. The air around this tree felt almost electric, charged with a purity deeply inside him, humbling. Dax approached the tree reverently, the weight of his past actions, the moments when he had used his power to prop the lies of the Radiance Church. He laid a hand on the trunk, his eyes slipping closed as the tree's energy washed into him-gentle yet insistent, an invitation to confront his inner darkness.

Memories burst forth-visions of battles fought, peoples oppressed beneath his former beliefs, the times he had turned a blind eye in favor of obedience. He felt the weight of those decisions, the twisted pride he once felt in being a soldier of the Radiance Church, a cog within their grand design.

But he also saw the glimpses of mercy, the surmises of doubt, the memories of times he'd instinctively protected those weaker than himself-even when he couldn't know why. And in that one deep, shining instant, he suddenly understood that inside him, Light and Shadow had forever been at war, each striving to gain mastery, whereas now-as he sat here before the Tree of Life-he could see a chance of harmony.

. . .

He drew a deep, shaking breath and let the energy of the tree course through him and strip away layers of guilt and anger ulcerating in his heart. Not an exorcism from responsibility, it was transformation-an opportunity for him to understand and accept his past as one part of a journey to bring him there.

He finally opened his eyes to find that the light around the tree had strengthened; his soft glow enveloped him with a new resolution: he had come for healing, but while the Tree of Life was not able to take the scarring away, it had given something more in its place-a realization, an opportunity to rebuild himself into a force for real balance.

Turning away from the tree, in him fell into place a quiet resolve: the power of the Empire was all about perception, the division of Light and Shadow into binary forces. He knew now, and would carry with him, that Light and Shadow are interwoven, each needing the other. They were constituent parts of a whole, not things separate to be conquered or feared, but a fit, just as he and Sylvia were.

Though the road through the Whispering Woods was one of discovery and change in vision, in fact, this was the real challenge yet to come: he had to return, unite those who would share with him in this New Understanding, rise up against the Radiance Church, and show them the truth it had shrouded for generations. This is something that needed to bring the Empire to its knees-up, not through vengeance but merely through knowledge and by the might of balanced magic.

. . .

As he reached out to turn and leave the grove, he faced the Tree of Life once more, its bark grayed with weather, its branches whispering softly back to him in farewell. And in a wordless promise, he whispered back to the spirits of these woods-that what they had shared with him he would honor, using his powers for balance, for harmony, for a world where neither Light nor Shadow was master over the other.

This also included his hope for a return to the world outside the woods as a new man: no longer Dax, the soldier; no longer the pawn of the Radiance Church, but Dax, the Shadow Mage, champion of Balance. Yet, with every step that he took deeper into the darkness of the Whispering Woods, he knew he carried within himself the first light of a fire that would never burn out.

PART FOUR
THE EDGE OF HOPE

Where the hour of darkness reigns supreme, hope swells as the most powerful tide of rebellion. Indeed, outweighed in force and on a crusade of personal sacrifice, Sylvia and Dax start leading their people toward a future without tyranny. Every triumph hard-won fills the oppressed of the Empire with hope, yet the journey remains fraught with hazard as the Empire closes in.

CHAPTER 38
A TEST OF CONVICTION

With every breath, the Whispering Woods breathed with him, the trees seeming to know that he had changed, their rhythm attuning itself to his very breath. There was always something inside of Dax, some gnawing disquiet, urging him toward the edge, but here-deep within the heart of these ancient woods-lay a stillness he had never known, seeping into his very bones, anchoring them.

The spirits swirled around him, their luminous bodies waltzing with each other in candle-like fashion across the night, their silence a drunken spell of approval. And secrets had been told, not of knowledge but of an understanding that could never be taught, only felt. The Light and Shadow that had divided him all these years were opposing forces, a part of a whole, equilibrium within nature: daytime and night.

Dax reached out, feeling the pulse of the forest emanating through his fingers, and knew his purpose had shifted. He was no longer a tool to be wielded, not a part of others but a champion of the balance, guardian of a truth the Empire had sought to suppress. A rugged path now faced him, lined with enemies in every direction, all of whom would do whatever it took to cling to power. Yet he also had behind him the Whispering Woods: an unvoiced entity full of its ancient wisdom and strength.

A turn to leave that had suddenly condensed into one last vision: the inner sanctum of the Radiance Church, whence leaders of the Empire were discussing their plans, cloaked in shadowed halls well away from prying eyes.

He called for the High Priest, Falk, surrounded by the ministers and the enforcers, where every face was cloaked in secrets and falsehoods-a reminder of corruption yet to be faced, a darkness cloaked under its veil of light.

"Dax," one whispered now, her voice barely an echo upon the wind. "The world awaits. The Empire has been culling the people deep within their minds with its lies. It would not be easy for them to see, even when it stands in front of them."

He nodded, his head heavy with the load of responsibility. His was a journey of waiting upon-to show and not to force, to will and not to will, what he had finally understood onto others. For the strength of Light did not consist in conquering, but rather in being able to light up. And the Shadow? A shield, a cloak-to shield what was in their trust, to guard what the Empire could never command.

. . .

With that, Dax began to trot his way back into the woods. The shadows this time welcomed him with open arms-no fear. With every step, he reminded himself of his purpose in doing so; the earth solid, true, beneath his hooves. He went through the Whispering Woods, and the wood seemed to part in respect as he went-an associate, rather than an adversary.

The ghosts of his old battles, the faces he fought and lost, came again before his mind. No more feelings of guilt, but rather of strength: every moment, every decision, had led him here, shaped him into the warrior he needed to be. He is no longer caged by regret but is liberated by purpose. Before him now, as the forest fell behind, lay the city: a tapestry of shadows and light, spires reaching toward the sky like fingers from a fist clutched. Everything the Empire touched, it tried to tame-twisting the natural order of the world to its whim. But he was here to unbind-to reveal the truth under centuries of the lie.

These people needed to see light and dark in their real color, not as a vehicle of tyranny but of harmony.

And there, at the edge of the forest, stood Sylvia, anchoring it for him, an equal resolve in her eyes as in his. She had learned, in turn, that delicate balance between Light and Shadow. Her journey to this had been running parallel to his. Her eyes met his, a silent acknowledgment of the path they now walked together.

. . .

"It is time," she said calmly, yet her voice possessed quiet resolution.

Dax nodded. The pulse of the Whispering Woods was still humming in his veins. "Yes, we carry the truth now, and the people deserve to know. They turned their backs upon the primeval forest as one, setting off toward the city so their footsteps fell into one rhythm. Gone was the bind of the Empire's illusions upon them, or even the weight of their own pasts. Free they were, and in that freedom lay a purpose-illuminated and pure as the morning light bursting across the horizon.

With every step, the city loomed closer-the shadow of the Empire over it, towering, yet no longer invincible. For Dax, the way to balance had just really started, but at least he knew he didn't have to walk it alone anymore. He was a Shadow Mage, but above all, he was an agent of Balance-a beacon of light and darkness-and together they would show the truth to all who could see.

CHAPTER 39
SHADOWS AND TRUTHS

The Whispering Woods swallowed Dax and Sylvia into their solemn silence, the weight of their revelations heavy as the thick canopy above them. For they had seen things-vision-like truths that would change their lives; an understanding which would make the way ahead more lucid yet more uncertain. The forest was a mix of shifting shadows and dappled light, almost a reflection of their journey in marrying two powers previously considered to be on opposite sides.

Standing close in this small clearing, each savored the wisdom given them by the spirits of the ancients-silent guardians of the woods. Whispers still lay in the air around them, with reminders of lost harmonies of the world and urging stewardship upon them.

"We have come so far," Sylvia muttered, her eyes falling on a gnarled tree, its roots digging into the ground in ropelike coils. "And yet all the while, it is as though we haven't started.

. . .

Dax nodded, her eyes straying off into the shadows cast by the big trees. "I had always thought of the Shadow as being some sort of shield, something that protected me. I never stopped to think that it could be a healing influence-easily as powerful in its way as the Light in its ability to wound.".

Sylvia's hand stretched toward her side, her fingertips brushing against the bark of the tree beside her. "The Empire taught us half-truths," she said, her voice tight with conviction. "They told us Light was purity and Shadow was corruption. They never spoke of balance-of harmony that had existed long before their rise to power. They used Light as a weapon, twisting it to serve their will.

Dax relaxed as he watched Sylvia, saw the weight she carried-years of teaching now shown to be lies, a truth she was now claiming for herself. "It is hard to forget the things they instilled in us," he whispered. "But we know better now. And maybe, if we're able, we will be able to make them see it too.

Sylvia's eyes closed to the world as she breathed in deeply, filling herself with the wisdom of the Whispering Woods. "I want to be that force of balance, Dax. Not some blind follower of the Light, nor one who fears the Shadow. I want to live within that harmony which they sought to destroy. And I want to help others realize that truth."

As her words died away, they seemed to hum with echoing resonance. Tall, towering trees, guardians of earth and silence, kept ward over an oath growing now between them. Spirits of the south wind whispered of ancient wisdom, of forgotten truths-but here, now, Dax and Sylvia were becoming enactors of that wisdom, a marriage of Light and Shadow.

They entered the woods, their footsteps attuned, placing them in perfect cadence. In the quiet, the only sound was the minor crunching of leaves as they fell underfoot. The sun had started to set, casting those amber tones of sunbeams through the woods to mingle with the shades into a living tapestry of gold and green. It told them once more of the balance they sought to restore-a view of what would be if they should happen to succeed in what they were doing.

It was on the walks that Dax felt the weight of his past beginning to shift inside. The spirits had taken him into his interior duality: he was a Shadow worker, a warrior of truth. Never in his life was there a moment spent being at ease with himself-not shunned, not exiled-but a guardian of the balance, a chosen one.

"Sylvia," he finally said, his voice breaking the silence. "We have to take this truth back with us, let others witness what we found here. The Empire is based on lies, on some corrupted vision of Light. If we can make them understand the real balance, if we can help them open up to both Light and Shadow-

"We can build a new world," Sylvia finally concluded, flashing her eyes with the vision. "Where man will not be divided by fear, blinded by illusion, and where magic is used to serve empowerment and never to control."

A silent, mutual glance marked a settling of understanding between them-sure, firm. They had fought as comrades, lost as comrades, learned truths that tore them down and built them back up again together. They were joined now by more than their resistance to the Empire: they had committed themselves to the restoration of the natural balance to the world.

They walked right to the edge of the clearing where the track forked right and left, one leading back into town, the other deep into the woods. They halted as one, a silent decision hanging between them.

"Ready?" Sylvia asked; her voice didn't quiver.

Dax looked at her, the determination in her eyes a mirror of his own. "We are ready," he replied. "The journey may be long, but we'll be walking it together, carrying the truth within us." With that, they hit the road back: the woods of whispers they left behind, replete with the wisdom they carried with them for each new beginning they made with every step as the trailing shades merged with the light when they walked into the world they'd change.

CHAPTER 40
A WORLD DIVIDED

There was a silence amongst the leaves-an expectant pause, it seemed-as if it waited for them to prove their resolve. The voice of the Guardians, an ethereal murmur, was silent now, but its challenge still lingered in Dax's and Sylvia's minds: a test of worthiness, one that would prod into the deepest corners of the most dreadful terrors and darkest memories, and the convictions that had brought them here.

His shadow magic stirred within him, a steadily pulsing hum that was the echoing cadence of his heartbeat. That thing which he had felt ashamed of, he now came to realize, was actually a balancing and stabilizing force-a counterbalancing power to Sylvia's light. Together, they were the balance: the very epitome of the Tree of Life-light and shadow as one. He knew it would be that which would see them through what was yet to come.

. . .

Are you ready?" Sylvia asked, her tone barely above a whisper, while her eyes met his steadily.

Dax nodded, his grip on his dagger tightening. "As ready as I'll ever be."

With a mutual nod, they strode out, passing the wall of trees almost as though it were little more than mirage.

In an instant, they were overwhelmed in thick, alien darkness that consumed every last photon of light around them. For a moment, Dax couldn't see Sylvia; he could hardly see his own hands. The pound of his heart quickened, and a primeval fear clawed through his brain, reminding him of every instance of isolation he had faced, every betrayal, and each loss that he had borne.

The darkness closed in around him, an anchor that weighed him down and pressed the breath from him. It filled his mind with the faces he had lost, the mistakes he made, and the soul-eating guilt. He was drowning, lost in some void of his own making.

"Dax," Sylvia's voice called out, clear and strong, cutting through the darkness like a beacon. "Don't let it consume you. Remember why we're here."

Her words steadied him, planted him, and called to the purpose that had brought him here. He reached for his shadow magic, willing it to flow through him, to allow it to wrap around him, not as a weapon, but as a source of strength. Then the darkness slowly lifted, and he could make out beside him the outline of Sylvia, her staff aglow with soft light leading them through the track.

They did not stop; they walked further into the bosom of the woods until it seemed the forest took them past every test of character: shifting, changing obstacles confronting them, making each of them face those secret fears and doubts that lay in their hearts. Every step was a test of ripping the wrappings off the layers in their hearts, making them raw, exposed-but then stronger.

They saw visions-sort of illusions-but as real as the earth at their feet. Dax saw visions of his past: the betrayal that had thrown him onto this path, how many he had lost on his journey. Still, he foresaw the future: a world where Light and Shadow would coexist, where the tyranny of the Empire had fallen to be replaced by a new order based on balance and harmony.

Sylvia's were different, yet as powerful. She watched the messages of the Radiance Church crumble before her-the lies uncoiling, releasing the knowledge of Light and Shadow into view. She saw herself at the helm of this new world, guiding others in how to grasp the true nature of their power: wisely and with compassion. The deeper into it they went, the less the obstacles were physical but personal, making them dependent not only upon their magic but also upon one another. Once they were separated, each being confronted with his or her worst fears.

. . .

Dax had to confront his terror of realization that he would never be free of the consumed darkness within him, that he would forever be an aberration, a means to an end, his life a tool to be used rather than a person. Sylvia had to confront her terror that her faith had been a lie-all she had followed-twisted and manipulated.

In those dark hours, however, they fell back on a memory of one another's words, a sense of the vigour in their team, a spirit of balance which had been theirs together. They pushed through the illusions, the fears, the doubts, emerging on the other side, stronger and more resolute.

They came to the middle of the Whispering Woods: a clear sky bathed by ghostly light. In the middle, the Tree of Life stood tall, proud, and erect, its branches towards the high firmament, its roots deep inside the ground. Its leaves shone with an ethereal brightness cast in soft, golden shimmer across the clearing upon the faces of Dax and Sylvia, astounded before it.

The air was thick with magic upon the Tree of Life, a site where the Force pulsed, alive, like life itself, with currents of Light and Shadow. Dax could feel it seep into him, fill the fissures of his soul, the hurts he had borne so long. A sense of peace, utter calm, swept through him, washing away the guilt and the pain, leaving in its stead a will of quiet steel.

. . .

Sylvia felt, too, the healing energy of the Tree course through her, filling her with a new sense of purpose, a deeper understanding of her place in the world. She was not just a wielder of Light, not just a rebel against the Empire; she was a guardian of balance, a protector of that harmony which the Empire had sought to destroy.

Before the Tree of Life, in the silence, now was heard again the voice of the Ancients--soft, reverential, and seemingly from the very heart of the forest.

"You have passed the test," the voice intoned. "You have shown your worthiness, your devotion to the balance of Light and Shadow. The Tree of Life has bestowed upon you its blessings. Go forth, and take back the harmony that was snatched. The Empire has marred the balance; now it is time to take it back.

A mute oath crossed over between Dax and Sylvia as their eyes met. Yes, they had found what they had set out to find in the Whispering Woods, but it was far from over. The world awaited them-a world in sore need of healing, in need of the balance they now possessed in their hearts.

Hand in hand, they started walking away from the Tree of Life, out of the clearing, onto the path that would be taking them outside Whispering Woods-carrying with themselves the blessings of ancient spirits, the wisdom of the forest, and the power of united Light and Shadow. And as they walked, the forest parted before them, its trees bowing in homage, leaves whispering down their benedictions. No longer were they simple rebels but bearers of hope, guardians of balance, and warriors of a new dawn. So let them also stand together against whatever the future holds, firm, steadfast, in the strength that comes from inside them, great to ward off all darkness and light up into the deepest recesses of shadow.

CHAPTER 41
THE ART OF WAR

As Dax and Sylvia emerged from the clearing, there was a ripple in the air that seemed to take place from some kind of unsubtle energy-a quiet reminder of the profound message from the Tree of Life. Each step they took was lead-heavy with a purpose, as if the very forest knew they had changed. They hovered on the rim of the clearing for several more seconds, looking at the Tree of Life-its branches swaying to some unheard breeze-as a final act of silent persuasion.

Conjured from the depth of Whispering Woods, they stood unflinchingly amidst an unsavory stillness. The whispering and murmuring of the forest in its sleep stood in anticipation of what was about to proceed. Sylvia's eyes had turned firm, steady, and bright with their newfound clarity. And Dax felt that, too-a steady determination, a subtle resonance now between them, ready to meet the world outside with the wisdom they had garnered.

. . .

Dax walked, his mind falling once more to the Empire and the Radiance Church-to those lies that wrung from him every doubt as to what had always been presented to him as sacred. Now, with the meaning of Light and Shadow literally explained to him, he felt closure brewing within his stomach-an inner silence that would no longer be controlled or defined by their twisted version of Light. Ready to challenge these very structures that had manipulated him since long, but not in anger; rather, the power of both sides put together in a balance.

Sylvia," he said finally, breaking the silence between them. "The road ahead. isn't going to be easy. The Church and the Empire have cemented their powers with those lies for centuries, and they're not about to give it up without a struggle.

Sylvia's face turned grave. "I know they employed Light in chaining people's minds, in veiling the truth. But we are no longer the same as we once were. We do know now that Light without Shadow is blinding, and Shadow without Light means darkness. And the people have a right to see that truth on their own.

Every step through the woods got more and more hazardous-thorns on the branches tore rags off their clothes, as if testing their will. Still, it would seem that everything only worked to strengthen it. The world outside was even more hazardous now that they were in possession of a truth that might unwind the very foundational structure of the Empire's rule.

. . .

The closer they were to the edge of the forest, the more weak lights they saw, flickering between the trees. They came out cautiously and found the Imperial patrol: the soldiers, bright in their armor, standing near the edge of the forest. They said nothing, postures tight, seeming on high alert. Dax and Sylvia shared a quick look; word of their being in the Whispering Woods had apparently reached the Empire. They would be in high need to be much more careful.

A woman's head with incisive eyes and an expression of severity lifted up, appealing for silent concentration, as her gaze then fell acutely upon Dax and Sylvia.

"You are far from the protection of the Radiant Church," she said, breaking the silence. "What brings you to these woods?"

With a deep breath, Dax could feel the steady rhythm of the Tree of Life pulsing through him. One more step, and he returned the gaze. "We come with a truth that has long been kept from the people, one that at its roots shall shake both the Empire and the Church which you serve. We seek no bloodshed but to shed light upon that which was in darkness.

Her eyes flashed, and she faltered. "What truth would that be?" she asked, a sliver of skepticism tingeing her voice, though curiosity wasn't too far behind.

Sylvia advanced forward, her voice unshaken: "The Empire corrupted the Light Magic into something it uses, not for curing or protection, but for maintaining control. They used

Shadow as a scapegoat to make them secure power, while we have seen with our own eyes that both Light and Shadow are indispensable, and there is no other real way to peace but through finding a balance between these two forces.

They eyed each other warily, the whispers building among the soldiers. The leader seemed flaccid, torn by loyalty to the Empire, yet the quiet doubt Dax and Sylvia's words had sown in her mind.

"Shall we believe such words of treason?" she said, but her voice shook a little.

He stared back without blinking. "You don't have to believe us. Just come along. See it for yourself: the Whispering Woods, and the Tree of Life-all these are much more than legend. They're proof that the Empire has lied. The very balance they fear will set us free.

She faltered; her eyes spoke volumes of the risk as she looked once more to the woods for the last time. Something in Dax's voice-the conviction with which he spoke-altered the tenor of her doubt. She gave one last signal, and her soldiers stood down. Very well, she said, an edge to her voice, both in defiance and reluctant curiosity. Show us this truth. But let it be known-if you are wrong, if this is some deception-you will suffer as no one has ever suffered. Dax nodded, feeling just a little tinge of satisfaction that he knew would be engendered by the seeds of doubt. That was all he needed for now. The glance trailed off across space between him and Sylvia till their gazes met, and she smiled determinedly.

· · ·

They took the soldiers further into the heart of the Whispering Woods-to the place where the truth about Light and Shadow lay in hiding. Uncertainty faced them at each bend of the path, and yet they knew the truth, fearless to walk. Further in the woods they thus went, with the whispers of ancient spirits once again-a soft chorus to urge them onward, reminding them of the balance they had promised to restore.

CHAPTER 42
BONDS FORGED IN BATTLE

The way back toward the middle of the rebellion was strangely quiet, that kind of silence that follows after a storm that finally has passed. It was as if everything in the world, walking side by side, touched their senses differently: each leaf, each stone, even the wind blowing. Dax and Sylvia stood ready, but this time not only as rebels but as vessels of the new balance ready to enlighten and activate the change that would break the cycle of control and suppression that had bonded their people in such a stranglehold.

Before them lay the city of Ashenfell-scarred, yet resilient. It was here that the heart of the rebellion yet stirred, an avid pulse of those who had suffered under the tyranny of the Empire and those in whose hands the future now lay. Yet as they entered, a new tension showed itself, one speaking of confusion and distrust, factions divided over what the rebellion was to do.

. . .

Now, they saw their fellows gathered in the Great Central Square; the buzz of angry argument leaking into the streets. Some wished to assume control with a new regime of order and watchfulness; others would reconstruct in peace, and only more violence served to continue the very mistakes of the Empire. It was a fissure none wanted to see, having once seen just such a split torn to its advantage by the Empire itself.

Dax pushed forward, his voice cutting through the chaos with silent command. "The balance we seek is not a location; it is a state of being. And we have seen firsthand that the more tightly we control, the tighter the chains. True power comes from the harmony we can create, not from the will we can exert over each other.

A hush fell upon the people as, in the weight of his words, it slowly dawned on them that what he spoke was completely alien to men who knew no other freedom other than victories against something. "The Tree of Life showed us that Light and Shadow are not opposing but complementary forces," Dax said. "The balance is inside each of us. In order to build this future, we have to understand one another, not be afraid of each other."

Sylvia stood now to join him, her voice low in tone but resolute. "So far, our journey has shown us that real change cannot be accomplished by overthrowing only to replace. We have to be united in purpose. The harmony we seek is in listening, in understanding, in lifting one another up. We must rebuild with respect, not with fear.

. . .

Her words hung over them, suspended until they could be absorbed into the lifeblood of the men, when a wave of energy ran through the assembly. Both Sylvia and Dax could see the shift: a light of recognition rising in faces hardened by war. They realized now it wasn't about something with which to wield, but a guiding principle by which to live.

Their vision calmed the silent revolution within the rebellion itself, as the divisions among its leaders were soothed and their cries of dominance and vengeance turned into one ideal of unity and learning to coexist. They all came together into a council, not to spearhead but to guide balanced in understanding, each and every voice and perspective valued.

And then, season after season, Dax and Sylvia watched change overtake the city of Ashenfell. The people who were shattered by tyranny and fear rebuilt-not just homes, but a new way of life. Schools appeared, some dedicated to Light, others to Shadow, in which the young of mind might learn about ancient wisdom obscured by the clutch of the Empire. There then began to appear sanctuaries of healing, that those who had been shattered by the darkness of the Empire might receive their cure in enlightenment from Light and Shadow working in conjunction.

Dax and Sylvia were inside, leading the people, no longer figures of rebellion but symbols of balance. The relationship thickened and forged in the very crucible of war was tempered by the wisdom they had garnered together. Partners of purpose bound not just by affection but by something more beyond that-a reflection of unity finally found after long searching.

・ ・ ・

Their only legacy was one of understanding, not one of conquest. It was a journey begun in desperate hope of halting the oppression, whereby in return came forth a vision of balance to echo down the generations.

CHAPTER 43
A BEACON OF FREEDOM

The pathway in front of Dax and Sylvia was just a little brighter, full of soft humming, which poured balm into the worn tranquility of their souls. By the time they saw the outskirts of Ashenfell, the coarse din of the city-strife and uprising-jolted into the stillness that lingered in their minds. That change, wrought in whispering woods, might be frangible, powerful, like an ember prepared to flare up and bring change to a world which had long forgotten the delicate balance of Light and Shadow.

They were greeted with a sea of rebels and those weary citizens whose faces were half-filled with hope, half-filled with mistrust. Recent successes had resulted in a fragile sort of peace, but the cruelties of the Empire ran deep within the marrow of bones. Some had joined the rebellion as a way of finding meaning through chaos; this reunification was at risk of being torn apart by those very same old terrors, that same anger, and those same ambitions.

. . .

Dax felt it in the crowd, the tension. He had felt it once before-a desire to fight, to strike back at the Empire for what it had done. Yet he knew now that to win solely by dominance was merely to continue the circle.

Dax raised his hand, and the murmurs died down. His voice, tinged with the wisdom conferred by the Tree of Life, rang out loud and clear: "Our journey brought us to the heart of the Whispering Woods-our quest for answers and healing at our backs. What we found there was much more than the truth which encompassed either vengeance or conquest; we have seen that true power is not of forces, but of balance.

Standing beside him, Sylvia added in soft yet firm tones, "We've seen the way the Empire twisted Light and Shadow to tear us apart, but Light and Shadow are not enemies; they are companions, bound in an endless dance. A world built upon this foundation must find its harmony first within and amongst us.

The crowd stirred restlessly, as if frowning upon this appeal for moderation and how it applied to their fierce rebellion. Conversely, in some faces, the expression softened-to the wisdom of the words from Dax and Sylvia-a gleam of hope in the wariness of the eyes.

From the crowd, an elder stepped forward, his face lined with years of hardship and loss. "And what will this harmony bring us, Dax? How will it heal the suffering we've endured, the loved ones we've lost?"

. . .

Dax's eyes locked with the elder's, his tone even. "Harmony is not a destination; it's a process. The Empire's strength was stitched from terror and oppression, and that strength was fragile, and we have seen that strength shatter. Let us not foster tyranny to take the place of tyranny. True healing, true freedom, lies in the establishment of a world wherein Light and Shadow dwell-neither as conquerors, neither as slaves, but as partners.

Sylvia's voice came, her hand upon her heart. "It is not only in Light that comfort resides, nor in Shadow that challenge does. It is in the unity of both that depth in our lives takes shape. We can build a new order, one that honors both-an order which refuses to wield magic as a weapon but uses it as a means to uplift each other.

Slowly, the murmur of the crowd took on a contemplative note. Those harsh lines of skepticism began to soften; the idea of harmony, though foreign to most of them, lighted within them a deep-seated longing. They had been so long entrapped in a circle of misery that unity and balance daunted and excited them.

Over the coming days, Dax and Sylvia started to work with the people, taking up more minor, profound leads among them. They formed a council of many voices from each part of Ashenfell. It is not a council that would rule through fear but a guiding light-one that embraces Light and Shadow, both as forces of wisdom and change.

. . .

And so, lessons in balance began to weave through the rebellion, still slow in evolving from an absolutely combative one toward a spirit of cooperation and understanding. Thus, Sylvia shared how Light Magic had become for her a healing force, finally free from all the control mechanisms of the Radiance Church in the old days, while Dax was sharing how Shadow can be a wellspring of resilience and creativity, a strength that overpowered none but supported instead.

As this balancing factor diffused its influence, the city of Ashenfell gradually began to change. Meditation houses, healing circles, and study halls-where one might learn of the history of Light and Shadow-increasingly came into being where there was once the bitter quarrels and cries for revenge. The town turned into one filled with children learning how to handle the mystical arts properly and not as a tool for fighting, but to create a harmonious balance.

Standing on a hillside one evening, peering down upon Ashenfell, the subtlety of change in the city astonished Dax. What had once been a fractured community slowly knit itself together-its wounds still showing, but healing.

Dax spoke softly to Sylvia, and with a ring of amazement: "The people are ready for this, more than I could have ever envisioned. Like waiting for the chance to break free from the old ways.".

Sylvia smiled, the same thought reflected warmly in her eyes. "Perhaps they were. Maybe all they needed was a reminder, a call for something greater. I think they always knew, deep inside, that Light and Shadow are not rivals. They needed only to see it is possible to accept both.

With the rustling wind the treetops waved, carrying away with it the whispers of the woods, a quiet reminder of the odyssey they had been on. Whispering Woods showed them the truth, and with it, this very truth now started to make its stay within the hearts of the people.

They stared down at the city below them, and both Dax and Sylvia knew that their work was far from over. The path to coexistence was long and serpentine, for there would always be those who envied power and wanted to control. But they were ready, both as heroes from a rebellion and as tour guides through a journey into a world where Light and Shadow could finally coexist.

And the vision of the balance was already burgeoning. As time passed, they were to water it, guard it, and let it bloom into so much more than a simple empire: a world in which the real power lay not with domination, but with balance, where Light and Shadow would dance forever, together.

CHAPTER 44
IN THE EYES OF THE ENEMY

And it was deepening within the Eryal Continent that the vision was now taking concrete form, which Dax and Sylvia had foreseen, their dream world in balance, synchronized with those on the way. Every village, every town showed traces of the Empire: walls defaced by battles, fields tainted by war, faces furrowed by hardship. Yet beyond this exhaustion and sadness, a flicker in the eye-a ray of hope towards life, to be more than just to exist-flickered. It was clear that Dax and Sylvia had not come to make them change; they came as carriers of a vision, which they must have glimpsed in the mystic profundity of the Whispering Woods.

In the town of Emberhill, villagers gathered, some hesitantly, wary of these strangers speaking to them about such things as balance and peace. Children clung to their mothers, while young men and women wore skepticism upon their faces, arms crossed in silent challenge to whatever promise these travelers might make. Sylvia stepped forward, her voice both calm and full of conviction.

. . .

"We're not here to offer an easy path or to erase the pain you've endured," she began. "We come with a lesson, one we've learned ourselves—a path forward, not built on conquest, but on harmony. A way to rebuild through balance, to find strength in both Light and Shadow, in all of us."

Dax joined her, his gaze steady as he addressed the crowd. "The Empire twisted Light to control, Shadow to instill fear. But we've seen both forces as they were meant to be—powerful, yes, but not enemies. True freedom isn't found in dominance; it's found in understanding. In balance."

Among them, an old shriveled woman spoke, her voice firm as the salting that weathered her features: "You speak to us of balance, but where is the reassurance which would protect us, when the only shield we have ever known is fear?

Sylvia met her gaze, her own fear bred into their psyches through years of repression. "Balance is not a quick fix; it is a journey arming us with resilience-a path teaching us to walk forward-together and not divided. Harmony is not something to control; it's a source of strength, and that's something we can all possess.".

The crowd's murmurs died away as the villagers weighed her words. Dax felt the weight of their doubts and hesitations but sensed, too, a quiet yearning beneath the skepticism-a yearning for a life free from the Empire's yoke, a world where they might finally be masters of their own fate.

. . .

Every city and village that they passed was either an uprising or gave reason to hope. The elders worn out by defeats listened to the word about balance with skeptical ears, while children saw them with wide amazed eyes without a trace of fear. It was these children who somehow felt that there was something right, instinctively sensed in their words the promise of a different future.

There, the first Circle of Balance was formed-a place where villagers could work out their differences that now would no longer be solved by violence, but rather by words. Younger and inexperienced trainers of Light and Shadow Magic began to train together, teaching one another and themselves how to cast for healing, creation, and unification.

Sylvia then started taking young Light Mages under her wing, teaching them to harness their magic with neither control nor fear but rather with compassion. She showed them Light could be balm to weary souls-a beacon of hope if it came with empathy. Her training made Light Magic bloom in life, weaved its way into healing gashes, both physical and emotional, within the community.

He took under his wing those who would follow the darkness, teaching them that the Shadow need not necessarily be about secrecy and destruction, but about its hardihood, its ability to give power and depth. He showed them it could link them with their inside self, with the unseen mysteries of the world, and that Shadow, too, might be a force of creation and insight.

. . .

Together, they inspired a new generation-a generation that viewed magic not as a means of conquest, but as one of harmony. Rumors of the Circle of Balance spread as far as to lands no man had ever laid eyes on. While unity was growing, the fear inspired by the Empire slowly began to wane, and belief in balance became one.

As Dax and Sylvia went forward, they turned out to be something more than the leadership of a rebellion: guides, mentors, and signs of hope for a new world. And in the power of that quiet revolution, the tide of their message ran down the length of a continent, in a movement too great for borders, too deep for differences.

One evening, beneath an open sky, their backs to the Whispering Woods, the beat of the earth beneath their feet-throbbed in cadence with that of Light and Shadow in him and her. So they knew full well the road onward would be riddled with hardships and doubts, but they also knew they did not walk it alone. The dawn of a new era was on the horizon, an era shaped by the balance and understanding they carried forward.

And with each step they took, so they knew they came closer to a reborn world, not of war, but of peace, where balance is not a mere idea but lived.

CHAPTER 45
CROSSROADS OF DESTINY

The soft carpet of fallen leaves deadened the silent, quiet footsteps of Sylvia as she walked through the woods, each one reminding her of today's battle-won and lost at the same time. A struggle that still is in the minds and hearts of the ones who remain: the wounded soldiers, the voids to mark where life once was, haunted expressions of faces whose memories are now filled with pain. Hard as she channelled light magic, the weight which came with the loss was never to be dispelled.

In the heart of that forest, the treetops parted above a grassy glade bathed by pale moonlight. The cool night air was almost holy in its quiet-a silence that gave her reprieve for this one swift moment. She sat on the ground, her hands pressed to the earth as if in supplication to the life beneath her fingers. She closed her eyes and let the stillness of the forest wash over her like a soft balm to the ache that went on and on.

. . .

In a few moments, she knew that someone approached her. Dax joined her, his feet light, respectful of the space she had sought. He sat beside her without a word, his gaze upwards in the sky. They sat this way for several moments, two figures within the vastness of the heavens, held together by battles fought and the weight they carried forward.

It was Sylvia who finally spoke, her voice little above a whisper. "We fought for this freedom, Dax. We fought to heal, to rebuild. And some days. I feel those wounds are just too deep, that every piece of Light magic in the world couldn't fix them. I wonder if it is enough.".

Dax turned to her now, calm yet incisive, a deep understanding in the quiet of his gaze. "I think about them too-all the people we lost, those lives we just could not save. It's their sacrifice that keeps us moving forward. Because of them, we create a world where their lives will be of consequence forever. We owe it to them to move on-when it seems impossible.

In Sylvia's eyes, there shone gratitude with a tint of sadness as she looked into his. "It's just.the weight of it: to always face the pull between Light and Shadow, between hope and despair, one does often wonder if he can bear that weight.".

Dax reached out and took her hand in his. His touch was grounding, steady. "You are strong, Sylvia-not because you're unbreakable, but because you feel this weight. That compassion you carry with you, that sorrow. it is what makes you who you are. And that is precisely what this world needs:

someone who feels the cost, who understands the weight of every life, every choice.

His words fell soft around her, a quiet reassurance, while every word sank deep into her heart to remind her of the very reasons she took this path in the first place. She wasn't fighting for a perfect world but one in which every life would have value-a place where hope could be real. And her doubt and her sorrow-they were not weaknesses but a reminder of the strength and resolve that brought her here.

The trees around them were still, the shadows deep but soft. As Sylvia sat down, her mind stilled, her thoughts lining up with a clarity that somehow was more than she had known he needed. She let go of her terrors, sending them off into the night, trusting for the first time on the journey-the bond she had with Dax, the vision they aspired to.

They stood in the silence, her hand still in his. There was comfort in the presence of the other, in the silent strength they found together. Dax's gaze drifted upward, his voice soft. "We cannot change the past, Sylvia. But we can build a future that honors it. We can teach others that Light and Shadow are not enemies but companions, that true strength lies in embracing both."

Sylvia lifted her eyes to the stars, her expression resolute as a quiet determination took shape within her. "Then that's what we'll do. We'll create a world where both forces are honored, where every life matters, where hope is real."

· · ·

They got up together, left the clearing with renovated purpose. Steady their steps were, hearts fortified by the understanding they had found. They knew the way ahead would be lined with challenges, that doubt and fear would rise again. But they also knew they were not alone. Together they were stronger, joined by a vision of a world where Light and Shadow can exist in harmony, joined within respect and compassion.

On their way back to the campsite, the first light of the day struggled through the trees-none too suddenly-and fell serenely upon the forest, painting in its gentle rays. The warmth of a new day wrapped itself around the promise that no matter how long the night was, morning would still break.

And in that instant, peace sat in her-a surety that however long the journey was, together they would face it. They would walk this path together, strengthened by the sacrifices of the past, driven by a common hope toward the future. This was no longer a far-off dream, a world in which Light and Shadow could coexist, but a promise-they would see it through to the very end.

CHAPTER 46
THE DEPTHS OF DESPAIR

As Dax and Sylvia pieced together a plan amidst the ruin of their rebellion, the air began to grow cold. Faces that had hardened through the years of war, yet softened in this brief period of peace, set again in renewed determination. This would be another kind of war-not one of opposition so much as one of persistence. This would be some amorphous, dark, and ancient enemy, an only partial presence hanging at the edges of existence and tugging at the seams that held their world together.

They gathered together in a quiet grove, the trees surrounding them, silent sentinels. Thick with oppressive silence, the leaves murmured on every now and then with a chill wind. Dax looked around grimly. "We have fought the Empire, fought oppression and control. Yet this. this darkness is something different. It does not strive after power; it seeks destruction. Where we do nothing, it's not going to be simply a comeback of tyranny, but it's going to tear it all apart.

. . .

Sylvia broke the whole silence by nodding her head, her face showing clearly the unease clutched in the hearts of them all. "This force is something the Empire may well have tampered with, unknowingly-something beyond their own corrupted ambitions. Whichever its origin, we can't face it with simple brute force. It requires us to understand magic itself on a level we've never reached before.

The group exchanged uneasy glances. This was no ordinary threat, and the path forward was unclear.

Elara came forward-a proven fighter and among their very few most trusted allies. "We shall need more than swords and spells. What they are up against was a corruption in magic itself, and so they needed insight-knowledge. There has to be something out there capable of helping them to find out what they are fighting against.

"There is a place," Sylvia began in a barely audible voice, "an ancient archive hidden somewhere within the massifs of the Stormpeak Mountains, a repository of knowledge gathered from time immemorial, even before the very rise of the Empire-secrets about the nature of magic as such, records kept by those who seek to understand Light and Shadow.

Dax's eyes slitted in thought. "That would be our only good chance. The path is full of danger, especially now that this shadow has begun sliding into the world. It is a risk, but if it will find us the knowledge we seek to counter this threat, we will be going.".

· · ·

As one, the whole group steeled themselves against the journey ahead-together. To the north lay the Stormpeak Mountains: rude, unforgiving, and until recently, unexplored. The legends spoke of eternal storms surging above the peaks, of blizzards so strong they could blind even the hardiest traveler. But it was a risk they were ready to run because they knew this new threat would not wait.

And so, the next day, they started. Dax led the party, Sylvia beside him, and the weight was upon their faces, features set with their resolution. Those behind them, similarly burdened but still hopeful, prepared themselves for what threatened their world.

The air was thin and keen, and the winds whirled around them in icy gusts as they went higher up the mountain. There was no life-no living thing anywhere to be seen: desolate landscape-worn rocks, twisted trees-were all the companions. The higher they mounted, the deadlier the air felt, it seemed-the mountain itself was alive and threatened them with some unseen menace, frowning on their approach.

Finally, after days and days of travelling under such conditions, they crossed a hidden cavern that opened from a yawning entrance into the very core heart of the mountain. Dax stepped forward, his flitting torch casting shades against the wall. There was a deep silence inside, almost palpable, like a weight heavy upon them as they proceeded further inside.

. . .

Inside, they found themselves surrounded by ancient carvings, symbols etched into the walls from a time when knowledge was sacred, closely guarded by those who had long since realized the true nature of magic. The Archive lay center in the cavern-a highly elaborate construction made up of crystals and spell-bound scrolls that contain preserved knowledge both tangible and ethereal.

Awestruck, she reached out a hand to touch a glowing crystal, pulsating inside with the pulse of magic. "This place. it's alive," she whispered, feeling the ancientness of the wisdom within its core.

Dax nodded as his eyes scanned through the inscriptions. "We have to find what this darkness is and how it came into existence. There is supposed to be a record of something here with information on how to counter a force that can corrupt both Light and Shadow.

And yet, the further they researched the records, the clearer it became that there was one more: The Void. While Light and Shadow were both co-dependent, entwined in a fine balance, the Void was a being of pure entropy-a hunger that wished to eat everything in reality, both tangible and mystical. It had once been cast out into the periphery of reality, but it would appear something cataclysmic, ages ago, had weakened its prison.

The twisted magic of the Empire must have ruined the barriers that kept it off," Sylvia whispered, her eyes tracing brittle pages of ancient tomes. "Playing with powers beyond their grasp, tearing at the seams in the balance, weakening the seals that kept the Void contained.

Dax clenched his fists, the weight of the revelation sinking in. "And now it's breaking through, seeking to devour everything—Light, Shadow, and all the lives we've worked so hard to protect."

Among them was mention of one ritual: a spell that would strengthen those barriers that constrained the Void. It wasn't a spell of destruction or of control, but one of unity. The required Light and Shadow were those which would be in absolute harmony with one another, their powers combined in such a way as to be unprecedented in its precision and balance.

Sylvia turned back to face him, her eyes now resolute and a shade of fear crossing them. "This ritual. different from everything that we've ever done-failing means the Void's taking the both of us, and the darkness will get free, spreading unabatedly.

Dax met her gaze, his eyes going hard with a firm resolution. "We've come this far, Sylvia. We fought against the Empire, and we'll go through this new darkness, one by one. We'll never allow the world to fall again.

In no time, they were in preparations for the rite, siphoning off from their aggregate powers, mingling Light with Shadow in fine balance in give and take. Energy crackled in the air as they worked; eyes never faltering, intent unblemished. Ancient words of the ritual poured from their lips-a chant which hummed at the very core of magic-to call upon the forces of Light and Shadow to mend the torn bounds and bring harmony once more.

As the last words of the ritual echoed in the cavern, a surge of energy burst from the Vault and sent a blinding light into the cavern. It shot upwards, weaving its way through the mountain, smearing across the whole continent, becoming one big, protective web. Dark corners of existence-the reaching tendrils of the Void-recoiled, the power of the barriers now too strong for them.

They fell to the ground, exhausted, Dax and Sylvia; all bodily energies spent, their heart full of relief. They had conquered the Void-held it long enough for their world to recover, for the balance to readjust.

In an instant, the cavern was lit up with soft light, as ancient knowledge stirred, the Archive pulsed in agreement with their endeavors. United against the darkness, together they presented the single most powerful armament-threatened cohesion-against the Void.

Many hopes were rejuvenated as they walked down the mountain, but full well they knew this was only the first of its kind of battles. They realized that balance is not a destination but a journey which one makes, nurturing the harmony between Light and Shadow with steadfast commitment.

. . .

Their message of unity was stronger, their resolve tried and found true. And so, from the heights of the Stormpeak Mountains, they descended, knowing they were ready for whatever was in store for them, armed with one vital piece of knowledge: together, they could resist even the oldest and strongest of powers.

CHAPTER 47
VEINS OF RESISTANCE

Uncertainty weighed heavy on Dax as he prepared for what was to be, knowing the rebellion's triumph was no longer as complete as it had seemed a little while ago. It was this new shade that bothered him more than the tyranny of the Empire could ever. His eyes turned toward the horizon-to the storm clouds gathering at dawn, dark, ominously lit. The spirit was untamed, though the doubt pulled deep, as he thought of the price they had paid so far, and the trials yet to come.

Sylvia was a beacon of comfort, soft in her approach as she came toward him shrouded in doubt, her face furrowed by as much exhaustion, though she was resolute.

We cannot let fear paralyze us," she said softly, though laced with a weight in her voice that spoke volumes for conviction. "We saw what happened when power was left to its own designs. This new darkness. it feels like unraveling, something that thrives on corruption, pulling apart the very fabric of our world.

Dax nodded, something in the weight of her words ringing true. "The Empire used Light to control and Shadow to oppress, but they were always wielding tools they didn't truly understand. This is different. It's a force beyond ambition or tyranny. It feels as if it's. reaching into the core of what we are.

He took a deep breath and turned to face their small assembly of allies-those who had fought alongside them, who had seen friends fall, who had watched cities burn and rise again. They were people who had laid everything on the line in the name of freedom and now stood ready to defend it once more, with the lines of war etched into their faces, as also the glimmers of their hope.

We are facing a darkness, not only coveting power, but one bent to twist the hearts and unwind the balance we worked so hard to build," he finally began on an even keel. "It is not just a fight over land, nor over rule-it is a fight over the soul of our world. Let it be so, this shall engulf in itself all that we hold dear.

The group fell silent, every member feeling the gravity of what he said. It was then that Sylvia stepped forward, placing a reassuring hand on his shoulder, before addressing their allies:.

· · ·

"We all know what happens when Light and Shadow are treated as tools for control. We've been down that path, and it led to oppression, to suffering. But we've also seen what happens when Light and Shadow are balanced, when they are allowed to exist in harmony. That's the world we're fighting for—a world where magic is a force of unity, not division."

Elara spoke first, undaunted as a warrior and strategist, throwing her chin up, her eyes narrowing. "Then we need knowledge-about this darkness, about its roots. We can't fight an enemy we don't understand.

A murmur of concurrence went around the circle. Knowledge had always been their armor against ignorance; now it was the only hope against a danger beyond anything they had ever known.

"There are rumors," Dax said, his gaze sweeping over his friends. "Whispers of ancient texts hidden within the ruins of the Forbidden Vale, a place once forbidden by the Radiance Church. I've heard tales of tomes that speak of forces older than Light and Shadow, records kept by those who understood the true depths of magic and its risks."

Sylvia's face became serious once more. "The Vale.they say that it is unsafe. But as it does hold what we need to find, there we must go. We go, together.".

. . .

Elara smirked, her usual determination evident. "Then let's prepare. We've faced worse odds, and we're still standing."

By stockpiling provisions and sharpening skills, this group set out on a course of action from which few returned, into the heart of the Forbidden Vale, knowing well it would be a perilous path, while heralding an intention with every step.

As they rode, the aspect of the land took on grimmer hues, forsaken in wars long forgotten. It was as though the shadows clung to the edge of their vision, and the wind was an utterance of intent. It was as if the land itself was against them, the very Vale aware of their presence to pry into its secrets.

At last they saw the mouth of the Vale: an enormous rift between two walls of tumbled stone. Then a wave of dread ran over them, yet they went on, heads high, eyes straight.

Inside, it was grotesque; the Vale was a haunted sight: twisted trees that groaned towards the sky, their branches grasping like skeletal fingers; a thick fog clung to the ground, shifting as they moved. They saw in the distance the remains of some ancient structure, its stones grooved with ancient arcane runes, evidence of an era lost to time.

A chill ran down Dax's spine as they approached. Colder, the air seemed to grow; a deafening silence surrounded them at the threshold of the ruin. There was a grand hall inside with ancient tomes, scrolls, and artifacts aplenty-myriad relics from times when knowledge was both adored and feared.

Sylvia approached a tome lain upon an intricately carved pedestal; these were pages yellowed with age, the symbols faint yet resonating with power. She opened it warily, and the symbols glowed faintly as her fingers brushed the pages. The more she read, the graver the expression that came over her face.

It speaks of an elder power, any of which are known to us-a force known as the Veil of Shadows," she hushed. "A force that feeds on one thing-imbalance-thriving where Light and Shadow have been corrupted, lost to their harmony. It was bound by ancient magic, locked away to protect the balance of the world. Dax's eyes went dark. "It was the tampering of the Empire that has to have loosened those ties-twisting Light and Shadow, breaking down barriers that kept this in check.

Elara stepped forward, her face determined. "Then we need to find out how to get those barriers back up-things we definitely need to know: how they were constructed and how we can reinforce them.

Days had been spent pouring over those ancient texts, unraveling the secrets of the Veil of Shadows and deciphering the rituals and spells necessary to maintain that balance. It was during that time that they finally came across one such ritual which called for both Light and Shadow to be used in conjunction-one that did require a very fine, balanced dance of forces.

. . .

A rite that might even restore the Veil once more to chain the darkness back to its prison-but at a terrible price: the sacrifice of energy, perhaps life itself.

Dax and Sylvia looked at each other; they knew what this could mean, and their total commitment was to the balance at any price.

It was on this day of days, after days of preparation, that they gathered deep within the Vale, its ruins shimmering silver in the light of the moon, heavy with pent-up power; and thus they started the ritual, voices rising, chanting in harmony with the very primal forces of Light and Shadow.

As the rite reached its height, the ground shook, and putrid fog began boiling-a noxious creature bucking against the bonds they tried to weave. The Veil of Shadows struggled in return; raw fury pulsed within the energy, trying to break free, to consume. The ritual required much concentration, and Dax and Sylvia put all their strength into it.

They called to being-the harmony they had learned to emulate, a perfect balance between Light and Shadow. Their energies wrapped into each other, forming a shield against tenebrousness closing in. It sprang back in a last access of vigour, caught in the bonds they had set on it and bound it back to those deep places whence it came. The stilled air broke its tension, and the veil of darkness that receded showed them deep silence. Weary yet triumphant, they looked to one another; within their eyes shone bright the knowledge that they had triumphed-at least for the time being.

The forces of the Veil were bound, but both were well aware that in the balance of Light and Shadow lies eternal struggle-a sensitive dance that requires unflagging watchfulness. As they re-emerged into the world once again, it was far from over, because all they had been changed into were guardians-protection for this fragile harmony bound by belief in something greater than rebellion or freedom. They stood watch over a world where Light and Shadow did not stand as enemies but as dancing partners in the never-ending waltz of life.

CHAPTER 48
FLICKERS OF HOPE

Sylvia stared straight ahead, straitlaced, as hard as steel in her heart. This new darkness was intangible, insidious, unlike any foe she had faced; it whispered not only of destruction but of corruption-to bend Light and Shadow alike to some twisted will. It is just that those very forces which she learned to love might be turned against her dream of harmony.

She breathed in with every word, gathering within her the profundity of the Whispering Woods and finding her strength in the wisdom of the Tree of Life. Its very ancient energy hummed deep within her, carrying along with it for her the memory of the connection between all. She felt that Light and Shadow were so much more than just powers but threads of a tapestry-a fine balance that keeps the world on its axis. This thought steadied her, gave her purpose, and, as it were, for the storm that was coming.

. . .

Alone, she knew she couldn't take on this threat. She needed allies-friends she trusted, who knew the cost of freedom, who had fought alongside her and shared the scars of victory.

The blur of her mind suddenly slammed back, hard, into focus, and back onto Dax, her most solid ally in the rebellion- a mage that once screamed passionately into the Shadow, before his finding balance through it. Together, they had smashed the chains of the Empire; together, they could face this.

Thus, Sylvia launched into an intensive round of collecting their forces: travelling to villages and cities alike, still showing the scars of rebellion, in search of those who had fought by her side, those who had seen the worst of the Empire's cruelty and knew what freedom was worth. She drew into her fold warriors, scholars, and healers-people from all walks of life who had embraced the ideals of Balance and Peace.

And at every stop, Sylvia had shared her vision-her understanding of Light and Shadow as interplaying forces. She spoke of the dangers of letting one power dominate the other, that this was a new darkness that sought to twist their hard-won harmony into chaos. She relit the fire in them once more as she reminded them of the ideals they fought for, and the responsibility they had toward those tenets.

News of that movement finally reached Dax, now busy with overseeing the reconstruction of a war-torn coastal city. With each word spoken that informed him of Sylvia's call to action, weighted by the burden of their shared responsibility in this solemn duty of protection they labored so arduously for, his heart beat faster. But he joined her at the edge of the town, where in a glance of their eyes in acknowledgment of the fire of the will within they shared silent understanding. For each had walked the path of oppression to freedom, through innocence to wisdom; each stood prepared for what was yet to come.

And so together they rode on, gathering their following as they went. Elara was a strong warrior who had lost her family pitilessly to the Empire; she swore her sword to their cause. Rion joined them-his great strategist mind with a heart for justice, thus already working out in his head the intricacies of this new enemy.

The small contingent of freedom fighters finally came out as a coalition: a fellowship whose aim it was to save the world from a certain darkness that threatened not only their lives but the real meaning of existence.

Soon afterward, he came across the fabled Ancient Temple of Duality, where it was said that inside, one could find knowledge about the primordial balance between Light and Shadow.

The carvings along these corridors told of an ancient struggle-one of darkness against light, each balancing the forces against each other. It was about an artifact, the Aether Shard, according to the writings in the temple-a shard of inestimable power that might amplify or diminish Light and Shadow alike. An implement of creation, it was also a tool for destruction because it was believed with it that the balance of this world can be changed.

Dax read from the inscriptions, his voice seeming to echo within the cavernous temple. "It is said that the Aether Shard can bridge the divide, has the power to mend the tear between Light and Shadow. or tear it asunder. In the wrong hands, it unravels everything.

Sylvia's heart was racing. It was the Shard that gave hope, yet at the same time was the one thing she could feel the new darkness sought to wield-to disrupt the balance and enslave it to its will. She turned to the group, her voice steady, laced with urgency: "We have to find the Aether Shard before it does. If not, the world will fall into darkness from which it may never recover.

Their journey was a race against time: to have to cross desolate mountains, storm-ravaged seas, into the heart of shadowed forests guided by the hint of ancient maps and inscriptions showing them where the shard was. They have been taken through many trials: fighting beasts twisted by the darkness, and parts of the Empire's forces that fell and now are thralls of this new enemy's will.

Sylvia and Dax worked in sync, their powers complementing each other in the repulsion of attacks and finding one's way through dangerous territories. Sylvia had used her Light magic to heal all the wounds and also to dispel hallucinations, while Dax's Shadow magic provided secrecy for them, a shelter from the enemy's prying eyes.

With every step closer to where it rested, they could feel its pulse powerful in the air, resonating with the very heartbeat of the world. They finally came upon the hidden valley where the Aether Shard lay-in a chamber deep within the earth. It shimmered with an ethereal glow, casting both light and shadow across the cavern walls.

Approaching it, Sylvia felt her heart simultaneously filled with reverence and fear. When she touched the shard, it welcomed her touch, radiating its warmth into her fingers as if reminding her of its greatness. She felt all the possibilities: creation and destruction, harmony and chaos. Again, she knew that with the shard lay either lasting peace or the spelling of their doom, should it fall into the wrong hands.

Dax rose in his seat, joining her, his eyes stuck to the shard, wonder in his stare, determination upon his face. "It is this that the darkness seeks to control-to break the symmetry, having both Light and Shadow as weapons and not as dance partners.

Sylvia nodded, her jaw set. "Then we won't let it. We'll protect the Aether Shard. We'll guard it, come what may. We will make sure that this force will be a force of balance and not some tool of tyranny. As one, they raised the shard, and through the power it contained, the stirring of Light and Shadow combined with their very core, guiding them with a will. They understood that danger was always close by, and the darkness would not stop until it regained the shard. They also knew they were strong enough to counteract this, to protect this balance for which they had fought with such effort.

As they stepped out of the cavern, the light of the Aether Shard led their way, so too did the hope for a new future where Light and Shadow coexisted in harmony. They were no ordinary warriors; they were guardians. They were protectors of a certain balance that extended so well beyond the realms of magic and powers. Having faced tyranny and overcome doubt, they now stood prepared to ward off the world against the darkness threatening to engulf it.

And though the fight wasn't close to over, there was something alive in their hearts, something nobody will ever put out. They would stand right at the eye of this darkness, armed with the understanding that real power was not domination but comprehension. Together, they would observe this puny balance of Light and Shadow prevail, be a hope unto all generations that are to come.

CHAPTER 49
THE BURDEN OF LEADERSHIP

As whispers of the encroaching darkness spread, so did the resolve of those who fought for freedom. In their ways, both Dax and Sylvia were a symbol of Light and Shadow, the weight of the world pressed heavily upon their shoulders-to think that faltering was impossible. No longer simple rebels, guardians of balance, champions of a new world standing at the edges of its own destruction.

They called upon those who had stood with them in the rebellion: warriors and scholars-all with one special strength or another, lending importance in bringing down the Empire. Elara, the fearsome swordswoman whose loyalty and fierce resolve had pulled so many lives from the mire, returned once more to stand by their side, her eyes afire with the very fire that had lent them such passionate favour during the war. Into this came Rion, a tactician with a mind sharp as an edge-an anchorage of steadiness in the storm of doubt and uncertainty.

. . .

United, they had traversed the Eryal Continent, rallying to their cause all those who had tasted freedom and knew well what was at stake. Whithersoever they had gone, they found the people responsive-standing and fighting once more, even with fear lingering in their eyes. To every person they met, be it farmer, healer, or mage, their message had always been: unity was their strongest shield; balance, their only path forward.

This darkness, hitherto only the stuff of rumor and legend, began to flex muscles in ways thoroughly unsettling. Figures robed in shadow prowl the nocturnal hours silent as ghosts. The skies, once soothing and tranquil, started twisting with angry formations of clouds, casting unnatural shadowing patterns on the ground below. This field, so rich and so vibrant, withered and died as the crops began to die amidst a sun that seemed to shine through with a pale, sickly complexion.

Dax felt an uncomfortable sense of familiarity stir in the plague-scarred lands-an echo of the Shadow, faint but twisted, corrupted. It was his own magic distorted, perverted, and an abomination to the natural balance. The shadows wrapping around him pulsed with dark vitality, one that would consume, not coexist. His own powers, so reassuring once, were stretched taut now, almost as if against an invisible force touching the land.

One night, as they set up camp on the edge of a dying forest, Sylvia approached Dax, a face clouded with concern. "This darkness," she said, "feels. wrong, different from the corruption of the Empire. It's like it draws power from the very core of Light and Shadow, trying to twist them both.

Dax nodded, his gaze fixed into the dancing flames. "I can feel it, too. It does not seek only to balance its power; it's about erasing the very concept of balance. If that happens... He did not finish, not needing to voice that which was so clear to them all: that their world, sturdy as it was, would be torn apart by such unyielding voraciousness.

Now they were seeking enlightenment about this Force in the Temple of Duality, one of the ancient sanctuaries. Those sayings, originated from times very long before the rise of the Empire, were inscribed on the walls of the temple. They told tales of a millenniums-old struggle between Light and Shadow-a great fight once almost consumed all. The carvings told of a third force: one of corruption and chaos that would tear the balance asunder and consume the two powers with its endless hunger.

Her finger traced the ancient writing as Sylvia's heart quickened with the implication: "The darkness is not just a force but a residue of some sort from an ancient evil trying to unbind both Light and Shadow out of the simple fact of leaving them ineffective and then consuming them all.".

In the very center of the temple, they found an ancient artifact-a crystal that pulsed faintly with both Light and Shadow.

. . .

It was known as the Veilstone, a shard of the original balance that once kept the world at peace. As the information they obtained from the temple showed, it would be able to bind Light and Shadow in harmony, protecting them from the destructive influence of Chaos. Still, work with it was to invest their powers in it-to risk everything on a chance of restoring the balance.

Now it was much clearer-but also much more ominous-in sight: the path ahead would be to carry the Veilstone directly into the jaws of the abyss, fighting this ancient evil in its own den. Such would take, besides the need for strength, unity-a binding of their powers which would try the very core of their souls.

They summoned their allies and initiated the pursuit, forging ahead, ever onward, toward the source of all that evil. The closer they came, the heavier the air was-thick with oppressing energy as if it wanted to choke the life out of them. The land shriveled, the sky gray, heavy, and unmoving- as if holding its breath. And last of all-the embodiment of darkness-a ravine entirely surrounded by some fog, that had taken to it all the light, even to the minutest particle, where shadows danced upon the air and coalesced into fearful forms that leaped out upon them and smote them, sucking their lives away.

Sylvia tossed her Light magic around their party, pinning them down into an uninterrupted attack, as Dax slung his Shadow magic to mask the traces of their movement, slicing easily through the night like a breeze.

. . .

And then, there it was, right in the middle of that valley: this huge vortex churning with darkness, torn from the very fabric of reality, out of which that malign force had been issuing which had been troubling the world. The darkness pulsed, reached out in tendrils of shadow, grasping at them, chill and cold to the touch, promising consumption.

Dax and Sylvia raised Veilstone overhead, their hands intertwined around it, as one, in a rush of their joined strengths with Light and Shadow. The crystal itself had responded by shining with fierce, blinding brilliance, pushing back the screen of darkness and lighting up the valley, shining clear light right into the very heart of the vortex.

But the darkness fought back, hashing out in anger and seeking to shatter the Veilstone, snuff its light, and consume the shadow. Its attack sent them both to their knees, and for an instant, it looked like all was lost.

And then, out of nowhere, came Sylvia's unmistakable, clear voice. "We don't fight for dominion; we do it for harmony! United we stay, joined by the balance that keeps us alive!"

Dax's voice added to this, words no more than a whispered breath into the void. "Light and Shadow: together, not tools of power, but as a force of life itself.".

Their words droned with the Veilstone; its light intensified, becoming one bright mass, shredding into the heart of darkness. The storm wailed, its very form breaking apart amidst the assault of regained balance in magical forces, and with one last tortured scream, it vanished, superseded only by silence.

Where once despair had saturated the valley, it now began healing-slowly, the land reclaiming its vitality, the air cleansing itself as the negative energy was slowly released into the atmosphere. The Veilstone, its task completed, dulled into a soft glow, its power gone, though the essence remains. Dax and Sylvia finally stood inside-just below the precipice, really-and stared out at a landscape they had saved. They had fought an ancient darkness, the breadth of their own powers, and the bonding between them.

United, they had made certain the balance of Light and Shadow would prevail to shine as a ray of hope in a world that would never forget their names. They returned home as heroes-to their people, not of war, but of harmony. Scars of the past remained, but even deeper and strong was the binding of the land and the hearts of its people, set into balance by their fight for its preservation. Whispers of darkness ebbed away while a song of peace wafted forth to be heard for many generations to come-a heritage from Light and Shadow intertwined, eternally in harmony.

CHAPTER 50
LEGACY OF LIGHT AND SHADOW

When the first light of dawn filtered into the stilled chambers, Sylvia and Dax stood shoulder to shoulder, looking out at the new members who took their place at the council table. These were no fighters but sentinels of the future, dreamers who had the sensitive job of governance. Henceforth, their task would be to guide beyond rebellion toward rebuilding of a society where Light and Shadow coexisted in harmony.

A low hum of murmurs filled the room-whispers of council members talking amongst one another of the weighty decisions facing the continent: dividing lines to be drawn, policies to take shape, war wounds still not fully bled dry. The Council was a composition of former rebels, regional leaders, and even scholars hailing from far-flung areas-a perfect representation of the diversity of the land.

Sylvia cleared her throat, calling the council to order. Her voice was composed, yet commanding, as she began: "We convene herein, not as conquerors, but as caretakers toward a dream where harmony and regard might serve as guides. Though the ghost of the Empire yet lingers on, it falls to us in common to light the way ahead with moderation and good faith.

Dax leaned forward, scanning the faces of the council members, both new and old. "We're not here to repeat the mistakes of the Empire. We're here to forge a different path—one that serves the people, that brings Light and Shadow into balance, without resorting to control."

Alaric was the round-faced elder councillor and was among the earliest loud critics to rise; in his boom of a voice: "The western regions hardest hit under the exploitation of the Empire, and they need immediate support to rebuild; their lands were our lifeblood during the rebellion.

Liana, a councillor from the coastlands, shook her head. "And yet, the eastern towns lie in ruins, their people homeless, orphaned, and bereft of livelihood. If balance is indeed what we aim for, then we have to help them, too.".

Sylvia raised a soothing hand. "Both are valid concerns, and both merit our consideration. It is just for this-that the Empire thrived on-that this council was formed: division. Balance has to be made, providing resources where they are most needed.

Dax's voice was steady as he added, "Unity can only be sustained through transparency and accountability. The people must see us as their representatives, not rulers. We'll assign resources based on need, not favoritism."

It was silent in the room as the words sank into the minds of the council member. Their faces were worm-eaten with responsibility, but that weariness covered a spark of hope and eagerness to do better.

Standing, Elara-so valued an advisor among them-started to address them: "This council is a rare opportunity to reshape the very nature of governance. Light and Shadow were never meant to be weapons against each other, but forces that complement and balance one another. Our new world must honor that truth.

One of the youngest councillors, a woman named Talia, who once was trained in the Radiance Church spoke. "The people fear Shadow Magic. It is to them a mystery, dangerous.

Sylvia nodded, catching the underlying meaning in the words. "The Empire controlled our lives through our fear of Shadow. Yet Shadow is within us, much as Light, which is our strength. We should tell people what it really is, and let them learn to live with it as part of themselves.

Dax's gaze was intense as he addressed the room. "The potential for harm exists in both Light and Shadow. We've seen how Light can be twisted into a tool of oppression. That's why we're creating education centers where both can be studied responsibly, to foster understanding and respect."

. . .

Elara rested a reassuring hand on Talia's shoulder. "Light and Shadow are interwoven, as our journey has shown us. We're here to shape a world that recognizes this interdependence."

It had deliberated by the hour while the council drew up a charter that would detail the shared values and responsibilities the group held so dear. Each word was painfully phrased, each clause weighed and re-weighed for perfection, to reflect their pledge to a just and equitable society. Sylvia was feeling proud as she watched this jagged tapestry of differences smoothly interwoven in the common aim.

As the evening eventually enveloped the city, it was finally closed and spilled them into light-filled, laughter-echoing streets. Folks began rebuilding or reveling in the ashes; Sylvia could not prevent an increasingly embedded core of purpose from arising within her as she walked with Dax.

"This council," she murmured, "something that none of us could have seen during the rebellion, and yet, here we are, shaping the future."

Dax's arm wrapped around her shoulders, his voice a steady reassurance. "We've given them a foundation. They'll have struggles, but we've taught them to question, to seek balance. And we're here to guide them." Together, they had watched over the city all night, its lights ablaze like a promise against the night. This was more than the end of a war; this was the start of an era narrated, not by control, but by hope and unity. Long after their journey was to be over, they stood watch, sentinels who made sure this balance they fought so hard for would prevail.

CHAPTER 51
A NEW DAWN

This was deep, ancient air, thick with some hum apparently at the roots of the trees themselves, surging in with a tingling thrill into the marrow of the venturer as he entered the Whispering Woods. Standing at the edge of the forest, Dax and Sylvia faced up square, eyes fixed upon the depth of woods that hid the Tree of Life. For within it is where their awakening hailed, where for the very first time they came to fathom the true balance between Light and Shadow. It is for its wisdom, in light of this new darkness, that they now seek it.

Full of perils, their journey was-a test of the wills. Then there were rumors about this darkness that would soon come-rumors which crept into every nook and corner of the free world. Those that had been freed by so many precious lives and hard work from the Empire faced yet another silent, hidden menace. Children stopped playing, the words of wisdom of the elders were given out sparingly, and in every hamlet, townsmen spoke in hushed tones to one another about shadows in dreams, plants of doubt and fear.

. . .

Exile brought a turbulent tide in the darkness of his past, a stirring betrayal, a loss within him. It was as if the shadows looming before him now closed in with the familiarity of a natural element parasitizing upon fears and doubts he had fought all his life. The Shadow magic surged within him, vibrating with the pangs of his heart. He had once been the outcast, the exiled mage who had been forced to face his power alone; now, he was leading, faced with the duty to protect those hinging their hopes on him.

Sylvia felt the tension in Dax, who instinctively reached out to her where their hands mingled in the midst of dark trees.

It was a journey of the ultimate change for her-from the preachings of the Radiance Church to her view of Light and Shadow. The Light magic that she could use was no longer a tool of control but was instead a beacon for balance and healing. She could, however, feel this new darkness challenging that fragile balance, tainting with whispers of doubt the purity of the Light. They plunged deeper into the woods, their hearts bucking in time with nature. Behind their backs, ancient spirits stirred: a quiet race of people, large of eye, who watched them with curiosity and caution. Sylvia felt their silent watchfulness, their soft whispers weaving through leaves in a symphony of voices speaking of battles fought, of heroes and villains, victory and defeat.

They knew her and Dax as the leaders of the resistance, at least, but also as searchers after a truth that went beyond mere power.

. . .

And finally, right in front of them, was the Tree of Life: tall, with a gnarled old body, its caliber seemingly exuding calmness and energy; the branches rose upwards toward the firmament, like arms in prayer. Whether the leaves shone with that soft glow inside them was an indication of the tender balance which this tree outlined. Then spoke the spirits of the woods, plunging deep into great stillness before the rise of the tree.

Children of Light and Shadow," it rumbled in a voice thick with the whispers of the wind that tussled with the tree tops. "You have come seeking answers, guidance against the darkness stirring anew.

"We have," Dax said, his voice even. "The peace we fought for is in jeopardy. The people we have liberated have been terrorized by something we do not understand-a darkness that somehow feels more personal, more intrusive than anything the Empire could threaten them with."

Sylvia nodded unflinchably. "This new darkness feeds upon fear and doubt, prizes open every fracture in the unity we've struggled to develop. We have to understand it-to see it for what it truly is-if we're to have any hope of defeating it.

The Tree of Life pulsed softly, its silent brilliance almost a form of acknowledgement. "This darkness is not a shadow," it spoke-a voice sewn from a thousand spirits. "It is the reflection of your own vulnerabilities, the manifestation of fear, greed, and doubt given form. It does not have one single master to give it life, no single point of origin. It feeds on the fissures in your world-on the breaks in the unity you have built. These words rang too much in his mind because the struggles of Dax himself seemed to resurface: years in solitary confinement, anger he once held onto, and the resentments he had carried. In this new darkness, Dax saw an echo of his own path-a shadow born of fear and weakness.

He realized that, to fight this, he had to turn to those aspects of his soul, not to allow the power of Shadow he was using with purpose to fall out of balance.

The same awakening stirred within Sylvia, and her view changed; what was used as a sword for purity now turned into an understanding tool that sheds light into the darkness and does not eradicate. She had grown up with a world of absolutes-light and shadow, good and evil. But the Tree of Life had taught her that it is only by embracing the spectrum between, seeing unity within duality, that one may find balance.

How then can we wrestle with something which does not have any body? " Sylvia replied in a pit of despair, "How are we to fight with an element which lives in us and sustains on our fear?

The tree's branches shivered, shards of light dancing around the clearing. "You must look within, for the darkness you face is not just of the world but of your own hearts. Only by embracing the balance within will you be able to guide others to find it. Only by facing your own fears, your own doubts, can you stand against this new threat as beacons.

Dax squeezed Sylvia's hand as his resolve was set firm. "Then let's face it, inside and out. We'll teach them to see this balance, to find the strength in their unity, not the fears in the differences that divide them.

The murmurs of assent from the ancient spirits around them fell into a unanimous hum, enchanted harmony impregnated with the power of the forest. So clear, yet full of personal obstacles lay the road ahead of Dax and Sylvia. They fully realized that to fight this darkness, they would have to first vanquish the shadows within themselves.

They now had a new will, a determination to return to the world for which they had fought so hard to liberate. One last blessing pulsed from the Tree of Life in silence, a silent promise: they would not go into the dark alone. The Spirits of the Whispering Woods would be with them, guiding them, their wisdom echoing in every shadow and their strength illuminating every beam of Light.

Dax and Sylvia came out of the forest, their hearts steeled for trials ahead. However, they would be much more than just warriors, for they were going to teach and lead people to understand that strength does not lie in the purity of Light, nor in the strength of Shadow, but in its balance. With each new step they took, they would be reminding the world that their unity was the most valuable weapon, which no darkness could ever snuff out.

CHAPTER 52
THE COUNCIL OF UNITY

Thick with tension, the air of the underground city nonetheless held an expectant quality to it, rather than one of fear. Anya navigated the cramped passageway, her healer's satchel riding secure over her shoulder, her fingers brushing the cool walls but lightly as she walked. Once, she had known only the sterile white halls of the Imperial infirmary, where the twisted form of the Church's Light Magic was used not to heal but to maintain appearances. Every nook and cranny here spoke volumes of resistance, hope, and unyielding spirit for those within these rough-hewn walls.

Since joining the rebellion, she had turned into a beacon of silent perseverance; her stories as a healer spread like bushfires.

They didn't search her out for that gift but for the comfort: a subtle warmth seeming to emanate from her fingertips, a healing of more than just flesh and bone. To a people who had suffered these many years, she was a beacon of hope, reminding them that Light and Shadow are not things to be used but forces to be felt and balanced. She walked downstairs toward the makeshift infirmary, her face turning at the several faces looking up to her in silent gratitude, the small nods of acknowledgment from persons she had helped. The underground city was a patchwork of hideaways: partially buried passageways hacked out of ancient caverns and joined together by narrow corridors.

It had been a haven for the disillusioned, a home for those who broke their chains loose from the Empire and who wanted to start anew.

"Anya!" a voice far too familiar called out to her. One of the former Imperial soldiers now turned to the rebellion, Kellan's wide frame took up much of the narrow hall as his face, always a somber mask, softened at the sight of her in relief.

"Kellan," Anya replied, sending him a reassuring smile. "How's the arm?"

He rolled his shoulder, flexing the arm she had treated after a skirmish with Imperial patrols. "Good as new, thanks to you," he said-there was a lot of honest gratitude in his voice. "We would be lost without your healing skills, Anya. I mean it.

She leaned forward and laid a light hand on his shoulder. "You're doing just fine, Kellan. We all have our own crosses to bear, and yours is just as important as mine.

. . .

He nodded; his eyes did not blink. "More news: today, another group joined us-scholars from the Imperial libraries. They have... documents, things that might help us expose the manipulation of the Church.

A spark of resolution flared across Anya's eyes. "Good. The more information we have, the better armed we will be against the Empire's lies.

She went further in, into the infirmary, her mind afloat with the images of the new alliance growing inside the rebellion. The resistance earned more substance each day, rich in variant types, skillful, and knowledgeable individuals. Each of the allies had something different to bear testimony to the breaking mask of the Empire and how strong the truth was compared with control. In the infirmary, she found the fighters, the citizens, and even the children stricken by all those traumas, which the manipulations of the Church had caused. It's a very simple facility fitted out with temporary cots and a scant supply of materials, but in Anya's hands, it was coming out to be a place of deep recuperation. An older woman, her face lined by years of suffering, clutched at Anya's hand as she murmured her thanks. "They told me I was cursed, that the pain in my heart was a punishment from the Light," she whispered, her voice thick with emotion. "But here. I feel peace. I feel whole.

Anya squeezed her hand, a soft smile gracing her lips. "The Light does not punish. It does not curse. It is the Empire that has twisted it into something it was never meant to be. Your pain... it is real, but so is your strength. And now you are free to heal, to be yourself.

Tears welled up in the woman's eyes as she nodded, some weight released from her shoulders that had burdened them for so long.

As the day wore on, Anya kept going from one patient to another, her heart swelling with the thought that now, in any case, she had some purpose.

It was not only a physical healing, but in the manner in which the Empire had rent asunder that was being healed-manhood and womanhood restored to people who had been denuded of these by years of oppression. Being able to perceive the subtle flow of energy within the universe was her special gift; thus, she did much more than mend bodies.

The terror and pain that still lay upon their souls, she could sense, and she attempted to seek a cure for them.

As night fell, Dax stepped into the infirmary, his figure silhouetted by the dim, flickering torchlight. There was weariness etched in his eyes, both in the battles he had fought against the Empire and the ones he'd fought internally. He had heard Anya at work and found himself needing to see it-to understand what she was accomplishing among these people, who were now looking to them for hope.

· · ·

"Anya," he said, his voice soft, but an edge of awe in it. "You are doing something quite remarkable here. People speak of you with a veneration seldom noticed.

Anlya finally looked up, offering him a soft smile. "I'm just doing what I can, Dax. We all bear our scars, some visible but most not. I can't go into battle like you, but I can help people find peace within themselves.". Dax nodded, understanding the depth of her words. "Sometimes the greatest battles are the ones fought within. What you're doing here, it's as vital as any sword or spell." There was a wordless communion between them, a recognition of sorts, that down different paths, they'd landed in the same place. Anya reminded Dax again that this was not a battle of arms and strength but one of healing-performing the repairs in the fractures left on people's hearts by the Empire. A low rumble echoed through the caverns; Dax and Anya exchanged a wary glance. There was a word that the Empire would attack, one last-ditch effort to put down the rebellion before it gained even more steam.

The rebellion was ready, but each new threat reminded them how fragile freedom was. "We shall stand together," Anya replied firmly, her eyes unblinking. "The people are stronger than the Empire gives them credit for. They've tasted freedom and will not let go so easily." Dax placed a reassuring hand on her shoulder. "And we'll fight to protect that freedom. Every person here, every soul you've healed, is a part of this rebellion. Together, we'll face whatever darkness the Empire tries to cast over us." Getting ready for the tasks ahead, to them it was not only the power of Light and Shadow but what lay at the back of either of them that mattered much.

. . .

It was not so much a rebellion, but one to heal the sores, bring about righteousness, and let people live life without fear. And in the gentle touch of Anya, in the unbreakable will of Dax-in the bravery of every single soul that joined their cause-a thing far stronger than any darkness: unrelenting hope.

CHAPTER 53
FALLEN HEROES

The return to the hidden chamber was an exhilarating and grim experience, as Dax and Sylvia had been walking upon the forgotten corridors of history, witnessed the echoes of a world bygone, and dug truths out of the varnish of dust and misconception. Working their way backward down the trail through the Whispering Woods seemed different, almost as if the very woods knew the weight of that with which they were now endowed.

Sylvia, her heart filled with an unshakable resolve, glanced at Dax. "We know what we're up against now," she said, her voice steady but filled with a sense of urgency. "This darkness isn't just a shadow to be cast aside. It's a reflection of everything twisted and misused in the name of power."

Dax nodded soberly, his eyes equally serious. "The Empire abused Light Magic, corrupting it into that abomination, but this darkness here. it's like the very entity of their tampering had come to life and sought vengeance on the world for allowing it to fester, unchallenged.

They came out of the ancient woods, the weight of their charge settling upon them. It was not only a matter of fighting this darkness, but wisely-to know of balance. The last prophecy on the stone altar told much, but it also left so many questions-open at least to interpretation-and how were they to make certain of balance within a world barely recovered from war?

Their journey full circle brought them back into the heart of the sanctity of the rebellion, awaiting people. Set amidst towering cliffs, veiled by thick forests, this underground city had been the hiding haven of the few who yearned for independence from twisted Empire control. As they entered the main hall of the city, a quiet murmur of attention spread through the crowd of people, eyes turned with anticipation towards them.

Kellan, the old soldier, one of the most trusted of Dax's companions, came running up to him. "Reports have come in from the outlying villages," he said, his voice tight. "Strange things are happening-crops shriveling in the night, rivers drying up. The people are frightened. They think the Empire's curse is back.

A chill ran down Sylvia's spine. "It's the dark," she whispered, "it's spreading, taking advantage of the fear and doubt the Empire leaves in its wake.

. . .

Dax's voice rose to the crowd now gathering. "It is neither some doing of the Empire, nor some simple kind of curse. It is something deeper: a darkness that feeds on our fears and twists the power of Light and Shadow to sow chaos.

Murmurs ran rife in a populace whose every voice carried apprehension. One elderly lady came forward, probably a leader among them, her hands shaking a little. "We thought the worst was behind us," she said, crackling. "We thought its fall would give us peace.

Sylvia stepped forward, her voice calm yet clear with conviction. "The peace which we fought for is real, but it is a fragile one. This darkness feeds upon our vulnerabilities, remnants of the fears and grief let forth by the Empire. But we have within ourselves the power to confront it, to understand it, and to bar it from taking hold.

She gazed over to Dax then, her eyes steady. "We cannot do that alone. We need each one of you-every soul that believes in the strength of unity, in the power of balance between Light and Shadow.

A hush fell upon the people when, with the weight of those words, these people-who had faced the repression of the Empire, who then found a glimpse of hope in this rebellion-were given yet another test. But as they look at Dax and Sylvia, their fears begin to break down, supplanted by a flicker of purpose.

. . .

Kellan nodded, a glint of determination in his eyes. "We've come this far together. If there's a way to fight this darkness, we're with you." He laid a comforting hand on Kellan's shoulder and spoke in an unshaken voice, "Together we shall find a way. This isn't treading the path against darkness; it is a journey for realization. We must keep in mind that Light and Shadow are not enemies; they are partners bonded by the fragile bond of balance.

They prepared for it over the following days.

Dax and Sylvia, assisted in these endeavors by stalwart followers such as Kellan and Anya, started to conduct ceremonies in their underground city and in villages sprinkled across the countryside. They explained the nature of Light and Shadow, the knowledge they had gained from the Whispering Woods and the Library of the Ancients to these assembled souls.

They gave stories and teaching that showed unity, highlighting strengths in embracing both forces and the importance of every individual in maintaining such a balance.

The ever-empathetic healer, Anya, reached out for the most traumatized, whose fear was further instigated by the darkness. She made small gatherings to heal not only wounds but the hearts burdened with such scars of their past. Her touch stirred serenity within-a reminder that as much as one could not rewrite the past, together they could press on and build on that strength.

. . .

It was one evening, with the lanterns ablaze in the central hall of the underground city, when Sylvia took time out and reflected upon the last prophecy: a warning against some darkness where force would be helpless. Indeed, they were into uncharted territories, being called upon to guide people toward embracing a balance that ran so contrary to everything the Empire had taught.

She looked to Dax then and whispered, "You ever get the feeling that this path to understanding Light and Shadow is never gonna end?

Dax chuckled, a wry smile playing on his lips. "Perhaps it's not meant to end. Balance- maybe this is what we pursue but never actually attain. But if we can lead people to live with that knowledge, well, maybe that's enough.

Their words were pregnant in the air, a quiet affirmation of their mission. They knew the battle ahead would test every belief, every lesson so well learned. Yet, they did know in each person lay the strength to confront the dark.

By morning, they had a different plan: to travel from suffering village to suffering village, explaining to villagers what it truly was. It wasn't meant to instill fear among them but resilience, so that they understand the only way to fight against it was actually balance-embracing Light and Shadow, not getting consumed by any one of these.

· · ·

The whole process was very cumbersome, yet complete with transformation, for both of them. In each village, they found people traumatized by the atrocities of the Empire some time back and leery of this new uncertainty. With discussions, teaching, and sharing their own vulnerabilities, Dax and Sylvia brought into focus the strengths from facing one's own darkness. And so they went forth, and as they walked, they noted, along the way, the results of their work.

Wherever fear had used to reside, it now glowed bright with embers of comprehension as an unprecedented resilience began to bloom. Persons now started talking not of survival but of growth-of a life with knowledge that balance was inside them, calling for tending. And with each village, the resistance grew-not just in number but in spirit. Where darkness had spread its whispers, now those whispered against the chorus of hope, a defiant reminder that even against fear there could be balance. Whereas earlier the reasons behind this journey for Dax and Sylvia slowly crystallized, now they were guiding, not just leading some sort of rebellion, but shepherding a people to greater understanding, and leaving behind them a legacy of balance that could face even the darkest shadows.

CHAPTER 54
ECHOES OF FREEDOM

Sombre yet enlightening, the journey out of Whispering Woods found Dax and Sylvia walking silently, lost in the realizations the Tree of Life had bestowed upon them. In them, each carried a new sense of the responsibility that vested in them, deeper than ever before. It is in the Whispering Woods that they realize the battle is not against some dark force from without, but with the echoes of the past, shadows cast by the untrammeled ambition of the Empire.

Clarity again set in by the time they reached the outskirts of the woods when he finally knew the shadows he was taming were not instruments of carnage but rather a balancing act.

The darkness in him, once the source of his fear and his sole interpretation, was now the path to conciliation. By his side, Sylvia's face reflected the same resolution, her eyes sparkling with the wisdom of the primordial wood. Her relation with

Light was no longer tainted by the dogmatism spread by the Radiance Church but glittered in the form of knowledge of unity, strength born from the acknowledgment of Light and Shadow.

The air was thick with fidgeting anticipation as they returned to the rebellion's haven; news of their leaving to the Whispering Woods had trickled out, and people were on their toes, awaiting their return. It was more than leadership they looked to in Dax and Sylvia-they were to bring a solution to this new darkness enveloping their world.

Before the crowning people, Dax raised his voice: "We sought the wisdom of the Whispering Woods, the ancient spirits, and the Tree of Life itself. What we came to know is that the darkness that threatens us is not just an enemy to be overcome, it is the shadow of our past, the echo of what the Empire has left behind, a result of using power without restraint.

A murmur of unease went through them; they had trusted in the surety of their victory, the finality of the fall of the Empire. To hear that its shadows yet lingered, its corruption had insinuated its way deeper than they had realized was to evoke both fear and determination.

Sylvia came forward; in clear, calm tones, she said, "The Tree of Life showed us something very real: true power does not lie in the dominance of Light over Shadow or Shadow over Light. It resides in balance, in understanding. We are not just fighting some kind of external darkness; we are fighting the temptation within us all to let fear guide our actions, to fall back into old patterns of control.

To this, Kellan, ever the man to stand by a friend and a former soldier, added with an introspective look on his face, "How do we go into battle against something like this when this isn't any ordinary enemy? If this is some kind of punishment because of past deeds, then what is to stop this from taking over?

A pause, after which Dax finally replied, "The darkness feeds on doubt and fear and the leavings of our old conceptions. It thrives on division, on mistrust, on our inability to come to terms with our own dark sides. To combat it requires willingness to look into the darkness within ourselves, to dismiss the part of our legacy from the Empire-to manipulate. Each of us is responsible for the balance within.

It was the voice of Anya, the gifted healer, speaking from among the crowd. Low and modulated, her voice was yet firm in quiet strength, having witnessed the wounds of the world. "Then, we must also heal-not just the physical wounds left by the Empire, but the scars it left on our spirits, the hurt it planted within our minds."

She nodded, her eyes locking with Anya's. "Precisely. The healing of our world depends on fighting, but more than ever on reconciling those parts of ourselves we may want to avoid. The Light and the Shadow are within us, and it's only by embracing each that we find real peace.

. . .

And all the people were silent, not to miss a word. It was crystal clear, and yet utterly impossible to fulfill-they had struggled with the sword, with strategy, with the will of survival against the Empire; now they would have to fight against introspection, against forgiveness, against resilience-the darkness living not only in the remnants of the Empire but in their very hearts.

Over the course of days, Dax and Sylvia held meetings within the sanctuary and throughout the villages. They spoke of no vengeance, but of recuperation. They called for talks about fear and doubt, about weight every one of them carried inside. Anya took the lead with her healing hands in group healings where the sharing of the load provides strength in unity.

Dax, now more enlightened by the wisdom of the Whispering Woods, held sessions of teaching in the balance of Light and Shadow. He said one should not fear Shadow, nor cover it up, but acknowledge it as a companion piece to life and to Light. Power, they explained, need not necessarily be derived from control, nor coerced from someone, but from mutual respect and understanding.

She spoke about the employment of Light, the use devoid of domination, showing how that is a force that nurtured, rather than subjugated. And often, her sessions took place in nature itself-wherein the forest became the classroom, each leaf and ray of sun representative of the beauty that comes with balance. One evening, as the sun was setting across the sanctuary, painting gold on the assembled, Sylvia's voice rose: an address of calm intensity to the crowd, "We are at a crossroads. We can continue on with our knee-jerk fight as we've always done, fueled by fear that breeds hate and division, or we can choose differently.

We can choose to face our inner darkness, to know our Light, and thus create a world where balance will no longer be an ideal but a way of life.

Dax laid a reassuring hand on her shoulder and nodded in agreement. "The road ahead shall be difficult, and at times the darkness may well seem to engulf one with doubt. But we are together and stronger. It wasn't the strength of one that brought down the Empire, but a will of the people, coming together as one, wanting a better world. Neither is this darkness any different.

The thunderous applause of the crowd reverberated through the space as if their clapping skimmed the surface of the sanctuary. An unspoken understanding of a consensus in decisions welling into the air, afresh with a new resolve: it was not for survival they were fighting, but to grow in healing, guardians of a balance that could change their world.

And as week followed week, Dax and Sylvia began to see change with their people: whispers of doubt and fear began to give way to whispered resiliency, of unity, of steadfast commitment on the path they had chosen. Instead of talking of fear, villages now spoke of hope-of resiliency-of something much more significant than anyone's personal fears.

. . .

Anya's work as a healer was never needed as much as it was now. She soothed those who still had been pursued by ghosts of memories of tyranny from the Empire-a way for them to find their inner peace. In the process, she nurtured a new generation of healers, people who knew true healing was of the soul as much as of the body.

With every step further in, both outside and in, Dax and Sylvia could feel the shift in the darkness itself: its hold was loosening because of their endeavors, the whispers of fear no longer having their tight grip on people's hearts and minds. The darkness was there, but it wasn't that strong; its influence being worn down bit by bit through a people who chose to stand as one.

He stood one evening at the edge of the Whispering Woods, staring outward over the horizon. Dax was determined, to say the least. "The world is changing," he finally whispered, and his voice was firm, with quiet resolution. "Not because we have defeated the darkness, but because we have learned to accept and love it- for it is a part of us.

Sylvia set a hand on his arm, and shining in her eyes was the enlightenment their quest had brought: "Balance isn't about erasing one force or the other; it's finding our peace within ourselves, creating a world where Light and Shadow can coexist together in harmony.

Those two guardians of a new era, those two souls joined in one through a common vision of hope and unbreakable power in balance, resilience, had found their way forward in silence. It was to be their guiding principle that would lead their world into the future, not one of fear, but one of unity and understanding of the deep strength found in the harmony of Light and Shadow.

PART FIVE
BALANCE FORGED IN FIRE

At the cusp of their triumph, the rebellion must still face even more crucial tests. In their transitioning from fighters to leaders, Dax and Sylvia will have to weigh justice against mercy in trying to rebuild broken trusts in a world scarred by war. Together, they will have to redefine what Light and Shadow are: a new base for society while working to not let the darkness of history repeat itself.

CHAPTER 55
THE LAST STAND

What was left of the Radiance Church stood in the shade of what once was their holy hall, everything broken to pieces: statues, relics, and faded tapestries telling about the fall of the Empire. Yet on a few remaining clergymen, no signs of repentance had appeared—only the seethings of their defiance. They had outlived the fall of the Empire, and their faith contorted and fractured, trying to respark their powers from the ashes.

Dax and Sylvia stepped out into the hall, their footsteps echoing in the silence. Around them, the remaining clergymen stared at them, eyes cold, faces pale, taut, and tight, shadows of what they once were, with control set in bones and flesh; their Light Magic was used to dominate and command. Now, they were desperate figures hanging onto a broken ideology.

"Perhaps High Priest Falk is gone," one of the clergy spoke up in a shrill hiss, "but the Light shall never bend for Shadow. We have seen the balance you speak of, and it is naught but illusion—a path to chaos.

Dax's eyes hardened; one step forward he did take. "The balance we speak of is neither illusion nor chaos: it is freedom-freedom to choose, to coexist, to show respect to Light as well as Shadow. Your teachings were based upon fear, on manipulation, but that time is gone. The people now have seen the truth.

Sylvia met the clergyman's gaze, her eyes filled with compassion. "The Light you used as a weapon has been reclaimed, and so has the Shadow. No longer a tool of control but as a force for healing, for protection. This is the unity we labored so hard to create.".

Amused, the clergy laughed, the tone of his voice devoid of humor. "Unity? You believe you can take away the fear that's ingrained within the people's hearts? Make them open their arms toward the dark willingly? We know this, man is weak. Man needs guidance; without it, they fall.

Sylvia shook her head. In a very even but firm manner, she said, "People don't need your fear; they need understanding, a chance to trace their path. The only way you think of darkness is to control it, but shadows are a part of life, much as Light is. True power is not about dominance; it's about harmony.

. . .

The mob of people gathered outside the hall watched in silence, tense. Dax could see in their eyes the uncertainty, the wariness. The clergy's words had found a memory among them, a reminder of the doctrines so thoroughly inculcated into the minds of men. Most of them had grown up under the teachings of the Radiance Church; still, a shadow of that influence fell upon their lives.

It was as if he sensed the falter in the crowd, for Dax spoke over the murmurs: "I know fear still resides within many of you, for we all learned that Light was purity and Shadow was danger. But think of everything we have achieved by standing together. The Light and the Shadow are not enemies; they complement and are part of a whole.

One of them quivered all over before stepping forward. "But we were informed that embracing Shadow would consume us, destroy all we held dear.

Sylvia held her gaze, soft reassurance in her tone. "That's what they wanted you to believe. They twisted Light and Shadow, turning fear into a means of containment. But we have seen otherwise. Shadow, when mastered, brings resilience, and Light, when unpolluted, brings hope. We need both to fully live.

The voice at the edge of the circle was a boy no older than fifteen years, his voice raised: "And what if they are right? What if this Union of Light and Shadow is impossible?

. . .

Dax came forward, tone firm: "Unity is neither easy nor simple. But just look among yourselves-at yourselves. In a few scant years, we've seen terror beyond our wildest imagination. Yet we're still here. We fought for freedom, and the right to make our own choices-to forge our own destinies. The power to make this happen lies within every one of you.

People quieted, engrossed in their thoughts. The clerics-their control over the people's minds tenuous at best-fumed. Making a last, desperate try, one of them stepped forward, and as venomously as possible, snarled, "They'll get you ruined. They'll bring onto you a chaos you can't even envision. They'll destroy all the Light built.

But then Sylvia's presence seemed to steady the crowd. She raised her hands and let herself shine with a soft glow of Light Magic-so soft, no harshness or brightness to it, warm and gentle, comforting rather than controlling. "This Light," she said, "is a force of peace, of compassion. And this Shadow," she gestured to Dax, who let the faintest trace of Shadow Magic surround him, "is a force of strength, of resilience. Together, they are balance-a promise that our world can be whole.

The crowd murmured; skepticism melted as they watched Dax and Sylvia together stand for the dream. The clergymen, who earlier had seemed so overpoweringly righteous to him, now seemed so little, irrelevant - the leftovers of a world that no longer was.

CHAPTER 56
RECKONING WITH THE PAST

The whispers started as a low murmur, similar to a faraway wind that just whipped above the treetops of the Whispering Woods. Dax had been the first to catch it-an air of unease, a sense of something, someone trying to cut through the borders of this hard-won peace. Beneath the attempted unity and harmony, discontent brewed, unseen, potent.

He looked out to the Whispering Woods, wherein apprentices under his tutelage learned the way of Shadow. Here, young mages might delve deeper into the use of power, the sensitive art of restraint, wisdom in self-awareness, and- quite importantly-balance. Yet, here, too, the shadows stirred within Dax.

Sylvia too had noticed it-the turning of the people's hearts. Her journeys across the Eryal Continent had shown her that most were content with this balance, but there were those murmurings from some who longed for the old ways-wishing to see once more the power and surety that was once held by the Radiance Church, and others dreamed of a world full of Shadow. Such divisive whisperings she saw as far more dangerous than any open battle.

They were seeds of discontent which, if not met, would undo all they built.

They summoned their closer allies-Elara, Rion, Anya the healer, and a few of the members of the council-deeper into the center of the Whispering Woods to speak about the shadows amassing over the horizon, which were not enemies at their gates but rather internal fears and ambitions within the hearts of the people they had set free.

"We fought to end the tyranny of absolute control," Dax said-the subtext of his tone somber with unspoken concern. "But the appeal of power is hardy. It speaks to people who feel invisible, who feel a need for order in a random world."

Sylvia nodded, her eyes wistful. "We cannot afford to let these whispers grow into a storm. We need to remind the people of the lessons that taught us the essence of balance-those that the Tree of Life and the Whispering Woods did tell us.

Elara crossed her arms, still as feral and pragmatic as ever. "How would one remind people of something so abstract? The concept of balance. the lure of power is instant, tangible. People understand control and dominance because these things promise swift results. Balance. it requires time, patience.". Anya, the coolest of the lot, stretched and laid a soothing hand on Elara's shoulder. "Perhaps that is why we need symbols, rituals. A way for people to remember. Balance is not just a lesson, but a practice. We need to make it a part of their life, something they see and feel every day.

It stirred within them. The peace they had won through fightings, but to maintain it called for weaving the balance into the fabric of every day. It wasn't good enough to continue to count on one's presence; there was a legacy to build, a means whereby individuals could wear the balance as easily and unconsciously as breathing.

Over the coming weeks, Dax and Sylvia arranged meetings all over the Eryal Continent. Not sermons or lectures, open forums for discussion, introspection, and sharing of personal experience with both Light and Shadow: "Circles of Balance" they called them-opportunities for people finally to speak their minds, to voice their fears, hopes, and doubts. Now, people would finally be able to see the harmony in practice between Light and Shadow for themselves. Sylvia would speak of the nurturing qualities of Light magic, using it to heal and grow; Dax would speak to the resiliency of Shadow, its strength in facing and overcoming fears. Together, they showed each force as a help, incomplete without the other. They made balance tangible, not an abstract thought, but a lived experience.

There were those few who resisted.

And it was on one of those nights that, in the Circle of Balance at the edge of the village that stood at the edge of the Whispering Woods, the elder rose to his feet, stark-faced. "You speak of balance," he said, tone fully rounded in disbelief. "But the balance is fragile. Too fragile for the uncertainty of real life. Sometimes, a firm hand is needed. We remember the peace under the Church, the order.

Now, one has free time, yes, but chaos, too."

Dax felt the sting in the man's words. Indeed, there was never ease in freedom. Where there is choice, there must be responsibility; where there is balance, there must be an understanding. Stepping forward, he spoke with firm but tranquil tones. "Indeed, balance is fragile, but so is life.

True strength doesn't hold onto control; it s more about embracing that fragility-peace is fostered continuously. Each of us must take an inner route and accept both light and shade in the heart. Then it was Sylvia's turn, her voice almost a whisper by comparison to his. "What the Radiance Church offered was not peace, but silence, an enforced quiet that stifles growth and understanding. True peace is messy. It's a process. It's something we all contribute to, every day.".

The stare of the elder softened; a glitter of comprehension stood in his eyes. Others around the circle nodded, faces with profound thought. They lived through oppression, experienced the freedom of rebellion, and now bit by bit, they come to see that balance is not an endpoint but a journey-a journey that requires patience, compassion, and courage.

. . .

And so, the Circles of Balance began to stretch to places where people came together, not in order to dominate one another, but to understand one another. It was a sign, a symbol of the world Dax and Sylvia had envisioned: one in which people would not be afraid to confront their shadows or be able to wear their light without pride.

As months slipped by, the whispers of discontent died; the people slowly began to personify a certain balance they had never understood. It was a family discussion, unabridged, of the tenets of Light and Shadow, and children grew up to know that power is to be shared and not held by any one person. The leaders listened to the voices of one and all regardless of birth and creed. Seated at the very center of the Whispering Woods, beneath the sprawling arms of the Tree of Life, were Dax and Sylvia, who watched the world they had a hand in building take root.

They knew well the work would never truly be complete, for balance was a continuing process-a sensitive dance that could be shattered at any moment. Yet, they had simultaneously known all the while that they were providing the seeds of resilience which, when tended to by the owners themselves in their self-help efforts, would eventually bloom.

And thus, with the seasons, Circles of Balance became a tradition, a living legacy of what they fought for-the harmony they were able to attain. Dax and Sylvia did not win the war; they changed a society, leaving in its wake a world-one which respects both Light and Shadow. It is a world wherein this balance is not just a word, but a certain way of life.

. . .

They stood together, their hands clasped; some silent understanding was crossing between them. It was a triumph of this world-outside of which the murmurs of separation fell away before voices of unity, outside of which Light and Shadow could dance in peace, outside of which hope was alive within the balance of all things.

CHAPTER 57
THE FLAME REIGNITED

Serious rebuilding of the Imperial City was in process. Amongst the still-smoldering ruins, the first contours of a new life began to take shape under the hands of the tired and yet inspired. Silent but resolute, people moved about, reconstructing their houses, making places for assembly, hammering out new symbols of unity in place of the once-shining Radiance Cathedral. Of course, it was a colossal job; however, all of them were driven by one dream: to find that world where Light and Shadow could coexist side by side, living freely from their oppressors, the Radiance Church.

Neither Dax nor Sylvia had left the heart of the city since the final battle. Every day, they walked among the people-listening to their tales, learning their woes, and being wary to give guidance wherever it was needed. They had become way more than leaders; they were symbols, not just of resistance, but of possibility, living, breathing embodiments of the balance they preached.

. . .

But with every encounter, it was they who carried the burden of expectation. The victory that came, which freed them from the clutches of oppression, had left a vacuum in its wake with structures and with new ideologies, new ways of thinking. The people needed more than freedom; they needed guidance.

As evening fell, the setting sun turning the concrete of the city to warm gold, so did Sylvia and Dax sit amidst a council-one that truly represented their fighters, their healers, academics, and others who were community leaders, some who have been instrumental in this rebellion. Its goal would be simple yet deep: to lead the people in constructing a society based on balance, compassion, and justice.

Sylvia spoke to them first; her eyes even, her voice firm in resolution. "We tore down the Empire, but the presence of it has still left its scars on us. We have to realize this isn't just simply going back to the way things were. We have to create anew, forged from the very principles for which we fought: freedom, choice, balance.

Rion, one of the most-experienced tacticians, crucial to the rebellion, leaned forward. "How will we keep it in balance? Even with the best of intentions, power does funny things. We have seen that first hand.

Dax nodded, keenly aware of the concern all too well. "We need checks, accountability-not only among us but also within ourselves. We fought for a world where people can choose their own path. That means accepting the fact that no one person or group should hold absolute control over others. Our role here is to serve, not to rule.

She said, "We must create awareness, teach about Light and Shadow, about balance. Radiance Church spread fear of the Shadow by using Light against them, to enslave the people. Such teachings need to be deconstructed, to show people that the Shadow is nothing to be afraid of, but to be understood, just like Light, cannot be used as an oppressive tool but as a means for growth.

In it, the words fell word by word, as the members of that council etched their faces with determination and caution, having seen in those days of rebellion the best and worst of men, aware of the razor's edge they were to tread the next few days.

The next to speak was Anya, the healer, who commanded respect because of her wisdom and her humanity. "We won their freedom, but too many still cling to the chain of fear-fear of what they have made them fear, fear of change, fear of one another. We need places where they could unlearn that fear.

Sylvia nodded dreamily. "Circles of Balance," she whispered; a light in her head suddenly flared bright. "Places where people come together, not to teach about Light and Shadow, but to experience them as a whole: share stories, share fears, and share hope.

. . .

Dax caught on; his eyes lit up. "Yes, sanctuary for them to understand the balance. They'll know neither needs to be feared if they see us, people they trust, pay respect to Light and Shadow alike.

The council decided upon this, and the Circles of Balance were born. Over the next two weeks, Sylvia and Dax organised the first of such events, where people were allowed to share their fears and face the lurking remains in their hearts of the indoctrination of the Radiance Church.

It is at these colloquiums that Sylvia evidences the nurturing aspects of Light for physical and emotional healing, while Dax evidences resiliency from within the Shadow to teach it, too, may be a source.

This reaction ran deep. Those who had shuddered at the very thought of Shadow as the very antithesis of Light now came to regard it as a part of themselves, no different than Light. They do not see Sylvia and Dax anymore as polar opposites but interdependent, each strong because of the other's existence. It's through the Circles of Balance that they learn the truth: strength does not come about by dominance but by harmony-the marriage of opposites.

Yet, as stirring as these congregations were, there was still a hard core that simply could not adapt to such a new ideal. One such was Elias, formerly with the Radiant Knights, his loyalty worn thin by so many years of indoctrination. He sought out Dax and Sylvia one night after a Circle, his face taut, a flicker of doubt dancing in his eyes.

. . .

I've followed the Radiance Church most of my life," he said, his voice shaking all but imperceptibly. "I have seen what Light can do when shown no mercy. But Shadow.it still sends a shiver down my spine. How am I supposed to trust in something I was taught to hate?

Sylvia set a hand to his shoulder, her tone soft yet firm. "It's natural enough to fear what we don't understand. Shadow is no good nor evil in and of itself-it just is. Like Light, it's a force, one that can heal or harm depending on the heart that wields it.

He finished his tale and said, "The strength of Shadow is resilience-to turn and face ourselves, to acknowledge parts of ourselves we'd rather ignore. It does not ask for blind devotion; it asks one to be acquainted with the self. You can find strength in Shadow if you learn to face your terrors without being consumed.

Elias nodded slowly, his gaze softening. "I'll try," he said, a note of hope in his voice. "I'll try to see Shadow as a part of myself, not as an enemy."

Instants like these were at once trying and a deep reward that their teachings were finally beginning to find root, that hearts and minds were slowly opening themselves to a different way of thinking. Every minor breakthrough that came along was a victory, reminding them that this was not a war against an enemy outside, but rather one against the divisions within.

. . .

Months melted away, years slipped by, and the Imperial City began to be less a terror placed at the heart of oppression but more of a haven to re-educate its people. The lessons of Balance rode to the smallest villages in towns and cities across the continent, teaching the ways of harmony. Circles of Balance began to place gatherings together-united in cause, not by power or fear, but by understanding.

Dax and Silvia watched their dream in progress, silent pride in the heart, knowing very well challenges were to follow, knowing that in the struggle to find a balance, it's a process and not just an event. But at the same time, they knew that something enduring had been planted-a legacy of survival, of harmony, of hopes.

As the evening wore on, and the town started coming out, beginning to fill up the new square, Dax leaned over to Sylvia. His voice was low, but firm: "We did it. Not by our hands, but by theirs. We gave them the means to make something better.".

Smiling back, Sylvia's eyes reflected the sparkle of the city lights around them. "Balance is something we cannot enforce, something they would have to choose every single day. And now they do have a choice.

They stood together, an unspoken understanding passing between them. It had been a long journey fraught with trials and victories alike, yet every step had been so very worth it.

They didn't fight for their freedom; they fought for the future-a future wherein Light and Shadow coexisted in harmony, a place where people could live free from the fear of their own nature. And when the city is abuzz with the sounds of life, laughter, and hope, they would know that they have done a great deal more than winning a battle-they changed the world, one heart at a time, leaving a legacy which outlived them.

CHAPTER 58
CONVERGENCE OF PATHS

Through shattered panes, the early rising sun cast fractured beams into the Imperial Palace. It was an omen, perhaps, that this world had only a few more scars to bear. Dax and Sylvia stood among the other Councilors, their steps echoing in that silent space as they prepared to go out and begin the first day of leading a newly free world. Today was to be the start of a new epoch: the marriage of such idealistic notions of balance and unity with the grim realities that necessarily accompany the rebuilding of a society on the ashes of tyranny.

The council was reconvening early, with determination etched in their faces, weighted responsibly. It is quite one thing to overthrow an oppressive regime; it is quite another to make a world where justice and freedom flower. All members of the council sat at a worn but sturdy table, each representative of the many diversities found on the continent: from former soldiers, healers, and scholars to farmers and artisans. And therein lay the cohesion and resilience of the people they served.

. . .

Sylvia began to speak, her voice smooth but firm: "We are here to serve, not to lead; to guide, not to rule. The test of our ingenuity is for the new society not to become that which until now has urged us on to destroy the Empire: we have to establish institutions serving the people-not controlling them; and we have to make quite sure that no single voice silences the will of a community.

The others nodded in turn, one by one. No one of them had balmed another regime born of fear or fattened on division. They all had seen enough agony and death, and none of them wanted to see a different future where Light or Shadow was twisted anew to serve tyranny.

Dax took a deep breath; in a low tone, he spoke with quiet conviction. "The cruelties of the Empire further extended to the manipulations of both Light and Shadow to divide them. If we are going to heal these wounds, then it is about time we start reshaping the perception of these forces. Let us create places to teach of both so people can examine their own strengths without fear.

A councillor, a former Radiant Knight who joined the rebellion once he saw the corruption in the Empire, raised his hand. "Dax, Sylvia," he began, "there are people still hostile to Shadow, and on the other hand, those wary of the Light due to how it was abused. How do we bridge the gap, to show that both are needed and neither can exist without the other?

. . .

Sylvia met his eyes, her face expressionless in comprehension. "Thus far, we have taught through the Circles of Balance whereby Light and Shadow are engaged on equal terms. We need to go a step ahead. We have to set up centers in each of the key cities-a place where people can think and study the two forces-not with stark lectures, but with feeling, touch, and understanding.

Dax then added, "And in the facilities, let us try to make that place where the two coexist-not as the opposites, yet one, balanced energy. Where people come to know that Light and Shadow could work together, it is actually parts of an integral essence.

The members debated, each voicing ideas and speaking to logistical concerns and rebuilding the infrastructure so that no one community should feel left behind. All they knew was that the Imperial Palace would stand, to unite them, but these would be enclaves of learning and balance, their heart of a new world, and testament to their vision of a harmonious society.

In every voice that spoke through-in each voice-Dax and Sylvia found empowerment, a wisdom earned through hardship as much as hope. It is a dynamic underscoring shared responsibility, reminding them again why they fought for a council rather than a single ruler. They didn't build a world that would depend on a few; they built it upon the contribution of all.

. . .

The question came sudden and small from the lips of one councillor, fragile but poignant-a healer who had seen the amount of psychological scarring from the Empire's reign: "What of those that still hold loyal to the teachings of the Empire? Those who looked upon the Radiance Church for protection, or those who cannot forget the past?

The room fell silent, the weight of the question settling deep. Dax chose her words carefully to try and address the complexity. "Healing cannot be forced. Those still hanging onto the ideals of the Empire need the time and space to come to their own place. We have to give them the option to come with us, not through any pressure or coercion. And if our vision is strong, then it will speak for itself.".

Sylvia added, her voice gentle but firm, "And for those who refuse to change, let us make it clear that they will not be persecuted for their beliefs. They have a right to their views, as long as they do not impose them upon others or threaten the peace we're building."

The way forward was debated by the council, and there was consensus that this had to be inclusive and patient. Some wounds would take generations to heal, and their job was not to sweep the past away but to offer a way forward-a choice for each person to walk his path within a framework of respect and understanding.

Then the meeting adjourned, and only Dax and Sylvia remained behind, observing while the other membership filed out of the council. The shared contemplative moment was brief, but both knew the enormity of what was to come, along with the strength of what had been forged.

Outside, the city slowly woke up; the early morning light cast long shadows across the newly cleaned streets from rubble. In walking, they found knots of citizens talking about plans they had listened to from the council. Some cleared rubble, tended to the wounded, or tried to rebuild homes, each contributing as best they could. There was an unspoken word-quiet resilience that kept them going day after day.

One square showed a crowd of young apprentices and children learning about Light and Shadow alike from a former Radiant Knight and a Shadow Mage. The Knight explained the healing warmth of Light Magic, while the Shadow Mage tried to teach resiliency, using one's inner strength against whatever challenges lay ahead. And the children watched, their eyes wide with wonder in that mixture of curiosity and reverence, learning that both have beauty and purpose.

Sylvia's heart swelled at the sight. "This is what we've fought for, Dax. For a future where Light and Shadow aren't feared, but understood."

Dax smiled, his eyes falling upon apprentices practicing small spells and 'ooh'ing and 'ahh'ing over the world around them. "They're the ones that'll carry it forward. They'll remember that Light and Shadow are two sides of the same truth, and they'll shape a world reflecting that balance.

. . .

It was a day full of turmoil and activity, but every single minute was not lost in silent resolve for rebuilding, or beginning anew. Dax and Sylvia resumed their rounds-speaking with the citizens, guiding and listening to problems weighing on people's minds and hearts. They drew encouragement from the resolute people-from their readiness to face even fear and prejudice for progress' sake.

With the sun now setting, they returned to the palace, in which the council had prepared a small dinner reflecting both the success and setbacks of the day. In the center of the hall, all by itself, one candle was burning, while around it was darkness, a sign of the balance they strove to keep.

Sylvia leaned forward, extending her hand towards the flame, almost: "This light. it is a reminder that the tiniest source of hope can light up the worst darkness.

Dax nodded, and his eyes did not budge. "And where there is light, there is always shadow. It is our duty to treat them with respect, to know a real force comes with harmony, not with dominance. The fire in them now was a much newer level of determination as they would look around the circle of council members, each face a mirrored image of their realization that their work had just begun.

They felt they had done the first steps toward building a world where Light and Shadow would exist side by side, under rights of choice that were free, and where freedom would be guarded not by force but by union. As night started to set in, Dax and Sylvia knew their journey had become more-a testament of the will to survive of the human spirit, a guiding star for people yet to be born, and a promise that no matter how black the future seemed, balance and harmony would prevail.

CHAPTER 59
A SYMPHONY OF POWER

Soft morning light filtered between the treetops of Whispering Woods, sprinkling on the forest floor in soft, diffused light, as Dax and Sylvia strode onward with a new sense of purpose. Something inside their hearts had been decided beneath the heart of those ancient ruins, and with each step, that weight was brought further into memory. No longer were they leaders of a mere rebellion, but undertook a mantle bigger than themselves to become watchmen for the fragile balance between Light and Shadow.

The leaves rustled louder, with only the soft calls of the morning birds that flew to the tops to break the stillness. Still, this was a deceptive tranquility; Sylvia knew that beyond the fringes of the Whispering Woods, their world-battered and scarred-would await them upon their return, its people in urgent need of guidance, healing, and hope.

Dax looked at Sylvia, and his eyes reflected the echoes of their decision. "The Whispering Woods acknowledged our decision," he said in hushed tones, lest the loudness of the voice breaks the spell of peace lingering around them. "The light we felt-that balance-it accepted our vow.

Sylvia nodded; truth deep-set in his words struck home in her very soul. "Now, the time has come to give back this balance to people. All they know is war. That is something we cannot take away by just words; they need to see and feel that Light and Shadow can walk hand in glove in harmony.

Their footsteps led them to a small clearing where the council had been waiting for their return. As they entered, already members of the council stood up, eyes relieved yet full of curiosity. Elara stood forward, for she had stood beside them since the early days of rebellion, her face lined by the vestiges of exhaustion and anticipation, a reflection of the very struggle which had brought them to this point.

"You both ventured into the heart of the Woods," Elara exclaimed in a tone full of wonder. "What did you find? What does lie at the heart of balance?"

Dax's gaze was nailed to hers, the weight in his voice carrying the weight of what they had shared. "We found a sanctuary-a place where Light and Shadow had been kept in balance, preserved by our ancestors. And that balance is not something given; it is a thing to be guarded, defended, upheld in every action we take.

. . .

Sylvia stepped forward, her face set. "The choice we have made is not an easy one. The world beyond these woods is fractured, divided by generations of fear and control. We believe the way forward is not through dominance, not through one force conquering another, but by embracing the balance we have found.

A murmur swept through the council, and then Rion-a arguably one of their most trusted strategists-began to speak. "But how do we show this to the people? How will we be able to convince those who had lived under the repression of the Empire that Light and Shadow can coexist?

Dax took a deep breath; his voice resounded with an air of conviction. "We begin by living it ourselves. We cannot expect others to believe in harmony when it is not reflected in every choice and every action by ourselves. We have to be the example-lived evidence of the truth we have found.

The enormity of his words settled upon them, as the members exchanged a glance. They all had seen the corruption that came with the unchecked Light under the Radiance Church, had seen with their own eyes how fear of the shadows had held so many back from embracing their own strength. Now, this journey of balance for Dax and Sylvia had turned into a journey which each soul would have to take in search of a world free from the tyranny of absolutes.

Sylvia leaned in towards the council, her tone warm but unwavering: "We shall not impose this balance. Instead, what we will do is build schools, give space to people so that they might come into contact-even with Light and Shadow-without fear or judgment. And by teaching, with the sharing of experiences, they shall learn the role each one plays and their place in the whole.".

She nodded as the council listened with great interest-words that echoed deep in the pit of their own longed-for freedom from the cycles of control and terror. Yet for most, the cruelty of the Empire was fresh in their minds, and embracing even those very forces used upon them was daunting. And yet, in Sylvia's words, there was unavoidable hope, another world offered-one that was defined not by oppression but, rather, respect to life's delicate balance.

And then, all in a high-speed discussion, came the forwarding of how it all was to come into being: how centers of learning were to be instituted both for the study of magic but also the philosophy of Balance guiding in the use of such magic; how sanctuaries would be given to those touched by Shadow Magic, finding a place of acceptance and understanding, and the places where the healing nature of Light Magic would be extended to all, irrespective of their gifts.

Throughout the hours that followed, Dax and Sylvia described to the council what the ruin meant: the carvings, the stories of old civilizations and their struggles for balance. There, every member of the council sat in respect, gathering experience from how people of the past balanced these tugging forces in every direction. And mirrored within those tales, their own struggles-ancient figures who have fought and fallen in their search for unity.

. . .

When the council had dismissed, every member wove his different ways, rejuvenated with a fresh determination. They carried not just a ray of hope for better days ahead but realized that the onus of balance lay in their hands. They were no longer constrained by the ideologies of the Empire but were creators of a new vision and stewards of a legacy which outlived their lifetime.

With the last of the council members gone, it left only Dax and Sylvia to themselves in the clearing, the soft, whispered rustlings of the forest around them a gentle reminder of the direction they had taken. They stood in silence, side by side, the weight of their decision and the world that they now carried in their hearts.

Sylvia looked at Dax, her voice barely more than a whisper. "We're not just leaders, Dax. We're the bridge between two worlds. And to lead others, we'll have to keep finding that balance within ourselves, every day."

The hardness in Dax's eyes softened, his voice quieting to a resolve. "And we'll face that together. The strength we need lies in each other, and in the people who believe in this vision. It's the only way forward.

Light of foot but sure, hand in hand, they left the glade. In front of them, there stretched the forest: the soft shadows of the morning danced across the way. They knew with every step that their resolution found here in the depths of the

Whispering Woods would fan out to reach those as yet unmet and shape the world ahead.

And it was there, deep inside that forest, with only themselves and the wisdom of yesterday guiding them, that they began to take the first steps toward the creation of a new world: one where Light and Shadow could stand together; one where Power would be chastened by experience, and Freedom would not be constrained by Mastery but by the resilient strength of Equilibrium.

CHAPTER 60
ROOTS OF REBELLION

The midday sun climbed high over Whispering Woods, casting warm rays through the thick canopy down to the forest floor in dappled patterns. The land was quiet, alive rather, with a different kind of energy-one where even trees and stones seemed to know the value of the day. The rise and fall within the tides of empires, the births of witness to battles in shadow and in light, came and went with generations into these woods, now finally able to rest easy in the promise of peace that had been won.

Dax and Sylvia walked through the forest, side by side, allowing the silence to extend between them as they digested the heaviness of what had passed. Their footsteps were unhurried, their gazes soft yet contemplative. Hard-won, the victory was, and with the threat of darkness having passed, both knew their work was only just getting underway.

They came into a quiet glade, and there, in the middle of it, stood the Tree of Life, sound and unshakable, its roots twisted deep into the earth. A tree of surprising strength and resilience, stretching wide as in arms to clasp the very soul of the world. Sylvia felt the warmth of it, knowing so well as in familiarity, the wisdom it had in store and the truths they had unraveled in their journey.

Dax was the first to break the silence, his voice deep in thought. "This tree has seen more than any one of us could conceptualize. It's a reminder that no matter how bad it gets in life, the potential of light coming back will always be there.

Sylvia nods, a soft, gentle, smiling curve of her lips curling over: "It reminds us that we are one with something greater, and the balance which we fought for is for all life and every end of this land.".

They breathed, silent, sopping into their psyches the stillness rising from the tree. It had been guide, shelter, and mentor. Here, at the heart of the Whispering Woods, they had learned Light and Shadow were not adversaries but allies, wherein the one power actually lay in harmonious conjunction and not in opposition to one another.

Dax nodded softly and then reached out his hand; Sylvia slid hers inside, and the fingers intertwined in silent solidity. Kneeling at the foot of this ancient tree, humming with the energy running through them, they closed their eyes and made a silent oath-one that this balance they had fought for would not break, but would be cared for and preserved, for the generations to come.

. . .

But with every rise to newer heights came to Dax clarity of focus, unhindered by shades of fear or ambiguity, the very shades of character that had always threatened him now his strong points, reminding him through each twist and turn that it was his choices that defined him, not his past. Sylvia had also started to feel a sort of wholeness, realizing that Light was not necessarily a force of purity but part of guidance, part of nurturing strength, and thus could coexist in unity without conforming with Shadow.

They emerged from the grove and back into the gathering-the resistance now joined by villagers and other people from far and wide-waiting for their leaders. The entrance of Dax and Sylvia was followed by murmurs of respect and admiration; reassurance that it was worth every sacrifice in this fight.

Dax spoke to them, and the crowd hushed. His voice was as clear as crystal, unshaken. "Today, we are one people, united in one purpose, a common dream. We have broken the shackles of the Empire, but that is just the beginning. We have a world to rebuild, a legacy to forge, a balance to preserve."

He paused to let the weight sink in, then he went on, "We have learned that Light and Shadow are not opposites, but dance partners in the balance of life. And we shall keep this in mind while we construct a world free of oppression, one that respects both sides of the self and one another.

Sylvia stepped forward, her eyes wandering across the crowd as her magic of Light shimmered softly with her words. "The teachings we shall set no more will be those that separate. Our schools, our places of learning, will be where everyone finds a welcome; the knowledge of Light and Shadow alike shall be passed on, and truth shall not be hidden but rejoiced in.

A ripple of realization ran across the sea of faces as each expression told a tale of relief and hope blended together. They had been freed not only from the chains of the Empire but also from the blindness and fear that once divided them. Now they were to be part of a world where magic became the bridge-the unifying tool-a testament to the harmony they had struggled to prevail.

They spent the rest of the day in preparation for what was to be done: resisters, villagers, and allies alike cleaned up the results of the battle, building foundations for a new world they would create. People told stories, tended wounds, comforted each other; their movements were haloed with silent intention. Dax and Sylvia walked among them, guiding, silent at times-as indeed during the quiet moments of introspective thoughts-but serving as a reminder of the strength that had seen them through the most fateful of moments.

When the sun started to set, casting a gold pallor on everything around, the gathering felt a silent gush of peace. Small fires lit, holding in their gentle light as people came into a circle, sharing a meal in token of their harmony. The quiet was comfortable, punctuated with soft 'hee-haws' of laughter, whispered words, and murmurs of thanks from time to time.

. . .

Sylvia turned to Dax with an air of quiet resolve, a stillness in her eyes. "We did it, didn't we?" she said softly. "We gave them a chance-a chance to be something better.

Dax nodded, a small, very rare smile tugging his lips upward. "We have. But now it's up to them, up to all of us, to protect it. Balance isn't something you can gain with one battle; it's a track you have to walk each day.

With the first twinkling of the stars across the sky, Dax and Sylvia again took time to ponder how long it had taken them to come there.

They fought for a world where Light and Shadow exist equally and each being should have rights to choose their fate. They forged a fellowship of unity, reminding people that the strong need to understand, be compassionate toward, and open their hearts to all shades of life.

Before them lay the New Era, its path lit with tough lessons from the past and a promise of a future written in the language of balance. Dax and Sylvia, for one final moment, looked upon the crowded people-their friends and families-before turning into the horizon, ready to lead this new world with the wisdom they had earned.

And the more they marched further ahead together, the more in their minds echoed the whisper of the Whispering Woods-a soft, soothing reminder that amidst the shadows, light somehow found its ways. In their hearts, they held a vow-a promise of unsealing to keep the balance, taking along with them the world they had saved and shielding the harmony that thus far had accompanied them.

CHAPTER 61
EYES OF THE FUTURE

The morning sun cast its first tender beams over the ruins of the Imperial City and lit a landscape alike torn by battle, subtly promising in its quiet a new beginning. The imposing structures of the city, which were to have spoken to the strength and control of the Empire, lay in ruin. With every broken building and shattered stone that the light touched, it almost spoke to strange beauty in remembrance that even in devastation, life may find a way out.

Dax picked his way through what was left of Radiance Cathedral, its halls silent as compared to when they rang with greatness, the high-pointed spires now rubble. Every step called to mind the fight that had raged inside these walls, powers pitted against powers, wills against wills. They'd triumphed-but the city broken around him seemed a heavy mantle of responsibility laid upon his shoulders. Victory brought them freedom, yet it left an aching void-a space to be filled with something more than this inanimate control which they had just torn apart.

. . .

Sylvia joined him there, her presence an anchor sure amongst the turbulence of his thoughts. Haggard with fatigue, her face shone with a faint reassuring glow of Light Magic that gentled the shadows clinging to the rubble around them.

She muttered, her tone sad, resolute: "Look at this place, Dax. How many lives it kept captive, how many minds it twisted to serve ideals not true. Now, it's just in ruins.

Dax nodded, and his gaze fell on hers. "Yes, but these ruins now mean something: they are the beginning of something new, something we get to mold. We didn't come here just to tear down but to build a world where Light and Shadow are not what divide us but make us one.

Sylvia's eyes softened then, and she reached for his hand. "Then let us make sure everything we do from now on upholds that cause. The people are free, but they have lost so much-homes, families, lives... We owe it to them that what we build now is done with compassion, with unity.

As they spoke, survivors of the rebellion began to gather around them-fighters, healers, former prisoners, and civilians who for years had been crushed under the heel of their oppressors. There was the line of exhaustion, there was grief, and cautious hope etched in the features, mirrored in the reflections, of one weight shared with another lying ahead.

Dax turned toward them; his voice rose above the quiet murmur of the crowd. "We shattered the chains of the Empire, but our job is far from done. Freedom is but a beginning-it is not the end. We must rebuild, not just the walls, but the lives that had lain crushed under the heels of the Empire. And for that, we need each and every one of you.".

The faces watched him, a mixture of relief and trepidation reflected on them. They were people who had struggled for freedom without knowing what that freedom would demand from them. All they knew was how to live under the Empire: a few options-one overriding choice-fear.

Sylvia stepped forward, her tone firm but clear and filled with compassion: "The Radiance Church turned Light Magic into an instrument of terror-a thing utilized for the terrorizing of and binding. This we can recover, redevelop into something soothing and not injurious. Light and Shadow are not opposing forces; they complement each other. It is time we learn to coexist with them.

A murmur of assent swept over the crowd, a ripple of understanding, really-for too long, they had been taught to fear Shadow, to treat it as if it were sinister and evil. Yet here was Dax, a hitherto shadow-shrouded idol, among them now as a beacon of hope and strength-a reminder that Light and Shadow together gave them this success. As the people went their separate ways to start the backbreaking task of rebuilding, Dax and Sylvia called together the leaders of the rebellion to form a new council. There was a need for something to fall back on, for some structure to supplant the void left by the dismantling of the Empire. They spoke of councils to represent each community, shared responsibility, and mutual respect. They wanted to see schools where people would learn about the Light and Shadow with equanimity, without the bias and manipulation that had once colored every corner of the Empire's teachings.

It was their leaders who listened closely, those who had been divided into class and region, even beliefs, which had come under the umbrella of rebellion and found themselves a part of something bigger-a vision for a just and balanced world.

They debated governance, laws, and a need for healing spaces where people could confront the trauma brought about by years of oppression. Respectful, yet not easy, this eloquent and fiercely committed conversation steered clear of repeating what history has stood for.

When the meeting was finally over, Sylvia stood slowly and spoke in hushed tones, "We are planting seeds-Dax, seeds that require time and attention to grow. It won't be easy, but I really do think they'll flourish if we fertilize them with what we've learned.". He met her gaze, his expression filled with resolution and tenderness in turn. "We have faced darkness together, Sylvia. Let us see this through. The road ahead will be long, but we have come to know how resilient people are, even incredibly kind. We can depend on them, and they on us.

With the council's plans now in motion, Dax and Sylvia walked hand in hand through the city in silence, mute testimony to a bond that had seen them through at their worst. They passed by survivors comforting each other, piles of rubble taken away by groups, and the healers attending to the wounded.

A snapshot of resilience, of what this future they were trying to build would look like: a place where individuals looked out for one another, and strength was drawn from unity rather than fear.

The sun was now slowly setting and casting the ruins in that warm, golden light. Dax and Sylvia stood atop what was left from the Radiance Cathedral, once a symbol of Empire control, now one of the resilience of the human spirit-to remind that even in the darkest of places, hope could still bloom.

Dax looked at Sylvia with quiet conviction brimming in his voice. "We can help make the something that would last, that brings out the best in people. It's the past, and one which won't be forgotten, but one we learn from. Sylvia nodded, laying her hand upon his arm. "Let's hope that the memory of what happened here can serve to remind us of what we overcome and what we need to protect. They stood together, looking out over the town-its buildings now silhouetted against a tapestry of soft light from the lanterns of its citizens, continuing the work deep into the night, untiring in the re-creation of what had been lost. They had won freedom, and with it the duty to create a world in which that freedom could flourish.

As night started to fall, Dax and Sylvia knew it was only the beginning. These were scars of the past that would take time to heal, and definitely the road ahead would be tough. They were ready, and they had each other. And it was with this vow that they walked shoulder to shoulder down from the ruins, carrying in their steps a hope for a time when Light and Shadow would walk in tandem-to a place where those of yore would not perish but live, where hope would never be doused.

CHAPTER 62
THE CHAINS BROKEN

This was a world standing at the threshold of change. The lands that had groveled under the jackboot of tyranny stirred with the tender whispers of freedom, as if taking the first breath after a silence so long held. The rising sun shone soft, golden upon the remains of war and revealed lacerations across the face of the land that reflected those that were borne by its people. But with the first light, the smoke of war was taken away to give novelty and development.

Rebuilding was a colossal task: every village, city, and town had stood a monument to the indomitable will of the human spirit. Communities all over the continent got down to work, rebuilding homes, schools, and markets. The streets, once patrolled by the Empire's guards, had given way to laughter and/or conversations.

It was lighter, filled with an almost palpable sense of hope and freedom in the air. Whereas cold fear once reigned, determination did now, and a sense that something more might not only exist but might be found.

Dax and Sylvia had become the spine of the rebellion, a symbol of this era. As much as they were leading the people to victory, both knew equally well that their job was a long way from where it should be. They walked among the burgeoning communities, guiding, comforting, and learning much as they taught. Their presence made them mindful that the path forward was one they would travel together, each a part of the greater whole. Rebuilding now had a rhythm all its own: craftsmen and laborers together raised walls abreast, telling the story not of a division but of unity. Even the marketplaces were gradually reopening to the hustle and bustle of traders and artisans. Many walls still showed the scares of war, but resilience shone in their faces as if the scares had converted into testimonials of what they had gone through.

This is not the time to forget but to remember-to remember losses and to construct a future which will not relapse into its mistakes.

Yet, in the quietness of the villages, this was much slower. To those who had spent their lives under the iron hand of the Empire, change seemed almost unreal. How open trusting was not possible among the people, as reflected in continued hushed talks and furtive glances. With views of growing cities and stories of hope and reunification before them, villagers likewise reached out to bridge, little by little, the gaps in a people torn apart by decades of isolation and terror.

. . .

Dax spoke to convened citizens, bringing with him the wisdom of his journey. "We have seen what happens when power isn't checked, when Light or Shadow is used without comprehension. Our world must be one where these forces can coexist, where freedom and justice guide our every step.

Sylvia, however, had learned more about Light Magic than the distorted learning of the Empire could provide, and thus was able to give solace to the wounded body and soul. Her Light was like balm, reminding one that true magic was never to be used in order to constrain someone but to be compassionate instead. With her, hope finally entered each village, free to take back their peace after all the destruction. It was a sign of the times they wanted to create: children playing and laughing in the streets. Children, as yet untainted by the cruelties of the Empire, were growing up into a world promising them choices and giving them opportunities to develop their talents, not exploit them. They were the first generation to know a life unshadowed by the terror of the Empire, and their joy was a reminder that, in the end, change was worth its painful price.

More than ever, it had been the aftermath of the rebellion that relaunched the eager study of magic. Scholars who, up to that moment, had been silenced were now pouring into just-opened academies, fascinated with the opportunity to start research on hitherto untouched Light and Shadow.

Free to operate independent of the Empire's influence, they could experiment and learn that Light Magic is not intrinsically good any more than Shadow is intrinsically evil. It was multicolored, just as people were multicolored-a part of themselves which, if used rightly, could serve all of humankind. And thus, Dax and Sylvia strolled side by side through such academies, envisioning in them the promise of a future whereby knowledge and understanding could shape the world, wherein the utilization of a magical gift was not the taking up of arms against brothers but a communal forward movement in growth and harmony. They listened to the scholars' theories and quietly watched with pride as these men and women tore down dogma that had once enthralled them, revealing truths that had been buried for centuries.

A council meeting was held in the great hall of the newly established capital, one that Dax and Sylvia attended, though one also crowded with hosts of representatives throughout the continent-from former rebels to newly elected voices of the people, every corner of the world. They spoke on governance, laws, protection of hard-won freedom. Every voice was heard, every opinion valued.

It is this council that comes to bear witness to the diversity and unity issuing forth from the rebellion: it is a body committed to cooperation, not domination.

Then Dax spoke before them, his voice low and proud: "We are not here to replace one ruling power with another. We come to create anew in honor of the right of every individual to live and pursue happiness. Our role is to guide, to protect, and to see that balance always prevails.

. . .

Sylvia added, her clear and strong voice firm, "The Radiance Church used Light to control and brought almost complete ruin upon us all. May this serve as a lesson that magic and power shall never be distorted with the intention of oppressing others. Light and Shadow shall be taught, respected, and understood; above all, they shall be executed with responsibility and mercy.

Yea, and the councilors nodded, in one second, in that one second, in the silent elapse of mutual understanding, united-not by power-but by purpose, not by fear but by hope. For within each of them was the weight of what had been taken, yet in each a mind which yet nursed hope that they might, together, honor that loss by making of it something worthy.

And so, bit by bit, as morning broke and evening spent itself among cities and villages, the continent began to change: scarred fields being plowed again, shattered homes rebuilt, bruised relationships cleared of bitterness. The people regained control of life-the small acts of rebuilding a further step toward integrity, each moment of kindness forming a thread in the tapestry of their new world.

Dax and Sylvia walked among them, giving strength when it was needed, giving words to comfort, and bearing witness to the resilience of the people they had fought to free. They were under no illusion that healing was anything but a process-one that would be undertaken in due time with patience, understanding, and steadfast devotion to the cause they represented.

. . .

But rather it should not be forgotten, yet a guiding factor towards opening up to the consequences of unbridled power, an object lesson in the need for compassion. The balance of Light and Shadow would go to be a cornerstone in the building they were partaking-a beacon for the later generations to learn from it, that harmony was not found in simplicity but in the acceptance of complexity.

Standing together, looking out upon the landscape they had freed, Dax and Sylvia knew pride, deep and profound. They had walked in darkness, borne the weight of loss, and emerged on the other side-not unscarred, but stronger. This would be their legacy, more than victory: the seeds of a future in which freedom, unity, and balance were really possible.

A new era had now begun, one that for the first time would secure peaceful coexistence between Light and Shadow and a regime to be held in trust in such a manner that the voice of every villager, even that of the most lowly commoner, was to be heard. Dax and Sylvia led the people together into the future they all wished, the one born from the ashes-resilient, radiant with hope.

CHAPTER 63
BUILDING A NEW WORLD

Morning twilight crept, softly dappled, across the reborn capital as Sylvia and Dax entered the newly reformed council chamber. Once a fortress of dread, with the dark fingers of the Empire casting long shadows, it was now a sanctuary of unity regaled by the people themselves. Ruby-tinted glass filtered the sunbeams into colors of warmth and energy as an enlisted mixture of signs of Light and Shadow filled the room, where harmony among those now enlisted would remain consistent in this new world.

As Sylvia stepped inside, silent and catching her breath, her eyes ran the walls that now carried emblems of both Light and Shadow, integrated, balanced. The memories of the struggle flickered back in her mind: the fights, the losses, the desperate hope of people hanging on to their freedom. It was here, amidst the dawn of peace, that the weight of it all seemed to fall into her heart, the taste of victory bitter set against sacrifice. They had fought for a goal, not to win, but to rebuild.

. . .

Her heart was torn by the loss and the promise of what lay ahead of them.

It was a council chamber full of representatives from across the land: farmers, scholars, warriors, healers-all gathered not in pursuit of power, but to advocate for their communities, eager to build a future free from tyranny and rooted in compassion, justice, and mutual respect. In their faces, Sylvia saw reflected the hope; her hopes resonated deep with the knowledge of the price they had paid for the right to be there. Dax stepped forward, his voice unrising yet firm, like some sort of soft anthem sounding through the chamber. "Today, we stand at the threshold of a new era. We have won our freedom, but the real work is before us. If we are to know true peace, we must give ourselves over to the work of unity and to a respect for the Light and the Shadow. Let this council be the common purpose that a promise to remember those we have lost, and a guiding principle as we look to the future.

Sylvia turned to the representatives present. With her eyes warm but with serious eyes, she spoke, "The Empire used Light Magic to enslave, and Shadow has, until now, been prejudiced by fear and misconception.

We have come to know that Light and Shadow are not about the enemy, but an entirety, necessary in their own respect, each commanding respect. Far from a council, it's the promise to protect this fragile balance-so each voice can find its voice within it.

. . .

A silent understanding filtered through the room, setting over the councilors almost like a summer breeze. Here they were, bound together, not by the idea of power, but by resilience-the spot where justice and balance would guide them forward. For most who knew nothing other than oppression, this new beginning was tenuous but fiercely inspirational.

And then the debates started, with one representative after another pointing out the special needs of his region. Villages and farmland torn apart by the war, the need to heal the scars the Empire gave them, a generation which had to live without this streak of fear-the talking went about schools where Light and Shadow Magic were learned together: harmonious villages with mutual understandings; a society remembering its history while neither erasing nor celebrating it.

The disagreement listened-Dax and Sylvia filtering the dialogue back through the core values: accountability, compassion, and balance. There were disagreements-fear of corruption, for one; the centralization of power, for another. Yet even within tension, a spirit of cooperation emerged-a will to create something better together.

Then it was the turn of Aldric to rise to his feet: an older warrior, his scars telling of a lifetime of struggle. His voice was firm, weighted with experience. "We've all lost friends, family, but rebuilding also means remaining watchful lest we become what we struggle against. Let this council be that beacon in vigil, a promise to our people that power shall serve and not control them.

. . .

Sylvia met his gaze, her eyes filled with understanding. "That is why we're here, Aldric. This council isn't about ruling; it's about creating a system where each life holds value, where decisions are made not through fear, but through shared purpose."

There was a hush of respect in the room. For they all had lived under oppression, and now they knew what freedom would demand from them: an opportunity to shape a world where the voice of every man would be heard, justice not as an instrument of oppression but a balm to heal.

As the speeches fell one by one, Dax stood again, his voice low, even, riddled with conviction. "Today, we take the first steps-but, all in a manner of speaking, our journey has just begun. We leave this chamber today, each of us carrying part of this legacy with us-a promise to remember those we have lost, to keep this fragile peace. Let this council live testimony to our will to survive, to live on, and to the principles we have sworn to live by.

Sylvia added, her voice gentle yet resolute, "Our role is not only to lead but to teach. Future generations will look to us as examples of unity, balance, and compassion. Let this council be a beacon, a reminder of what we've overcome, a legacy for those who follow."

In one motion, the members of the Council rose, ready for the long journey ahead, knowing well they were not only survivors of tyranny but guardians of a new world: a world where Light and Shadow could coexist, where justice would bring men together rather than set brother against brother.

Later in the night, Sylvia and Dax went on a night walk down city streets abuzz with light from lanterns and murmurs of laughter. They stood at the central square, where children played, free-spirited antics; elder ones told stories of struggle for survival now overcome; neighbor spoke with neighbor, trust now earned. It was a rebirth of the city, testimony to the world for which they had fought, for its right to be.

Dax turned to Sylvia, a soft smile in his eyes. "Today, I felt the strength of our vision—a council which values each voice, which honors each life. If we can nurture this, then perhaps we may have a world where succeeding generations would not have to fight the battles we have.

Sylvia smiled warmly but firmly. "I think we can, Dax, but it will require vigilance, compassion, and humility. We have to teach them-to guide them-so that they know not only what freedom costs but also how beautiful life is when lived together in harmony. They walked together, down through the outskirts of the city toward the horizon, as the sky sewed on a thousand-star latticework. Standing shoulder to shoulder, they stood together for what they had overcome, bound together by a dream that had seen them through every trial.

The road ahead would be rough, but they were ready, forged in the strength of the people that they had freed and the promise of a world remade in balance. They then faced the city, walking shoulder to shoulder in wordless reassurance, their hearts full of hope. Far from the close of their journey to that fragile balance, one thing they did know all too well was that every step was worth its price.

The city of Sunhaven stood as a beacon of unity and hope in the soft morning light-a promise that for as long as Light and Shadow are to be in harmony, so bequeathed would be the legacy of peace.

PART SIX
A LEGACY OF LIGHT AND SHADOW

It was a rebellion that had succeeded, but the peacemaking job was only just beginning. So it was Dax, Sylvia, and their allies who laid the bedrock for a world where Light and Shadow would finally balance in harmony. And their legacies would live throughout the ages of time, guiding beacons ever toward unity, resiliency, and the courage to remake the world.

CHAPTER 64
HEALING THE WOUNDS

As the morning sun shone bright, that torn city square gradually became a hotbed for whatever new life it would produce. The craftsmen labored with a purpose, hammering out signs of unity, reuniting families tearfully and in laughter, voices arising this time not in panic or in pain but in friendly debate and laughter. Thus, a city rebuilt from the ruins of oppression stood tall, standing as a testament to resilience and collective dream.

It was among such hustle and bustle, amidst the presence of even healers, teachers, and counselors all alike, that Sylvia realized how deep the gash ran within this city-across the realms of the body and spirit. It is in refreshing hearts and minds, not in rebuilding the structures, that true healing lies. And so, she called together the healers of the town so that they might make a fresh start toward founding an institution where, in utter dedication to balance and restoration, individuals could confront and release the burdens of their past.

. . .

As Sylvia spoke to the healers, her voice took on a quality of warmth and determination: "We all have inner shadows, scars not just in our skin but in our hearts. The Empire hurt us deeper inside our skin. This sanctuary is the place where Light and Shadow will combine to free us from those burdens-a place of peace and renovation. No one is healed alone.

Moved, tears in their eyes, yet with firm resolution, the healers listened. Many were the wounds they had attended to, the price of rebellion; Sylvia's dream gave their work a meaning it did not have; not only would they knit bones and flesh, they would soothe souls, taking care of life and a balance extending beyond the body.

With plans for the sanctuary well underway, Dax called the council together to discuss the new form of government. Gone would be days of Empire decrees from on high; this new council would be constructed on a foundation of inclusion and respect. Arguments turned hot as its members called into question, debated laws, and invoked freedom, justice, and mutual responsibility in their endeavor not to allow the evils of the past to raise their heads again.

Dax leaned forward. His tone was firm, yet reminding: "Freedom is fragile, and it's our duty to protect it. The laws we set down should not just govern but inspire: a lesson to all that every person in this world has a role and a purpose. We're all connected, no voice louder or lesser than any other.".

. . .

With grave ascent, in a solemn agreement, nods from council members acknowledged this would be a promise in need of more work and commitment. Thus, schools that taught balanced Light and Shadow Magic, plans to rebuild farms, and regional councils were discussed in order to make sure every voice is represented from every part of the continent.

During the night, Sylvia withdrew into this freshly consecrated retreat and, along with the healers, instructed them in the hybrid arts of Light and Shadow-sorcery methods that she did with them, while Shadow Adepts were building meditation rooms-ritualistic places to cleanse old wounds. Sylvia explained, "An inner demon is not a monster to fear but a part of oneself that needs to be comprehended and changed.

Soon enough, the sanctuary wasn't just a haven of recuperation but a place of stillness and poise within. People learned to accept their parts and began drawing strength from their journeys of self-acceptance. In due course, Sylvia would come to recognize such change the time to leave arrived-lighter steps, eyes clearing.

Meanwhile, Dax frequently visited the city's outer districts, where remnants of the Empire's rule still lingered. He spoke with farmers, artisans, and families piecing their lives back together, encouraging them to see themselves as part of a larger whole. "We're not only rebuilding walls," he told them, "we're building bridges, trust, and a world that values each one of you."

. . .

Where evenings converged into sharing tales in the city square, strangers previously apart now shared laughter, bread, and stories among themselves, strengthened by common ills and a shared sense of home.

Dax and Sylvia would also appear at these functions, content to stand in the background and listen to the hopes and dreams of those for which they had fought. It was in moments like these that they could find great contentment, knowing the seeds of unity had been sewn, grown, and flowered into something real.

It was the first night the city had ever celebrated the remembrance festival-those lost to the Empire-a tradition long forbidden. The night sky came alive as lanterns, each carrying a wish or a memory, rose like stars. It was the only thing Dax felt comfortable doing without Sylvia.

She turned to Dax, speaking in a barely audible tone: "They had come so far. This city isn't just rebuilt; it is reborn.

Dax squeezed her hand softly; his eyes were warm. "Yes, for they believe in it as we do. They know that balance is a gift not just received, but lived.

And so, they started walking the streets of the city, passing the New Sanctuary, the Council Hall, busy schools, saw old and young, the former rebels and those grown under the Empire, bright-eyed children who would grow up with harmony and not fear as the premise for their world.

. . .

They watched from the small hill that overlooked the city, lanterns still going up into the air, softly lighting the sky. In Sylvia's eyes was a spark for resilience, a hope, and unity that they had struggled to keep alive.

"This," she whispered, "is the world we have hoped for; Light and Shadow dancing, the treasure of liberty, the realization of every man's own strength.

Dax nodded, a peaceful resolve settling within him. "And it's a world they will carry forward. We've given them the tools, the vision. Now, it's theirs to nurture, protect, and make their own." As the last of the lanterns vanished into the night, Dax and Sylvia stood in dumbstruck silence, surveying the city below them alive with life, laughter, and lights-a promise of a future they had struggled so desperately hard to create.

Down the hill, they walked their hearts keeping an unsaid promise that they still had a long, long way ahead in guiding, shielding, and fostering this newborn world. Morning drew its veil, and the city awakened anew, promising harmony, balance, and peace. The world was healing, and for the first time in a very long period, hope-a small, fragile thing, yet so strong-lay securely in their grasp.

CHAPTER 65
VOICES OF THE PAST

Above her, the evening sky stretched upwards as Anya walked back from the shadowy grove, whirling in mind but beating in heart with anticipation. But the encounter with this woman just haunts the lines-just as every word is the echo of an unsaid truth. The glowing, ghostly grove had stricken deep into her, a quiet reminder that all of the world she had grown up in was but a single chapter in a continuing story.

Emerging from the grove, Anya found Kai and Elara staring back at her-curiosity marked upon their features. They had watched her disappear into the depths of ancient ruins, her eyes holding questions within them they did not ask.

"What'd you find, Anya?" he heard Elara ask in a soft tone that mixed curiosity and apprehension.

. . .

Anja inhaled sharply as her mind reeled with the words of the woman she had just met. "I don't know exactly what I found," Anja said, "but something. something strong is alive in the shade of times past.".

Kai's question-mark eyes darted a sideward glance at her: "Well, did the legends spring to life, Anya?"-teasing, yet a thread of seriousness tautened in his voice. Tales of Light and Shadow, of Dax and Sylvia, those entwined with their lives, weighted each telling with mystery and awe.

"Maybe I did," Anya said softly, her gaze somewhere else. "But it felt so real to me-a warning, you know? She said the cycle doesn't stop. The past doesn't ever die. Weird, huh? You know, thinking of how all that struggle our parents and grandparents went through isn't really over?

Elara's face was grave and held deep the extent of Anya's unease. "We've grown up in a world free of oppression, one where Light and Shadow are balanced in their core. But I assume that does not mean the darkness is gone. That just means we're responsible for keeping it at bay.".

This silent understanding of the three friends seals an unspoken acknowledgment of how fragile their peace had been, tenuously held together by sacrifice and memory of those who went before. They were the weight of those stories, of lives devoted to a cause which had reshaped the world. And as they walked in step, the track leading back to the village felt less an end than the start of a journey. As days passed, the words of that weird woman kept ringing in the conscience of Anya. She now listened more closely for the whispered softness in the air, the way the windCarries secrets nobody else but she seemed to hear. Nighttime dreams, shadowed groves, figures lost in the twilight, and the closing in of darkness met her.

And yet, in the fear was a strange clarity, a crystallization of something within her, that her place in the world was no longer the same, something more beyond what she so far could grasp.

It was one evening that she confided in her mentor, an elder by the name of Maelis, who had survived the rebellion and yet held much knowledge from a lifetime of both Light and Shadow. Maelis listened to all the woman of the grove had said, Anya's fears and curiosities laid open.

As she watched, it was almost like it was her speaking to her, like she knew what she was supposed to do, and it's something Anya doesn't. "I just," Anya said in a voice full of wonder and confusion.

Smiling serenely, she laid her wrinkled hands over Anya's. "You are right to feel that, child. Though the past is behind us, its shadows stretch forward, entwining with the paths of our own. You are young, but the wisdom of the past runs in your veins. Remember, Anya: balance is not a place that one reaches; it is a path-one that one walks day after day. Anya nodded, her resolution hardened with every one of Maelis' words echoing within. Never was she again to be satisfied standing off and listening to the stories of old. The legacy of those that fought and suffered in the name of freedom was hers for the taking, and she was evermore bound in duty to see it through.

Yet in the same breath, she knew her journey was going to be rough; trials lay ahead that were going to try not only her magic but also her heart. In the days that followed, she and her friends began to train with a newfound fervor, learning to meld their magic, to entwine the forces of Light and Shadow together as they had learned from those who remembered the days of the Empire. Kai, his mind quick and keen, soon mastered the intricacies of merged magic, using his insight to help them train.

The compassionate one, sensitive to the emotional shades, Elara knew only that person is strong-not by power-but when he was tuned to harmony.

It was a friendship forged in innocence and flying free, now harnessed and heavier with purpose. They realized, too, that they were no longer just children from a world finally at peace but were growing into its protectors-the next watchmen and women who guarded the balance bought with such costly striving by their ancestors.

And so, beneath the openness of the sky, they started to train. By day, they would cast their spells in practice, perfect the control of the elements: Light and Shadow. By night, they sat around the fire and listened while tales of old were told whereby a lesson was learned in each story or memory.

· · ·

But sometimes, as she sat and watched the fire dance, Anya's mind would fall back on the warning of the woman: a silent determination that settled deep in her stomach. She didn't know what the future held, but one thing was certain: she would be ready. She and her friends would defend life's balance, stand against the dark should it ever rise again, just as Dax and Sylvia had before them.

Children of the rebirth into the world, born of a new era driven by hope and toughness, they would be ready for the trials ahead when the time came, armed not only with magic but also with the bond of friendship and experience from those who had gone before them. In their hearts, the light of freedom, the shadow of sacrifice, and the indelible stamp of the spirit of balance. And as the wind, still whispering, again stirred the leaves of the ancient oak, they knew they were where they should be: wardens of a yet unfolding future, ready to defend the world that they loved.

CHAPTER 66
THREADS OF LEGACY

The sun climbed over Sunhaven and cast its share of warmth upon the village, settling a sense of quiet resolve over her people. Morning eventually passed much as any other: simplistic tasks, one neighbor laughing with another, people humming in comfort with community working as one, but something was in the air, some vague residue from the tales of the previous night. The memories of Ivor's words were still fresh in the minds of Anya, Kai, and Elara as they woke up, knowing full well that those stories were no longer tales but an inheritance, a summoning to be prepared for anything.

Characteristically, the village square was not abuzz with its morning chatter. Small clumps of villagers stood together in contemplative discussion, remembering Ivor's words about how Dax and Sylvia had to make their sacrifice. To many, the memory seemed a lot more like a plan for times to come.

. . .

Slowly, almost reverently, Anya, Kai, and Elara felt themselves being drawn back to the square-together, it seemed, some unspoken companionship of shared purpose hung in the air-to step into something much larger than themselves, a role out of age and experience, from which came willing hearts that understand and protect a hard-won balance that so deeply underpins their world.

Upon arrival at the square, some elders were discussing preparations for festivals over the just-won freedom from the Empire. Festivals, as a rule, are fun; this time, however, it would be an affair of a much deeper significance. This time, it would be in commemoration of those who fought for them, helped things balance out, and gave the younger generation a better chance to grow up unraveled by fear. The elders wanted this festival to be one of festivity and a reminder-to renew their pledge into a world where Light and Shadow can go together in harmony.

Elara watched the elders from a distance, her voice now contemplative as she turned to Anya and Kai. "It feels... important, doesn't it? Not just the stories, but what they left behind. I really don't think they ever wanted us to forget, to take this peace for granted."

Kai, ever light, nodded with unwonted gravity. "They fought so we didn't have to. But maybe, somehow, it's our job to keep that fight alive-not with swords or magic, but seeing that balance is always there."

. . .

Anlya turned to her friends, her face set. "Then let's do our part. The stories aren't just memories; they are lessons. Dax and Sylvia showed us what it means to protect balance, to stay vigilant against anything that threatens it. Maybe it is about time we really understood what that means.

With silent concurrence greeting their common resolve, they began to walk towards the Whispering Woods.

They could feel the pull of the woods, that place wherein so much occurred, where secrets had been kept, where the ghosts of those gone before yet echoed. It was within these woods that Dax and Sylvia had found their strength, learning what it is to use Light and Shadow with wisdom. And herein lay the answers that would be found by Anya, Kai, and Elara.

Morning light bathes the Whispering Woods in soft lucidity, casting long shadows dancing amongst the trees, in a rhythm as timeless as the land itself. Quietly, they enter in respectful silence, the weight of the place, the knowledge that this is hallowed ground, settling upon them. It was more than just any other forest-it lived, breathed, and reminded one of the balance between the fates of Light and Shadow.

The deeper in they went, the more it became familiar to her. She had been here so many times in her childhood, and then later with friends, but it felt so different today. Quiet energy saturated the air, humming deep inside her; it was almost as if the forest was waiting, knowing they came for something bigger than themselves.

. . .

Until finally, they came to a small open area, the trees parting, it seemed, to allow the sun to break through to a circle of stones said to be one of the places people long ago would go to consult the wisdom of the Whispering Woods. Elara closed her eyes and felt how the energy enveloped her-the low hum of the forest speaking to her in its own language, which she did not understand yet somehow knew deep in the marrow of her bones.

Kai stepped forward, laid a hand on one of the stones; his touch was light, reverent. "I think they were here, Anya," he said softly, looking at her. "I think Dax and Sylvia stood right where we are, facing the same shadows, carrying the same hopes.

Anya nodded, her eyes aglow with that quiet understanding inside. "And they found their way here: to the strength to build them a world, to give Light and Shadow ground on which to step-neither of which needed to be feared.

Elara's eyes flashed open; her gaze was even. "Then let us do the same. We don't have their experience, their power-but we have their lessons. Let's learn from the balance they created.

Hand in hand in the circle, a silent promise was exchanged in the darkness. They knew they were young, and it was only the beginning of their journey, but they knew too that this was far more than just stories about Dax and Sylvia; it was a responsibility-to protect this balance in memory of the two and thus become guardians themselves.

. . .

As they went back to the village, the weight of their journey fell over them once more, yet different this time, in a new sense of purpose and quiet strength. Whatever was next, they would be okay; they were no longer scared. They had each other, the stories, and most of all, the balance Dax and Sylvia fought to keep intact.

Then the festival arrived, and Sunhaven was filled with music and laughter in a strong, vibrant claim to the peace they had won. They felt Anya, Kai, and Elara grow closer to those who went before them as the villagers danced and sang. They came to understand through them-the shadows cast by the lanterns, the radiating warmth of the light-that the concept of balance was not an idea, but a living, breathing thing-a tender harmony which they finally found themselves a part of.

Standing together on the edge of the celebration, they faced toward the village-where younger children sat around, listening in on stories, elders sharing in wisdom, and the whole village celebrating, not only their freedom but also unity, which made it possible. Amongst it all, the voice of Ivor soared again with the sagas of Dax and Sylvia as words wove their way deep into a history that would be remembered for ages. Anya, Kai, and Elara stood in quiet acknowledgment, a legacy shoved their way, and they knew they were ready for whatever was to come.

The more the festival wore on, the more an unruffled silence took hold of the three friends; it slowly dawned on them that Dax and Sylvia had indeed been the past, but the bedrock upon which their future was going to be built. And as night wore on, they vowed silently: to protect the balance, to hold hallowed the light and the shadow, and to press on with the dreams those had left behind them, giving reason to fight for a world now worth living in.

CHAPTER 67
THE PATH TO PEACE

As the days passed after Dax's warning, expectant silence fell on Sunhaven. The villagers performed their tasks with quiet resolve, the hearts of those from their leader now hardened. The whispers of the wind were still unnerving but no more fearful; instead, they reminded villagers of mutual strength: their unity and strength found in each other.

The children, especially, had taken Dax's words to heart; they spoke of the "new darkness" in hushed tones, of their own desires to face such, before turning play into small acts of defiance while imagining the casting of Light and Shadow spells against unseen foes. Among them, Anya, Kai, and Elara felt themselves being pulled together-each feeling the weight of the stories they grew up hearing brought to life with Dax's cautionary words.

By the early evening, when the village was in purple twilight and the sky was gloomy, it was in such a time that the three friends succeeded in disappearing from the square. They went further on to some well-known place-the ancient oak, in the shadow of which they had spent their boyhood years- drawing very long shadows across the fields. Indeed, many secrets and dreams had been discussed in the shadow of its sprawling branches. Tonight, however, was something different.

Anya, her eyes filled with a spark of determination, broke the silence first. "We've heard about darkness our whole lives. But this... this feels different. Dax isn't the kind to scare people without reason."

Kai, ever the pragmatist, nodded contemplative. "It's like he knew something was coming. He has gone into parts of Whispering Woods that we never even imagined. If he said this darkness existed, then it was likely to be something beyond what they went through during the rebellion.

Elara spoke with a softness, her gaze to the far horizon, the quiet conviction held tight. "Then we have to be prepared for them as they were. Dax and Sylvia, they did not fight only for themselves; they fought so we can grow up unraked by fear, so we may live in a world where Light and Shadow are more than weapons but a part of the balance.

Anya looked to her friends then, the weight of their words settling upon her. Young, yes, but they had inherited a world which had seen its darkness and its freedom; they were not the leaders Dax and Sylvia had become, but they could still protect what had been hard-won.

. . .

Kai looked around, an idea sprouting and sharpening his gaze. "Maybe it is time for us to go to the Whispering Woods ourselves. We hear the stories, we know the legends. Yet there is much we don't understand. If there's something dark a-coming, maybe there is something there that can help us.".

Elara nodded, determination brightening on her face: "The woods are more than a place of old magic; they are part of our legacy. If we're serious about the protection of what's ours, we should go there and take a look ourselves.".

A cold thrill coursed down her backside, exciting yet daunting. Turning to her friends, her voice was very low, almost a whisper. "Then it is sealed. Tomorrow, we enter the Whispering Woods."

A decision was reached, and as they parted ways, a thrill of anticipation mixed with the weight of great responsibility coursed through each. As young as they were, they were heirs to Dax and Sylvia's memories-to the memories of a thousand others who had given their lives to create the world they now enjoyed.

The three of them set out toward the Whispering Woods the next day at dawn, by which time no one in the village was yet awake. With silent footsteps, forced by their racing hearts from fear and excitement, they came closer to the dense trees, which stood before them threateningly, like a barricade. That is what the woods have always held unto themselves: mysterious and a place where only the bravest dare tread. This was a land of spirits, ancient sorcery, and forgotten times and the thinnest of borders between worlds.

They were swallowed by silence the moment they entered the forest-air inside was cooler, the light was dimmer, and the sounds of the village fell away into a near-ethereal stillness. It would appear that the trees watched them, their branches dancing softly, rhythmically, as if in welcome and test alike, into their abode.

Kai took the lead, his eyes scanning the ground as if he were searching for some hidden path or markers. Anya stepped close behind him, every sense high, heart pounding with a mixture of wonder and terror. Elara fell into the back, the weight of the energy of the forest settling upon her skin, soothing yet disturbing.

They trudged through an eternity before they finally reached a little meadow bathed in that weird, ghostly light. Right at the very center was a kind of stone altar, writhing with ancient carvings; on its surface throbbed some faint luminescence. Anya approached warily, extending her hand to the thing as if being dragged by some invisible thread.

As her fingers reached out and touched the cool stone, she felt the surge of energy within her rush forward. Visions of battles fought, of heroes and sacrifice, and of Light and Shadow locked in an eternal dance were given life within her mind. She saw snatches of Dax and Sylvia, their faces set with resolution as hands clasped hands to face the darkness together.

. . .

The vision faded, and Anya caught her breath. She looked toward her friends, her voice barely above a whisper. "This is where they came, where they found the strength to keep fighting.

Kai, his eyes wide with awe, placed his hand on the stone beside hers. "Then maybe this is where we'll find our strength, too."

Elara stepped forward and said firmly, "We are the next generation. And whatever it is, it has to be faced-together.

The few stood silent, laid hands upon stone, and felt the weight of their legacy, the power of the past coursing through them. Under no illusion, their road would be littered with troubles, that the whispers of darkness would test them. Still, they also knew that in them stirred the strength of those before, those who had faced the shadows and light.

The whispers of the wind followed them out of the clearing-a soft murmur of encouragement, reminding them that they were never really alone. Sons and daughters of freedom, heirs to a tradition of hope and survival, they did not know what was waiting for them, but they knew they were ready to face it altogether.

The return to the village was in quiet determination. The air was different, the shadows not forbidding; even the forest, as fair as seemed, understood their purpose. They had taken their first step, and with each passing step thereafter, they knew how much more prepared and assured they were for whatever the future had in store for them. And then, with the sun setting over Sunhaven-once afternoon had poured over the edge of the field-hedged village-the villagers again came together. It was as though the leaves spoke to them in their rustling, of some presence that stirred beyond the reach of their sight. They were not afraid, however. In the hearts of their young, in the valor of the next generation, they saw the promise of a new dawn.

CHAPTER 68
VOWS OF GUARDIANSHIP

In the golden light of the setting sun, Sunhaven glimmered in pastel shades, as if all labors of the day were yielded unto a serene hush falling on the lands. Anya, Kai, and Elara sat near the edge of the village where the open fields flung themselves toward the blue-distant hills, and the sky was laid on with colors of amber and violet. The silence was almost hallowed, as if the very air surrounding them held its breath to fix with the soul the purpose uniting these three friends.

The time gone since they returned from the Whispering Woods had been a time of preparation: Anya delving deep into the wisdom of the elders, Kai into the study of ancient texts, and Elara into deeper communion with the land. As much as they were learning, they knew their answers still lay hidden, waiting to be found.

Elara broke the silence; her hand lay on the wildflowers growing at her feet. "Do you feel it?" she finally asked, her gaze unfocused, as if listening for something just beyond the reach of her hearing. "The air…different tonight.

Kai nodded, his fingers tracing the symbols he'd studied in his book. "Yes. It's as if the whole world is…watching, waiting.

Anya looked toward the horizon, her eyes large with wonder, yet set with a steely determination. "The feeling of darkness we've had-the whispers, the signs-it's drawing closer. We do not know what it is yet, but it does get harder to ignore.

A silent understanding passed in the glance they shared: this was different, something their village had never faced, some strength that would push against the very core of their beliefs-a darkness that would tip the balance they wanted so desperately to keep.

Kai took a deep breath, and the tension broke. "We have spent weeks gathering our knowledge, preparing in our own ways. But perhaps it is time we drew everything together, compared what we have learned, find out if there is a common thread.

They stopped beside a gentle stream, where the gurgle of water over smooth stones serenaded their conversation sweetly. Anya pulled out a dog-eared notebook full of jotted notes from the village elders' stories-fragments of history which she prayed would guide them. Kai laid out his book of symbols and spells, while Elara held a small pouch containing various herbs and stones, each representative of some part of her connection with nature.

Anya began to speak, her voice low, yet firm. "The elders remember the time before the Empire, before magic was controlled and distorted into a means for earning power. They spoke of a balance that once came naturally, a harmony between Light and Shadow which kept all in balance. But they also spoke of an imbalance that always starts so subtly-a whisper, a feeling.

She looked to Elara, who nodded. "The spirits of the woods... they speak in whispers too. They have shown me visions of a world where Light and Shadow are interwoven, where neither can exist without the other. But they've also warned of something else: a force that feeds on fear, which grows in the shadow of doubt and division.

Kai looked down at his symbols, tracing a finger over one Circle bisected by a line-the unity within duality. "This symbol," he said reflectively, "is one I come back to time and again. It's not just a question of balance; it's a question of integration. What we are picking up on with this darkness is not so much a force as it is something which thrives on separation-on pushing Light and Shadow apart, not putting them together.

His voice tailed off, and in that instant the weight of his words sunk deeply into the soul of each. They realized that the darkness ahead was not to be vanquished but rather a test of how much one had thought about Light and Shadow and his capacity to take either of them inside himself or not.

Setting her eyes on Anya now: "You said the elders spoke of a balance that was once natural. Do you think. could this darkness be a manifestation of the world's imbalance? That it is a shadow born from the divisions we have allowed to grow?

She considered this, her heart heavy for the insight. "That makes sense, after all-if we're to protect the balance, we need to realize that our job isn't about defeating something in the first place, but healing-to bridge the divides inside of us and in the world.

Kai glanced at each one of them, a fire starting to gleam within his eyes. "Then that is what we must do: not only fight but bring everything we have learned into focus-be living embodiments of Light and Shadow in harmony. Perhaps if we can find that within ourselves, we shall gain the strength to face what awaits us.

Their words melted into silence, and new resolve was filled into the silence. It is in this coming of age that they realized their journey wasn't to defend home but to turn themselves into the very symbol of such balance they so loved. And were they to stand against the darkness, then they would have to be like a guiding beacon of unity-a force that reminds the world that Light and Shadow are not enemies but partners.

. . .

They rose from their spot beside the stream when night began to fall, their hearts steeled with resolve. The first stars pierced the night sky and cast soft diffused light upon them as they headed back toward the village. They moved in quiet strength, a resolve going beyond the scope of fear and uncertainty, for they were not preparing for battle but to be an embodiment of balance that shall see them through whatever was to come. In the following days, they prepared even moreso, this time with a different degree of unity running through their veins. Anya fostered her knowledge in the old tales, searching for deeper truth in the wisdom of their forefathers. Kai studied the symbols and the spells, finding a way how Light and Shadow could both be taken to balance.

And with that, Elara would disappear into the woods for hours on end, while the whispers of the earth-the spirits-guided her ever deeper into the connection with the balance of nature at hand.

But this change within them did not go unseen by the village: a quiet power, some might say, flowed from their bonding. They were more than three friends; they were growing into guardians they had always been meant to be, stewards of the balance that Dax and Sylvia fought for.

As morning lit a new day, the whistling of the wind grew loud, reminding them that this was only the beginning. They could feel the pulse of the world around them, the thin line of balance that held everything in check. And they knew, with whatever would come, they would rise, bound and committed to the balance that they chose to keep. Now they walked together, side by side, having the torch passed from those who came before them, ready to fight for the legacy that would maintain the balance: now their own legacy of Light and Shadow.

CHAPTER 69
NAVIGATING THE FUTURE

With cold breezes always blowing across Sunhaven, some latent tension wove itself in the air-as if it were almost some tune out of reach. The village seemed to go in its usual flow: children playing, elders sharing tales, workers each attending to their tasks in earnest. Yet, beneath this visible calmness, some unseen movement brewed an unspoken apprehension. Its murmurs had grown from murmurs to a force put into motion, to which even the smallest child was accustomed.

In turn, the village council had summoned all voices to one venue. In the main hall sat the leadership to the farmer, the artisan, and the learned ones in Light and Shadow, all cross-legged and quiet murmurs of many individual conversations, as people settled in their chairs, faces a mixture of concern and curiosity.

Anya, Kai, and Elara sat in the back, their young faces set in a mixture of awe and a determination: weeks by now, having attended meetings and listened well to absorb their lessons of balance and harmony, the_need for vigilance. But then the stories of the elders, lately the warning from Liora, changed something inside each one of them-instilling in them a sense of responsibility that they had not felt before.

As the gathering began, Elder Liora rose before them, her figure lit by the soft glow of lanterns placed round about her, grasping in her hands a staff of wood from ancient times, with patterns of the journey of Light and Shadow carved upon it. Beside her stood Tarek, the lines on his face evidence of a life weathered and strong, his very presence lending a sense of unyielding stillness in the room.

"We are here tonight," Liora said without delay, her voice soft, yet full of command. "To speak about what's gone on in the shadows of our world, whispers-yes, but more than this, there are signs the balance we fought so hard to get is in danger. We can't afford to ignore them."

A murmur ran through them, and the villagers looked at one another with concerned expressions. The period of peace had been so long that the idea this might be threatened was not quite real and was peculiarly terrifying.

"We have known peace since the fall of the Empire," Tarek added, his voice level-equal, though laced with undertones of urgency. "Peace is fragile, especially when it depends on a balance. Gone are the forces we once fought against, but balance is more than fighting against darkness; it's a journey, continuous-a pledge we make with every new day to keep harmony within ourselves and in the world that surrounds us.

One spoke-one villager, a blacksmith named Arin. Voice gruff, yet respectful, he spoke, "But what if the darkness comes once more? We are simple people. We are not mighty like Dax and Sylvia.

Liora's expression softened; her face was a mask of sympathy, yet unyielding. "Indeed, we may not be as strong as those heroes of yore. But in each one of us, the power of Light and Shadow prevail. The Balance is not the power of a few; it is an individual responsibility. And within unity, we find strength.

It was then that Anya began to feel her will ignite. The stories of Dax and Sylvia were fresh in her mind, not just as fighters but as balancers of life's sensitive scale, which was always attained en masse and never by the victory of a few. She looked up at Kai and Elara, and it seemed they, too, shared this very feeling.

After a moment of thoughtful silence, Liora continued with, "We shall strengthen our defenses, not with arms, but with insight; and we shall teach every generation about Light and Shadow, not as myths, but as their reality, which is to abide among them. And we shall be prepared against every evil which would wish to suppress our peaceful coexistence.

Kai stood up, his hand raised, and went on in a firm voice, "Elder Liora, what if this darkness isn't like before? What if it's something new, which we have not understood how to fight yet?

With that, the room fell silent, and all eyes were on Liora. Reflective, she seemed an image of deep thought. "You're right to ask that, Kai. Each form of darkness takes on its own shape, molded into what it is by various desires and fears. Whether we fight against a familiar or an entirely new foe, our strongest assets are understanding, fortitude, and harmony. We have to be flexible for whatever shape it may come in.

While the council prepared and made plans, villagers talked in low tones of what dangers they may face. There were to be meetings for those that knew the old magic to teach the young how it was done, how it once worked to protect them. Others would be taught how to read the signs of nature when it becomes imbalanced, so they may be the first to indicate the disturbance.

In the boys' and girl's young minds, the wisdom of the council filled their spirits, brimming with resolution. They well knew this protection of the balance meant not about acquiring some skills or understanding how the magic was working, but vigilance and readiness for courageous action upon a given moment.

With one raise of her staff at the end of the meeting, her voice settled and leveled, an anchorage, sure and steady, to the people inside. "Remember, the legacies of Dax and of Sylvia live on within each of you. You are the protector of this world, guardians of balance, stewards of peace. Let not the seeds of fear find purchase in your heart; cling fast to hope and let us recall that we are stronger in unity.

Renewed determination had them leave the gathering, each to his or her own realization of how to play their part in keeping this harmony they had grown to revere. New duty settled deeper in the children, especially Anya, Kai, and Elara-the feeling one gets when one is not a mere observer of a peaceful world but an active co-creator in its preservations.

Later in the night, the while village lights began to go off one by one, the three friends were sitting in company under an acute-dotted sky, looking toward the depth of the dark above. The endlessness of the sky-an unlimited sign of both the beauty and mystery of the world they inherited.

"We should be ready," Anya whispered, her voice low with that steely silence of one who has finally found her purpose. Kai nodded. "We may not know what's coming, but we'll face it together."

Elara placed her hand over theirs, her touch a silent vow. "Whatever it is, we'll protect Sunhaven. We'll protect the balance."

And thus, with words unspoken by three, who sat close and silent, an oath joined heart with heart, to them fell the torch of equilibrium.

CHAPTER 70
HARMONY IN OPPOSITION

In the serenity of morning light, Sunhaven was a testament to endurance, fields full of new life, and people to overcome the day with renewed determination. The restoration from having been torn apart was slow, gradual- not only in the walls and roads of villages on the Eryal Continent but even within the hearts of those who suffered such great bereavement. They had built this peace with their bare hands: brick by brick, field by field, each one a promise for the following day.

Dax and Sylvia strolled across the square of Sunhaven-to faces that welcomed them and had seen the worst of terror and bravery. The villagers of this place, who once shook with fear under the shadow of the Empire, now proudly though silently stood, carrying the onuses of their survival. Children ran across, the sound of their laughter filling the air with a promise of hope.

. . .

They paused on the outskirts of the village, which was in morning assembly-farmers, artisans, teachers, and healers all together, sharing news and tales and planning times to come. It was more than a village-it was the heart of a whole new world to come into being from this union for the sake of balance between Light and Shadow.

Dax spoke for them all, his voice steady and deep with warmth: "We have traveled a long way together, we ripped the chains from our backs, and now we stand on the bedrock of our own making. Yet true freedom is never an achieved state of being but a condition to be nurtured, guarded, and passed on to our children.

He studied their faces, the villagers', and the will in each that had pulled them through the dark; they were not survivors alone but makers of the future they had fought for.

Sylvia stepped forward, the level of her tone inviting.

It means that in using Light Magic, the Empire sought to control and to divide, but we know Light and Shadow are not tools of power, they are parts of a whole, each with their own strength, each a reminder of what it means to be human. Now, it is our work to teach that balance, to live it. Its our task to ensure that the next generation would never have to fight the same battles we did.

They listened intently, their countenances softening into comprehension. They had learned the cost of division, the price of fear, and with a new era before them now, they stood ready to forge onward, carrying the lessons of Light and Shadow alike.

During the day, Dax and Sylvia had been working with villagers, sharing in the mundane of life and helping where they could. They spoke to farmers about the strength of the crops, to healers about the wounds yet to be tended, and to artisans rebuilding the town's structures-to take them from relics of oppression into unity and a symbol of hope. They even joined children and told them stories about the battles fought and the world they were building together.

One elder, a former soldier who had fought in the rebellion, pulled them aside, his voice low but filled with reverence. "What you've given us is more than freedom," he said. "You've given us a way to hope again, a way to believe that even when darkness comes, there is strength in unity." As the day headed towards its end, the people came again-to fire up a new ceremonial flame in the middle of the square: a ritual to the passing of an era and the beginning of another, a commitment to the peace they had forged.

And in the dance of the fire, faces came into being around the blaze, illuminated by hope on every face, by memory of that they had come through, by will to defend hard-won peace.

His voice barely more than a whisper, Dax watched the dancing flames intently. "This fire is our freedom: it must be tended to, nourished, and strengthened by all. It is not an end, but a beginning to what we shall create.

. . .

Then Sylvia added, "Let it be to remind us of the road on which we came and what lies ahead. Let it be the beacon to those coming behind us to guide them to live by, have faith in, and guard.".

And then as night fell on Sunhaven, villagers melted into the shadows, hearts set firm within the taciturn decisions of men who know the beauty and brittleness of liberty-the fact that the test of time was in store, the fall of dark once more in some form or another-but so was the knowledge that they could face it.

Soon after, Dax and Sylvia, side by side, took a walk through the village. Above them, the stars shone bright in the sky while all the muted noises of evening muted. They stopped on the outskirts of the village and looked across the land they had fought so hard to protect, finally at peace.

Sylvia's eyes lifted to the stars, a soft smile curling her lips. "This peace. just the beginning. Fragile, but ours. As long as we remember what we've been through, as long as we stand together, I believe it will hold.

Dax took her hand, his grip warm and steady. "We'll be here to protect it, to guide them. And when it's time, they'll be ready to carry it forward."

. . .

The firelight from the square cast an easy pattern on the streets as they faced the village once more, guiding them along. Moving on, hand in hand, Dax and Sylvia went forward with a soft echo in the night, with the silence of their footsteps carrying the burden of all they had endured, the promise of what they would still build.

A new dawn breaking-a day of peace they had labored to attain, a balance they had opted to safely maintain. It would be into this new world that together they would step: guardians of a fragile but abiding hope-a legacy unto themselves and to all those who would come after them.

CHAPTER 71
PROMISE OF A NEW DAWN

As the first light of morning peered over the treetops of the Whispering Woods, stillness gently kissed the ground, painting an ethereal glow upon the ancient forest. The tall branches moved with one accord in the morning breeze, while the leaves shimmered where they captured the soft light. Sylvia and Dax followed the well-worn path through the treetops to the council meeting place at the edge of the forest-a place that once had seen fierce battles and that was now reclaimed as a sanctuary of unity.

This was the day, unlike any other. The councilors would gather to lay the cornerstone of a new civilization-a world wherein Light and Shadow did not exist in parts but interwove a tapestry of times to be passed on to the ages. The moment weighed upon Sylvia's heart. The war may have been over, but the guarding and protection of this fledgling peace had just begun.

. . .

They were there, awaiting them at the ring of standing stones where the council would take place: newly appointed ones-young men and women from the four corners, carrying with them in their hearts the same ideal Dax and Sylvia had lived through. Warriors, scholars, healers-all of them earned their place in the circle through hard-won resiliency and commitment to a balanced future. Dax looked at them, the pride shining in his eyes.

He stepped forward, his voice not shrill, yet piercing, and words of eternal memory were spoken: "Today we charge each and every one of you with a responsibility born from years of struggle and sacrifice. The balance, real balance, is not easy to keep. It doesn't take just strength but requires patience, modesty, and respect to all powers, both those of Light and of Shadow. It is this council that has to be ever vigilant, a living, breathing testament to what we have accomplished, and guidance for those who follow.

Sylvia's eyes gleamed warm and solemn as she joined her voice to Dax's before the council. "The Empire brought us to fear Shadow and to worship Light blindly. We have come to understand since that these are not opposing forces-the one, an enemy of the other-but complementing ones. Leading this world requires us to let go of these divides. Each one of you is a guardian to this unity, one who has come to realize true strength does not stand in domination but in harmony.

There was something silent in the air as her words began to sink in, and this council did not exist to rule but to tend to and foster the tender shoots of peace. That a society was guided by balance-alien and shifting-was new to people who had never known anything other than life under the Empire's control.

The fire stayed in the center throughout the day, surrounded by discourses as each council member spoke his vision about his region. Some had visions of rebuilding homes and farms, cities left devastated by war, while others spoke to educating children who had grown up in fear-of teaching Light and Shadow together so respect would be fostered for both. They envisioned school as a place of learning and healing, a place where magic was taught as a means to connect, not control.

Dax and Sylvia listened intently, cutting in only to keep them on track, around to accountability, compassion, and shared responsibility. There was disagreement-organic, some council members afraid of corruption, others questioning how to guard against another divisive doctrine rearing its head. Yet even in the tensest moments, the ghost of cooperation hung around, reminding them of the unity that had brought them into this room.

Aldric rose, his voice loaded with the weight of a lifetime of battles fought alongside Dax. "We've all suffered loss, sacrificed to this future. Let this council stand as a monument to that sacrifice-a watchful beacon. Let us not forget that power is to serve the people, not to control them.

Sylvia nodded, her eyes locked with his. "That's why we're here, Aldric: so that the world we'll build is one which will hear every voice, every life. We are not here to rule but to guide-into a manner wherein decisions shall be made respectably and with mercy, not in the manner of one force dominating another.

The members were seized with respectful silence; the words began to dig deep into the souls of the people. All knew the price of tyranny, and all knew what freedom called for from them. This was to be a society wherein justice was going to be a healing balm, not punitive, and not divisive.

When night fell and the deliberations finally came to a close, Dax stood again, his voice firm and reserved, his words still unrelenting. "We have taken the first steps today, but it is far from over. Each of you carries a part of this legacy, a promise that those we've lost are remembered and that this peace is cared for. Let this council live as a testament to our resilience and a guide to the principles we've chosen to live by.

Sylvia added, her tone soft but resolute, "Our task is not only to lead but to inspire. Future generations will look to us as examples—not just of courage but of balance and compassion. Let us ensure this council remains a place of unity, a symbol of what we've fought to achieve."

The other councilors stood, their faces set with the weight of new responsibility: no longer mere survivors of the Dark Age but also custodians of the new one-guardians of a world where Light and Shadow could coexist, where justice would be utilized to build and never to break.

· · ·

As night began to fall, Dax and Sylvia walked through the city's distinguishing streets: paper lanterns casting an inviting, warm glow around them; they stopped in the square and watched people come together-families and friends who laughed and shared tales under the open sky. It was a rare sight, one Sylvia savored, for it was a true reflection of the unity they had dreamed of.

He turned to her slowly, the quiet pride and hope shining in Dax's eyes. "Today, I feel the strength of our vision: a council that indeed values every voice, indeed respects the story of each individual. If we can foster this, maybe we can create a world where people are not still fighting the same wars.".

Sylvia smiled serenely but resolutely. "I think we can, Dax-but vigilance and compassion are required. We need to guide them, help them understand the value of freedom, the joy of harmony, the importance of balance.

They walked together up to the edge of the city, beyond which stars dotted the horizon, signaling the beginning of yet another chapter onward. Standing side by side, they were the icons of trials undergone and the vision that had pulled them through. The road ahead was hazardous, but they were ready, strengthened by the power of those they had freed and the promise of a world being reborn into balance.

Guardians of hope and unity, on their way back to the city, were able to see clearly by the end that their respective roles had now turned from warriors into mentors: protectors of a legacy to guide many future generations. Far from over, their journey toward balance was creating with each step taken a new certitude: what all they were building was worth every sacrifice they had to make.

CHAPTER 72
GUARDIANS OF BALANCE

And finally, when morning dawned over Sunhaven, the first light of day seeped high in the windows of the council hall and painted delicate lines of gold across the faces of the assembled representatives-farmers and healers, scholars and soldiers, the voices of Eryal's future seamed into their faces with stories, the scars of battles fought, and hope yet to come. It had not been a council; it was one chorus of life, joined in a common pursuit, ready to forge the way onward.

Dax and Sylvia stood right in the middle of the council, their faces set. No longer mere rebels, warriors-the world they aspired to was not relieved of tyranny but one of coexistence: a frail tapestry of Light and Shadow, of strength and compassion intertwined. It is to be the very heart of that vision, a living testament to a balance they strove to create.

Discourses started, their voices ebbing and flowing with the tides. Issues relating to governance, resource allocation, and what continental structure the land should continue with overwhelmed the major concern of every one present within the convention. Tense but firm was the mood; every delegate spoke of something different, molded by the problems within their homelands. Sylvia could feel in each voice the weight of responsibility to remind her powerfully: every decision would shape the world they were trying to create.

Of primary concern it is that those eastern lands laid waste by war be our first concern, " said Alaric, a stout councilor from the eastern steppes. "Their fields lie barren, their homes in disrepair. Unless we extend an olive branch, dissension would flower.

"And the western territories?" she said, Liana, leader of those from the coast, stood against him. "They provided for the rebellion, and sacrificed their own resources. Are they less in need of relief?

The thumb of one hand turned upward, Sylvia raised it for silence. "Alaric, Liana, your concerns are valid, but let's not forget why we are here. This council is here to make sure no region, no community, gets left behind. We're not here to fight over resources; we're here to share, to pull ourselves up together. If we choose unity over division, then in time, every region shall prosper.

His voice was sure and strong, laced with the conviction in his words: "We fought together for freedom, and now we must fight together for peace. The Empire fell due to the differences between us being exploited; that cannot happen again. Every voice here counts in matters of balance and justice.

The silence in the room turned reflective. Each representative seemed to take the weight of his words-the reminder of shared history which had led them to this very moment. So far they had come, yet so conscious were they that if peace were to be real, eternal vigilance and accountability were called for.

Elara stood forth- scarce a girl, yet honored member of the council, once powerful ally in rebellion. Her voice was clear, words even.

A world we can forge: Light and Shadow side by side, with a voice for every soul. And toward that end, we must confront our deepest fears, those that have sculpted us into what we have become. And should we be in pursuit of the path forward, then the understanding must come, not by the enforcement of law but by a culture embracing Light and Shadow. A murmur of assent went through the room, and Talia-one of the delegates who had once been in training with the Radiance Church-voiced the sentiments of many. "The use of Shadow Magic still upsets many people. For generations we were taught to fear it. Whatever are we to persuade people that Light and Shadow can really exist in harmony with one another?

Sylvia turned to her then, her eyes warm yet firm. "We know that feeling of fear, Talia.

. . .

It was instilled in us by those who sought to control us. But Shadow is not malign in itself-it is a part of us, a force that, as is Light, can heal and protect if used wisely. Our journey showed us that neither force need dominate; together, they create balance. Now we have to teach our people a different lesson: harmony is not to be found in suppression but in acceptance.

Dax nodded. "There's risk in any power- Light, Shadow. The Radiance Church manipulated Light to enslave and Shadow to terrorize. But here, we get to do it different. We open schools where both these arts will be taught along with each other. And our children will grow up understanding them to be partners, not enemies.

They felt his words fall like weights upon them as they listened intently to the members of the council. It was not a question of policy and division, but of an entire different way of living based on mutual respect and the wisdom of living in balance with nature.

After much deliberation, it was in that council that there would be laid an agreed document of governance for the continent, named the Charter of Balance. The common pledge to justice, transparency, and protection for Light and Shadow alike was consecrated therein. It would be that charter that would make sure the hard-worked balance achieved would live for generations.

The words faded, and Sylvia's mind began to wander to how it all brought them to this point. Turning to Dax, remembering all that happened to them, the fights, the losses, those who didn't make it-a turmoil in her mind. In the council chamber so filled with voices of hope and determination, she felt a profound feeling of closure.

She rose and, her voice ringing with command, told them, "We fought not only against tyranny, but to create something of worth. That dream is what this council is for: to make sure every life here counts, every voice heard. Let us not forget the cost of freedom and let it guide us as we forge a future whereby Light and Shadow can walk together.

Dax added in quiet strength, "We are not just rulers, we're guardians. And the future that we're gonna forge here will be watched for generations. Let this council be a beacon to unify, to show a balance. Let it remind everybody of what we've overcome-and what it is we're trying to create.".

One after another, the members of the council stood and pledged their loyalty to this new vision, and, little by little, the enormity of what Dax and Sylvia had endured began really to sink in. They were no longer rebels, fighting against oppression, but protectors of a newly reborn world, a world in which Light and Shadow might coexist as friends.

Later, after dark had fallen for a good while, they strolled down quiet streets, hand in hand, the lanterns' soft emanations lighting children's laughter, whispered conversations of families rebuilding. And Sylvia drew a deep breath out toward the horizon.

. . .

"This council. It's more than I ever dreamed," she breathed. "We've come so far, and yet there's so much more to do."

Dax laid a reassuring hand on her shoulder. "We've given them the chance, Sylvia. We put them on the path. The council will change, just as we have. There are still hard times ahead, but they're ready. We've taught them to question, to balance. And we'll be here to guide them. They attained the outskirts, standing as one, staring out into the distance they had sworn to protect. Above them, stars stippled the sky, silent testimony to the road behind them. No more warriors, they became the wardens of a dream: a world in which balance was not a want but a sure way of life.

They turned toward the city now, side by side, hand in hand, knowing well they were very far from the end of the journey. But for the first time, they walked in quiet confidence, knowing they had set the world right toward wholeness. The way ahead would be long and rough, with the intelligence of the past and the promise of the future, but they were ready. In the soft dawn light, Sunhaven spoke to the balance-a promise-so long as Light and Shadow were in balance, so would their legacy survive.

CHAPTER 73
THE TIES THAT BIND

But as the sun, now setting, cast its warmth upon the city, still the council had to face yet another inordinately difficult job. Tonight was different, though, because tonight they were facing the inescapable future-the consensus they had won, and how to hold onto it in a world that was in transition. The rebellion was over, but the shadows of division, suspicion, and fear still clung to the edges of this hard-won peace. Dax and Sylvia knew full well it was one thing to free a people from oppressors, but quite another to raise a world where balance could be passed from generation to generation.

The circle sat in representation for all those other aspects, each part of the varied contour: farmers tilling the land, healers restoring both body and spirit, scholars who chronicled and preserved knowledge, and artisans who put meaning into their work. Each representative spoke for their people, their own perspectives different from one another, shaped by struggle and hope, and relentless wills toward a finer future.

• • •

Elder Liora, whose wisdom had considerably guided the council, began that evening's discourse with a soft yet commanding presence. "We have fought for a world valuing the balance of forces," she said, her eyes slowly circling the room. "Yet peace, much like balance, is tender. It would demand a common vigilance, a dedication to something greater than our selves. Tonight, we must choose how to protect the freedom we have won.

A murmur of assent surged around the room, before sober silence fell once more as the weight of her words settled upon the council. They knew full well how insidiously freedom might be nibbled away, how the seeds of dissension could find fertile earth if left unchecked.

Dax leaned forward, his tone firm yet soft, "Our unity was forged in the fire of rebellion, but we cannot depend on memory to support it-the memory of struggle. We need something alive, living-something to make sure Light and Shadow are taken into consideration as one, and every voice, no matter how small, is being heard.

Sylvia nodded, a conviction and compassion tracing an edge around her tone. "We have seen how easily power can be twisted, how fear and ambition can corrupt even the noblest of intentions. We have to provide a base that listens to the balance between freedom and responsibility which brings in strength and vulnerability of every single individual.

• • •

As discussion unfolded, each of the council members took a turn in sharing his vision for maintaining the unity they had struggled so desperately to achieve. One farmer of the plains spoke of needing local councils so that decisions could be made by those closest to the land and its people. One healer did mention a few amenity centers for healing mentally and emotionally-a place where people can actually face their traumas and learn to heal together. One artisan spoke about cultural gatherings and festivals honoring the memory of this rebellion so that the spirit of these ideals of balance, resilience, and hope remain a part of life.

So the council realized that each formed a part of the symbiotic relationship of the whole, a vision of the future wherein governance was to be in partnership-not hierarchical-and wherein the principles of balance extend beyond those of magic into the whole of living.

Elder Liora spoke again, her voice heavy with the burden of years. "Let us make it a custom to remember so that what we bought with such a high price will never be forgotten. Once a year, there comes a day of retrospect and festivity when people come together in honor of both Light and Shadow, share their stories with one another. A day when it would come to mind that freedom is not a reward but a vow.

Sylvia ended with a ringing voice now inspired by his, "And on that day, let us call forth those who walk both paths-mages of Light and Shadow, healers and warriors, scholars and artisans-to share in their knowledge and to teach the young what it truly means to live in balance. It is in this way we shall be certain the generations hence are not only fully aware of the danger of division but also the strength of unity.".

Pride swelling, Dax scanned the faces in the room, finding in each face the resilience that had seen them through the darkest of times. It was more than a council; it was a community of leaders, bonded by an unspoken vow to protect the harmony they had fought for so hard. He rose, the room hushed, and spoke in quiet strength. We are the guardians of a legacy bigger than each and every one of us. We will grow, together, a world in which balance will not be given due respect, but will don each form of life. It is this future we fought for-a world where Light and Shadow are companions, not foes; a world where freedom is dear and well-guarded.

Finally, the meeting was brought to a close with an air of determination. The councillors emerged from the chamber, carrying away in each heart the revived pledge to that dream all had sketched in their minds-long since ceased to be an aspiration, now an action-something, a pledge to keep that fragile balance for ages to come.

They stood there in silence a few moments, Dax and Sylvia. Then Sylvia took Dax's hand, her eyes soft yet ablaze. "This is the world we dreamed of, Dax. Now we have a shot at making it real.

Dax squeezed her hand, his heart filled with both pride and a quiet resolve. "We'll protect it, Sylvia. Whatever comes, whatever shadows rise, we'll face them together."

. . .

By the time they finally emerged into the city, the stars were already breaking through above, shining soft upon the land they had taken back. They strolled down the quiet streets, hand in hand, with the hum around them in vibrations of life- a song of resilience, a song of unity, a song of hope.

Together, they would lead their people to balance Light with Shadow, to hold freedom dear, and to make balance more than a word but a way of life. But they also knew full well that many trials lay ahead, and they were ready, in the power of their bonding and the legacy they carried. And as they stood there, looking out over the city, Dax and Sylvia felt the comforting weight of the future settle upon their shoulders: a future they would protect with every part of themselves, a world that should rise from the ashes of the past-a legacy of balance and harmony that would flame forth to generations yet to come.

CHAPTER 74
ETERNAL BALANCE

As morning stretched over the Eryal Continent, stretching across the sky in an awakening of gold and violet shades, Dax and Sylvia stood atop a hill overlooking Sunhaven. The city wore the noose of fear and oppression, shining new under the morning promise. The roads pulsed rhythmically to life as voices were raised to drown them in laughter, quiet conversations filling the morning air. While it was still streaked by the scars of old, those formed one huge scar tissue of history, telling their tale of stubborn will to survive and unequalled strength in unity.

They watched the villagers move about in the square below-the morning sun's long shadows sometimes seeming to dissolve into the light.

A strong reminder of the balance they fought for-an ideal come alive. He sees it in the kids running and playing around, uncontrollable giggles, and in neighbors hailing one another-people who earlier had to live with fear in their hearts. Here, trust and peace had flowered, free from shackles of the shadow of the Empire.

Sylvia's eyes spoke volumes of the break of dawn outside and the depth involved in that odyssey they found themselves in. "We gave them so much more than freedom," she whispered, firm, shining with quiet pride. "We gave them a way of living- a manner to embrace both Light and Shadow so that strength could be drawn in unity.

Dax's eyes softened at her words: "And they're ready, Sylvia. They've seen darkness, and yet they have chosen to stand together, to protect each other. They're not rebuilding a city; they're building a legacy.".

They walked down the hill again, into the bustle of city streets, people greeting them, but as friends and comrades, not as fighters, not as leaders. In this world, Dax and Sylvia were its products no less than farmers and artisans and healers that had struggled so hard to restore. Symbols, yes- but rooted in shared humanity.

District by district, people went through the town, day after day, in which people came into contact with councillors, murmurs of the people, soft sharing in the renewal of the people's simplicity. They talked about what was to come within the hall of councillors: schools to teach in Light and Shadow Magic as a force to complement and never oppose; healing centers to the soul in need; quiet places of sanctuary in which one can reflect and grow in peace.

. . .

Later that night, they joined the council to perform a more solemn ritual for all souls lost, for those who gave all that they could grasp this chance for peace. This was done in the middle of the city, at a newly-erected monument: unadorned, yet deeply-interconnected signs of Light and Shadow in witness to their unity.

First to speak, Dax was solemn-voiced, and the crowd fell silent to listen. "Tonight, we remember those who gave everything for this future, those who believed in a world they might never see. Their strength lives on in each of us, in the lives we build, in the choices we make.

The soft, even voice of Sylvia added from the center, "They are not gone; they are in the air we breathe-in the earth beneath our feet, in the love we carry onward. Let this monument stand for witness, shouting aloud to all that Light and Shadow are not the forces of segregation but unification forces. Let us live in courage, compassion, and commitment uncompromisingly toward balance in their memory.

A hushed silence befell the multitude, and heads bowed in silent vow to forge ahead headlong with resolve toward a shining morrow, their bond forged from the very values that brought them to this place. It was one of those reflective, thankful, and together-strong moments when each and all were tied in their collective memory.

. . .

And when it finally did, jubilation erupted through the city: families congregated in the square, recounting stories, singing together with friends, and peals of laughter spilling into the air in a sound that had for so long been suppressed and was now evident with the freedom forged among them. Far removed from unity, this shall never again be an ideal but one of blood running inside the heart of Sunhaven. And so, as the night wore on, Dax and Sylvia knew comfort lay once more in the shade of the Whispering Woods-to the trees that had seen much of their journey. Above, stars glittered across the still sky, their soft, diffused glow cast down upon the forest to guide them to the Tree of Life.

His roots below were wrapped about the nether-world, his topmost shoot touched the heaven, wherein all peoples dwelt in his shadow, remembering the covenant sworn of old.

Sylvia placed her hand on the tree, feeling the steady pulse of life that flowed through its roots—a quiet testament to resilience. "This balance isn't just something we've created," she whispered. "It's something we've returned to, something that was always here, waiting for us to remember."

Dax sat down beside her and laid his hand beside hers on the gnarled bark. "And now it's our gift to the future-a world whereby Light and Shadow can walk side by side, where power isn't used to control but to guide, to shield.

They were quiet then, easily silent; the cohesion between them forged from more than battlefield adrenaline, forged from the love and trust in a commitment unbreakable to the world they had dreamt of. This was their legacy, not the monuments, not the won battles, but the peace they nurtured- a peace which would live long in the hearts of those they had inspired.

As the first hints of light from another dawn painted over the world they redesigned, Dax and Sylvia turned back toward the city. The challenges would come, for night would fall with the tides and rise anew. But they were ready: they had stood guard together over a balance in protection of a fragile, resurgent peace, their lives sewn deep into the tapestry of this new era.

And so they strolled together, hand in hand, sure-footed, their mission clear. It was a world to tend and nurture and guide. Whatever the future held, they knew they would share. More of this life path lay ahead of them, but it was a path they were to continue traveling in love, resilience, and belief in the strength of unity. But when the first morning light struck the earth, Sunhaven rose, meaning that delicate balance won with such struggle.

For as long as Light and Shadow dance their fated dance in harmony, so would the memory of Dax and Sylvia be with them, etched not on cold stones but in every heart which treads the path which they broke.

ACKNOWLEDGMENTS

I'd like to start off by thanking the readers out there who have been supporting my work. It is your love of elaborate world-building and heavy morality that inspires me. Your passion was the reason I wrote this book.

I would also be eternally grateful to my family and friends, who constantly encouraged me and believed in my work. In fact, their support was really highly instrumental in keeping me on track through the challenges of the entire writing process.